I want you to love me.

Justin had no reason to believe her. No reason to trust her again. Sarah had betrayed him. She had rejected what he had given her.

She had borne another man's bastard and then asked him to teach the child to be a man. She had lain in another man's arms and then asked him to love her again.

No explanation. No apology. His throat closed, hard and tight, aching with the force of what he felt for her. What he had always felt. His eyes burned with tears he had never shed, not once in the horrors of the past six months. He denied them now, but somehow she knew....

Dear Reader,

Welcome to Harlequin Historicals—stories that will capture your heart with unforgettable characters and the timeless fantasy of falling in love!

There are few writers better than award-winning author Gayle Wilson when it comes to storytelling. Highly acclaimed for both her Harlequin Historicals novels and her Harlequin Intrigue titles, Gayle stays true to her powerful and emotional style with *Lady Sarah's Son*. Set during the Regency period, this is the story of long-lost sweethearts who are brought together again by a marriage of convenience. Although a secret from Lady Sarah's past still haunts them, the passion and love that they have repressed for so long will not be denied....

Fans of medieval romance will no doubt enjoy *The Hidden Heart* by Sharon Schulze. Here, an earl on a secret mission for his country falls in love—*again*—with the beautiful owner of the keep in which he is staying. Jillian Hart returns this month with *Cooper's Wife,* a heartwarming Western tale about single parents—a sheriff and a troubled widow—who marry to protect their children, but find a lasting love. And don't miss *The Dreammaker* by rising talent Judith Stacy, a feel-good story about two people who work side by side to realize their individual dreams, not noticing that the dream of a lifetime is right before their very eyes.

Enjoy! And come back again next month for four more choices of the best in historical romance.

Sincerely,

Tracy Farrell, Senior Editor

P.S. We'd love to hear what you think about Harlequin Historicals! Drop us a line at:

Harlequin Historicals
300 E. 42nd Street, 6th Floor
New York, NY 10017

GAYLE WILSON

LADY SARAH'S SON

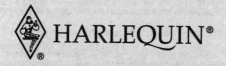

HARLEQUIN®

TORONTO • NEW YORK • LONDON
AMSTERDAM • PARIS • SYDNEY • HAMBURG
STOCKHOLM • ATHENS • TOKYO • MILAN • MADRID
PRAGUE • WARSAW • BUDAPEST • AUCKLAND

ISBN 0-373-29083-7

LADY SARAH'S SON

Copyright © 1999 by Mona Gay Thomas

Visit us at www.romance.net

Printed in U.S.A.

Books by Gayle Wilson

GAYLE WILSON

is the award-winning author of over fifteen novels written for Harlequin. Gayle has lived in Alabama her entire life, except for the years she followed her army aviator husband to a variety of military posts. She holds a master's degree and additional certification in the education of the gifted from the University of Alabama. Before beginning her writing career, she taught in a number of schools around the Birmingham, Alabama, area.

Gayle writes historicals set in the English Regency period for Harlequin Historicals and contemporary romantic suspense for Harlequin Intrigue. She was a 1995 finalist in the Romance Writers of America's RITA awards for her first historical, *The Heart's Desire*. Her first contemporary, *Echoes in the Dark*, won the Colorado Romance Writers 1996 Award of Excellence and was awarded third place in the Georgia Romance Writer's prestigious Maggie Award for Excellence.

Gayle and her husband have been blessed with a wonderful son, who is also a teacher of gifted students, and with a warm and loving extended Southern family and an ever-growing menagerie of cats and dogs.

For Angela Catalano,
who rescued my very first book
out of Harlequin Historicals' slush pile and,
through some time-warp miracle, is now my editor
at Intrigue. And who, through it all,
has always been my friend.

Prologue

Ireland, 1809

She had never before watched someone die, Lady Sarah Spenser realized, her eyes focused, almost unseeing, on her sister's shallow breathing. The rise and fall of Amelia's chest was now so slight it barely disturbed the bed-clothes.

Sarah had lost her mother when she was only a child, but that death had been something the women who came to help had talked about in whispers, their mouths carefully hidden behind cupped hands. The experience of her mother's death had been vague and somewhat distant, the pain of it abridged because she had not understood until it was long over what had happened.

She knew their mother was not there, of course, but perhaps she and Papa were away in London. She had thought *Maman* would soon come home, as she always had before. Laughing, her beautiful French mother would sweep into the nursery or the schoolroom, bringing an armful of presents and wearing a smart, new bonnet from the shop of London's most fashionable milliner. By the time Sarah realized *Maman* was not ever coming home again, the ache of missing her was familiar and bearable.

She wasn't sure Amelia's dying would be, and yet she had been forced to accept there was nothing she could do to prevent it. David had finally, at her insistence, called in a surgeon. Although the doctor had succeeded in delivering the baby, which the midwife had been unable to do, he had simply shaken his head in response to Sarah's repeated entreaties that he stop the relentless seep of blood.

So much blood, she thought. More than it seemed her sister's slender, graceful body could have held. Now that it was obvious, even to her untrained and inexperienced eyes, that Amelia could not live out the night, Sarah had been thinking of all the things the two of them had shared through the years. Laughter and tears and a thousand whispered secrets. The throes of their first infatuations. Dreams of their futures.

Two motherless little girls, left in the care of an increasingly cold and disinterested father, they had comforted one another. Sarah, the older by a scant two years, had always tried to take care of Amelia. She had failed only once. And this—her sister's lonely dying—was the result of that failure.

So white and cold, Sarah thought, taking the thin fingers into her own, mindlessly trying to warm them. To hold death at bay a little longer. Just as she and the wet nurse David had found had tried to warm the mewling newborn and keep him alive. Now both appeared to be battles she was destined to lose.

"Don't be angry with me, Sarah."

The whispered words shocked her out of her despairing reverie. Her gaze lifted quickly from her sister's hand to her colorless face. Amelia's eyes, which had from childhood sparkled with an irrepressible gaiety, were wide and dark in their sunken sockets, the skin around them yellowed as old bruises.

"I could never be angry with you, dearest," Sarah said softly. She forced a smile, suspecting that her sister knew her too well to be deceived by its falseness.

"I'm going to die, aren't I?" Amelia asked, her voice so low Sarah strained to catch the words. They seemed without emotion. A request merely for information, devoid of fear or concern.

Her throat too thick to push words past its constriction, Sarah nodded. It was too late for lies and deceits. There had already been too many of those. And Amelia deserved the chance to make whatever peace with their Heavenly Father was necessary.

Of course, there had been little in Amelia's sixteen years that might have displeased Him. No sin other than loving David Osborne enough to bear him a son out of wedlock. No sin other than being young and therefore vulnerable to Osborne's ruthless machinations and flattery.

"Poor Papa," Amelia said.

A tear slipped out of the corner of her eye. It traced a path across the bridge of her nose and down the cheek that rested against the white pillowcase. There was little difference now in their color.

Sarah wiped the moisture away with her thumb, aware again of the unnatural coldness of her sister's skin. "Don't cry," she whispered.

"Where's my baby?"

"Asleep," Sarah said, wondering if that might be true. Even if it were not, even if that poor scrap of an infant had already crossed the veil her sister was approaching, there seemed no point in burdening Amelia with that knowledge.

Sarah and the wet nurse had taken turns holding him, trying to warm the fragile body with their own. The nurse had managed to berate the landlord vigorously enough to procure a bucket of coal for the fire, so that the rooms David rented had at least a modicum of heat. Not enough to warm the baby into activity. Or to keep the cold breath of death away from her sister's bedside.

"David?" Amelia whispered, her eyes searching Sarah's face.

Out, Sarah thought bitterly, remembering the single word he had flung at her when she dared to question where he was going. She had begged him to stay, but her pleas had had no effect. Despite how she felt about him, her mind tried to formulate an acceptable excuse for Osborne's unacceptable behavior.

Why *not* another lie? she reasoned, meeting those entreating eyes. What could it matter now? Osborne had done nothing but lie since they had met him. Since *she* had met him, she amended, and had introduced him to her sister. A fatal introduction.

The Spenser line had run exclusively to females in the last generation, and there was not even a distant male cousin to lay claim to her father's extensive holdings. It had long been accepted that Sarah and Amelia would be heiresses, and since their father had married so late in life and was almost seventy, their inheritance might not be so far away.

And so, charming and devastatingly handsome, the Irish ex-soldier had first courted Sarah. Finding her heart irrevocably engaged, Osborne then turned his attentions to Amelia, who was not yet out. Despite his limited opportunities, David swept Mellie off her feet before Sarah or her father had realized what he was doing, far too late to prevent what happened.

After all, there wasn't a deceitful bone in Amelia's body. Or so Sarah would once have said. That was, of course, *before* her sister had willfully planned an elopement with an Irish adventurer twice her age. Amelia's note, its script large and unformed, reminiscent of the schoolroom she had so recently abandoned, had been left on the pillow of her bed.

The marquess of Brynmoor, driving his favorite team to blood-frothed exhaustion, had attempted to stop them, of course. Osborne, however, had been too clever to be caught by an enraged father. Instead of following the Great North Road to Gretna, the couple had made for the coast to board a ship bound for Ireland. And had disappeared.

It was then Sarah's world had come crashing down, all the stability she had known wiped out in an instant. As a result of Amelia's elopement, an enraged Brynmoor had declared to the world that his youngest daughter was dead. He had even held her funeral, having an empty coffin interred in the family vault.

Stunned by her father's insane rage and the bizarre nature of his reaction, Sarah had attempted to tell the cleric that her sister wasn't dead, only to be assured that Amelia was indeed alive in Christ and that she would see her in heaven.

The only other person in whom she might have confided was too far away to help, fighting with Wellington in Spain. And committing the sordid details of her family's situation to paper had seemed impossible—even when her fiancé's letter of condolences arrived. Justin's brother had written him about Amelia's death. By the time Justin's response reached her from Iberia, Sarah had already decided that her sister was truly lost to her forever.

Then, almost two months ago, Amelia's own frantic missive had arrived, begging Sarah to come to her. Sarah never considered refusing the appeal, although in order to fulfill it, she had been forced to lie to her father for the first time in her life.

She had invented an ailing relation of her mother's who had supposedly invited her for a prolonged visit. Her father, slipping further into madness with each passing day, accepted the story without question.

When Sarah arrived in Dublin and found that Osborne had not even married her sister, she knew she couldn't leave Amelia to bear her child alone. Not even when confronted with Osborne's quickly rejected attempt at renewing his flirtation with her. Such was the man who had lured her sister to her death.

"David's gone to buy more coal for the fire," Sarah said, telling the lie without a quiver of remorse. She was becoming too adept at lying, she thought, so she added another for good measure. "He was worried the baby wouldn't be warm enough."

Her sister's fevered eyes held hers, wanting to believe, Sarah supposed. Still wanting so desperately to believe in the man on whom she had thrown away everything, including her life.

"Take care of him," Amelia said.

Osborne? Sarah thought in disbelief, and then she realized what her sister was asking. Mellie wanted Sarah's promise that she would care for her child, that wizened speck of humanity, whose hold on life seemed as precarious as his mother's.

"I will," she vowed softly.

"Don't ever tell..."

Amelia's voice faltered, and her eyelids closed as her breathing shuddered, the ominous rattle in her throat audible. Then her lids slowly opened again, her dark blue eyes more focused than they had been in some hours.

"Don't tell them," Amelia begged. "Don't tell anyone. Not even Papa. I could not bear for them to know what I've done."

"No, I won't," Sarah said quickly, gripping the icy fingers in her own. But there wasn't enough strength left in them to allow Amelia to respond. Another tear slid weakly across the path the first had followed.

"They'll think so badly of me," her sister whispered.

"No, dearest. No one will ever think badly of you. I won't let them," Sarah promised fiercely. "No one will ever know."

Again Amelia's eyes held hers, assessing the depth of that fervent vow. "Swear it to me on *Maman*'s grave," she said. "Swear to me no one will ever know what I've done."

"I swear it," Sarah said quickly, still clutching her fingers, which seemed to be growing colder. More lifeless.

"On *Maman*'s grave," Amelia demanded, something of her old spirit in the too-bright eyes. They appeared almost as they had always been—sparkling with life and promise.

What did it matter, Sarah thought, what promises she must give, as long as they eased this passage? She would never betray Amelia's trust. Never spread gossip about her own sister. Or destroy her family's good name. It was a pledge easily made, and so she took a breath and gave Amelia the oath she had demanded.

"I swear it on *Maman*'s grave," Sarah vowed.

Amelia nodded, the movement of her head barely discernible. Then her eyes closed. And she never opened them again.

"Because I can't possibly take him with me," David said. His pleasant features were not even strained or angry as he repeated his refusal, unmoved by any of her arguments.

"He's your son," Sarah said, cuddling the infant against the softness of her breasts, far more secure now in that maternal role than she had been two weeks ago when he had been born. "You can't really mean to abandon your own son," she said.

She looked down on the tiny face, relaxed now in sleep—an infrequent occurrence. Perhaps she had lost the battle to save Amelia, but her sister's baby had proved to be far more tenacious in maintaining his fragile hold on life than he had appeared.

The wet nurse—thank God for her, Sarah thought— had been both skilled and patient. After two weeks of unflagging care from the two of them, it seemed that the baby would survive. But it also now appeared that David Osborne had not been in the least concerned with the outcome of their struggle.

"He'll have you to look after him," David said easily, his engaging smile touching the corners of well-shaped lips. "You'll make a much better job of it, Sarah, than I should."

"I can't take him home," Sarah said. "You don't know—"

"Unfortunately," Osborne interrupted, "I *do* know. I know your father, my dear. Well enough to assure you I don't plan to show up on his lordship's doorstep and present him to his grandson. As much as I'd like to see his face if I did," he said, his smile widening, apparently amused at the thought.

"But what am I to do?" Sarah asked.

Her eyes were drawn again to the baby's face, which was really not unattractive when it wasn't reddened and scowling with crying. At eighteen, Sarah had little experience with babies. And more than enough experience with her father's mad rages. She, too, was having a hard time imagining showing up on his doorstep, bringing Amelia's illegitimate baby home.

"You'll think of something, I'm sure," David said. "I trust you implicitly. I know Amelia would have as well. As a matter of fact, I'm certain she had much rather leave the upbringing of her son in your hands than my less competent ones."

Sarah took a breath, deep enough that the infant she was clutching stirred. She looked down in time to watch his eyes open. They were as blue as Amelia's. As blue as her own. That midnight hue was a Spenser characteristic, its prevalence among her ancestors documented in the portrait gallery at Longford. The baby yawned, tiny rosebud mouth stretching wide to reveal pink gums. His eyes seemed focused on her face. As if he were interested in it. As if he were trying to communicate with her.

To tell her that David was right? That Amelia would much prefer her son to be in Sarah's inexperienced hands than in the irresponsible and profligate care of his father? A father who had demonstrated an inability to care deeply about anything other than his own pleasure.

After ruining Amelia's life, David had been cruelly inattentive to her, at least during the last weeks of her difficult pregnancy, when Sarah had been with them. And uncaring, it seemed, about her death. Sarah had had to make arrangements for the funeral, although David had rather strangely sent for a priest when he learned Amelia was dead. Since her sister had not been Catholic, the entire episode seemed out of place.

Almost as out of place as this baby would be at Longford, Sarah thought. It seemed, however, that she had no choice but to take him there. She had promised her dying sister that she would take care of him—a deathbed oath made on her mother's grave.

Sarah could have, as yet, no idea how much keeping that simple pledge would change her life. And when she finally did, it was far too late to turn back.

Chapter One

England, 1813

After returning from his first survey of his inheritance, the new earl of Wynfield gave in to a rare display of despair. He sank down gratefully in the chair behind his father's huge desk and put his head in his hands.

Those who had served under Justin Tolbert would have been surprised by that gesture. His men had never been allowed to see anything but Wynfield's steady confidence and courage. He had demonstrated both in numerous battles, especially when the odds weighed heaviest against his regiment's success.

He hadn't been Wynfield then, but simply Colonel The Honorable Justin Tolbert. The title and the inheritance that went with it had, during his years of service, belonged to his brother. And now everything of that inheritance was gone, except the title Justin had never wanted or expected to bear.

The once verdant fields of the home farm lay fallow. The tenant cottages had been allowed to decay into a state of disrepair that would not only be expensive to remedy, but was dangerous as well. The gloomy picture his late father's man of business had painted for him in London had not begun to approach the reality he had faced on his homecoming.

Homecoming, he thought bitterly. *What a bloody hell of a homecoming this has proved to be.* It had begun, almost as soon as he'd stepped foot on shore, with the terrible news of Robert's death, followed by that brutal assessment of his financial ruin.

Justin had cherished the dream of returning to this lush corner of England. It had carried him through the deprivations of the long war the British had waged against the Emperor. He had lain in his tent at night dreaming of the very landscapes he had visited today, laid waste now by neglect and mismanagement.

First had been his father's neglect, which he supposed he had been aware of on some level while he was growing up, although he had been too young and unthinking to realize the implications. At the old earl's death, his brother Robert had inherited not only his father's title, but apparently his weaknesses as well. For excessive drink. And for betting impossibly large sums on impossibly stupid wagers.

Robert and their father had been immensely popular with the proprietors of the London gaming hells. Judging by the reception Justin had received today from his gape-mouthed tenants, they had frequented those far more often than they had their ancestral holdings. After his father's death, Robert had evidently not come back to Wynfield Park at all, preferring to spend his time in the capital or in one of the fashionable resorts, wherever the wagering was the most reckless. And once his brother's downward spiral had begun, it ran its course very quickly.

Less than two years after inheriting the title, Robert

was dead, the victim of a senseless, drunken duel. It had been an ''affair of honor,'' for which none of Robert's friends could quite remember the originating insult. What they had all remembered, with appropriate horror, was that his brother's less inebriated opponent had managed to put a bullet into Robert's heart.

That had been the first blow of Justin's homecoming. The second had been the realization of his current fortunes. The estate, which had been in his family for over two hundred years, was now so heavily mortgaged that it was virtually worthless.

Even if the physical work of restoring it had not loomed so hopelessly large, given his current state of health, there were no funds with which to make improvements. And no one willing to extend further credit that might have put his inheritance on the path to solvency again. All of that had been explained to him in London, but until he had seen the devastation with his own eyes—

''Shall I ask Cook to hold back dinner, my lord?''

With the first word of his butler's question, Justin lifted his head out of his hands. His hazel eyes considered the figure in the doorway. A door he damn well wished he had remembered to close, he thought bitterly. The last thing he wanted was for the story to get about that he was shattered by the situation he was facing. Keeping up appearances had been one of his father's primary concerns in life. Justin could only suppose he had inherited something of that desire as well.

He truly didn't want his neighbors' sympathy, despite the seriousness of his plight. He also knew that if he were to have any hope of pulling things together, he must appear full of confidence, even before his own servants.

''I shall only need time enough to change,'' he said.

''Very good, my lord,'' the old man intoned solemnly.

After Blevins began to walk away, however, it appeared he was struck by another thought. He turned back, meeting Justin's eyes with an almost speculative gleam in his.

"If I might be so bold..." he said in preface. When Justin didn't deny him permission to speak his mind, he continued, "Your lordship might prefer to dine here. I have often brought your late father's supper to this very room. *If* the earl did not wish to be troubled to dine more formally."

The butler's eyes were steady on his face. Justin could detect no pity in their rheumy depths or in his voice, although he knew Blevins would certainly be aware of what he had discovered on today's disheartening tour. And perhaps even aware of how badly his leg ached.

It was strange how a limb that was no longer present could hurt so damn much. Of course the stump of the amputation, which ended a little below midcalf, was as yet unaccustomed to the socket and leather harness of the new foot the London bootmaker had fitted for him. It was an appendage that gave Justin mobility, if nothing else. Certainly not comfort.

The simplest movements, those that had once been natural and unthinking, were not only painful, but perilous as well. Justin had told himself, with the same dogged determination that had seen him through five long years of war, that in time he would adjust to the awkwardness and discomfort.

And if he could not, then he would be damned if anyone would ever know. He had made that decision the moment the surgeon had given his clipped verdict that the shattered foot must come off. No one would ever be allowed to know how deeply Justin felt that loss. And *no one* included Blevins.

"I shall need time to dress," he said again, injecting a hint of coldness into the soft words. "I should be ready to dine within the hour. *In* the dining room, thank you, Blevins."

The old man's eyes held a fraction of a second too long on his face, the prerogative of a valued family retainer. There was absolutely nothing untoward in his voice when he nodded agreement with those instructions. "Very good, my lord," he said. He turned, leaving the study as silently as he had entered it.

Behind him, Wynfield's mouth tightened in disgust. He'd been rude to an old man who had only his best interests at heart. Perhaps he was more like his father than he had realized.

Putting both hands flat on the desk in front of him, Justin pushed his body out of the chair, getting the unwieldy artificial foot under him. The pain in the still-healing stump, which the damn thing had already rubbed raw, was a reminder of the number of times today he'd climbed down from the open carriage in response to some entreaty or inquiry from one of his tenants.

It might have been a request to take a look at a leaking roof or a fouled well. Or an invitation to comment on a fine new calf or even a baby. Nothing that couldn't have waited until another day, but Justin had not once refused. That was his duty, of course. To see to the welfare of the people who lived on his lands. And no matter what else anyone might say about him, Justin thought grimly, he had never been accused of shirking his duty. Not even the unpleasant ones.

Such as dressing for a dinner he would eat alone, when all he really wanted to do was take off this torturing contraption and lie down on his bed and wait for the pain to subside enough that he might fall asleep. What he was going to do instead was change his clothes and dine in lonely if elegant state in the dining room of an estate that was falling down around his head.

"You stupid ass," he muttered, his voice low enough that his derogatory comment couldn't possibly reach the ears of any servant loitering in the hallway outside.

He closed his eyes before he took a step. When he put his weight on the foot they had fashioned for him in London, he found the pain to be every bit as excruciating as he'd anticipated.

"Proud, stupid moron," the earl of Wynfield whispered, and then, with the same courage that had distinguished him on the Peninsula, he began the long, limping journey to his room.

"Wynfield's home."

Lady Sarah Spenser's eyes lifted from the small curly head her gloved fingers had been guiding down the steps of the village church. Her prayer book was clutched in the fingers of her other hand, or she might have been tempted to lock them together to keep their sudden trembling from being so obvious.

She settled instead for moving them in a small caress over Drew's curls before she looked up. Within Lady Fortley's eyes was a gleam of malicious satisfaction, probably there in response to the telltale drain of color from her own cheeks, Sarah thought. Apparently the old gossip had seen in her face exactly what she was hoping for when she had sprung her news.

"Indeed?" Sarah said simply. "I hadn't heard."

She lowered her eyes and allowed her fingers to increase their pressure on the back of Andrew's head. Obediently the little boy descended another of the broad front steps.

As Sarah was poised to follow, Lady Fortley added, "So tragically changed, of course. Poor man."

Sarah's eyes rose again to her tormentor's face.

"Or perhaps you didn't know that, either," Lady Fortley said, smiling, her voice imbued with an unctuous kindness.

A patently false kindness, Sarah recognized angrily. However, she was no more capable of walking away from this conversation now than she would be capable of pushing Andrew down the stairs. Or of pushing Lady Fortley down them, which, God forgive her, was an action she could consider with no small degree of pleasure.

"Changed in what way?" she asked, gratified by the calm serenity with which she managed to ask the question. After all, her heart was pounding so wildly she wondered it wasn't making her mother's cameo broach vibrate.

"Why, so grievously wounded. You really had not heard?"

Why should she have heard? She had broken all ties with Justin Tolbert more than four years ago. Shortly after she had brought Andrew back to England, and the gossip had begun.

"I don't know how he shall manage," Lady Fortley continued, shaking her head. "Fortley says he's probably come home only long enough to sell the place, though who he'll find to buy it is beyond me. Gone to rack and ruin. Rumor has it that it's heavily mortgaged as well. Mortgaged to the hilt, Fortley says."

Sarah's eyes remained focused on Lady Fortley's face, but it was her mind that was racing now. Caring for Andrew and her father and his properties had left her little time for indulging in a social life, even if the district had offered her the opportunity. She had vaguely been aware that the Wynfield estate was falling into disrepair, but because her own responsibilities were overwhelming, she hadn't had the time or the energy to keep up with what was happening to her neighbors.

Since she had been deliberately excluded from the affairs of the county, and since her father was no longer able to participate in them, she had had no warning of Justin's return. Which was exactly what Lady Fortley had been counting on.

"Perhaps then we shall finally see someone in the Wynfield pew next Sunday," Sarah said.

She allowed her eyes to hold Lady Fortley's a moment longer, and then, touching Andrew's curls again, she marched him down the remaining steps and toward her father's waiting carriage. As she walked, Andrew ran ahead of her, free from any restrictions on his behavior now that they had left the throng crowded around the front of the church.

Words and phrases from the confrontation echoed in Sarah's head, almost keeping time with her steps. *So tragically changed, of course. Poor man. Grievously wounded. Come home only long enough to sell the place.*

Justin, she thought, feeling the sting of unwanted tears and blinking to control them. This was her Justin Lady Fortley was talking about. Justin, whom Sarah Spenser had once loved more than she had loved her own life. The very thought of whom she had denied herself, as she had been denied every other pleasure, during the last four years. Denied everything but doing her duty and keeping the promise she had made to her dying sister.

Nothing had changed, Sarah told herself, angrily rubbing an escaping tear off her cheek before anyone saw it. Nothing had changed because nothing could ever change. Like all the other unpleasant realities she had faced up to four years ago, she would in time learn to deal with this one. Justin was still as far away from her as he had been during the years he had spent with Wellington. Just as much out of her reach. And there was no sense crying about him like some lovesick ninny.

Nothing had changed, she told herself again, watching Andrew clamber up the steps of the carriage with the help of the footman. This event could not be allowed to disturb the even tenor of the life she had established for herself and for her sister's son. Nothing at all had changed.

Justin, her heart still whispered. Justin was home.

As the earl of Wynfield rode through the wide tract of forest on the eastern edge of his estate, he felt nothing of the despair he had experienced last week. Instead, he had had a heady sense of freedom almost from the moment he'd swung into the saddle and touched his heels to Star. The animal's unquestioning obedience to his unspoken commands was reassuring, and as they crossed the rugged terrain, Justin's confidence had grown.

Mounted on the gelding, his body didn't betray him with its unaccustomed awkwardness. And if Star were aware of any difference in his master's technique, he wasn't letting on. The horse seemed as glad of the gallop as Justin was.

He had already slowed his mount, however, not only to give the gelding a breather, but because the woods here were too dense for their previously exhilarating pace. Now that he knew riding was one pleasure that wasn't to be denied him, he had nothing to prove anymore. Not to himself or to Star.

He had almost reached a broad clearing in the very heart of the forest, a clearing he had forgotten, when he heard the shouting. Boys' voices, he recognized. Thin and piping, and they were coming toward him. The sounds at first seemed ordinary, comfortingly familiar. After all, he and Robert had often sneaked off to play with the tenant children in these very woods, which joined the Wynfield lands to Longford.

Probably not much had changed about the activities of the district lads in the intervening years, Justin thought, a remembering smile on his lips as he listened to the excited shouts, which were growing louder. In this same clearing, the boys of his generation had once built a fort and spent long summer afternoons playing at war.

His smile faded at those words. *Playing at war.* Which, as he certainly knew, was not a game. And not for children. As a boy, he had thought battle was all flags and glory.

Now he knew, of course, what it really was. Death and maiming, of both horses and men. The ghastly sounds of their dying and the unmistakable stench of hot blood. The roar of the cannon so loud he would be deafened at the end of the day. His arm so weary from hacking with his saber that he could no longer lift water to his parched mouth. His throat raw, his voice hoarse from trying to make his orders heard above the din.

Deliberately, Justin erased those images from his head. The first child had entered the clearing, followed rapidly by a stream of others. The children were so engrossed in their play that they took no notice of the horse and rider.

As he watched them, feeling old and rather avuncular, Justin gradually became aware that whatever was going on was not a game. A variety of missiles, rocks and roots and sticks was being thrown at the little boy in the lead. As Justin watched, a rock, thrown by one of the largest of the pursuing boys, struck the child they were chasing the back of the head.

Although they were almost upon him, the victim whirled and began picking up the fallen objects, lobbing them back at his tormentors. His throws were short and ineffective, but one had to admire his spirit, Justin thought. Apparently, however, the others didn't feel the same admiration.

"Surround him," shouted the boy who had thrown the rock.

Like well-trained troopers, his followers did just that, encircling the still-defiant victim as he pitched whatever he could find on the ground back at them. The boy who was giving orders broke out of the circle and began to approach him.

"Now you're in for it, you little bastard," he said.

Enough, Justin thought, especially given the disparity in size between the two. He touched his heel to Star's flank, sending the gelding charging toward the children. The boys on the outer edges scattered at the sound of his approach, and the two in the center looked up in amazement as he pulled up just before it seemed Star might crash into them.

"That's quite enough," Justin said.

He hadn't raised his voice, the tone of command unconsciously the same one he had used on countless battlefields. His voice rang with authority, however, and not surprisingly, it had the same effect on these boys as it had once had on soldiers.

The larger lad looked up, eyes widening at the sight of the horse looming above him. Justin knew that he and Star would appear as threatening as St. George approaching the dragon, lance in hand. The spectators had already backed away in terror, avoiding the hooves of his mount, which Justin was controlling almost without thought.

"What's going on here?" he demanded.

Their eyes round with shock or awe, the boys remained silent for a moment. The larger of the two in the center of the circle had scrambled back, getting away from the horse, but the smaller child had barely moved.

"What we're about here ain't nothing to do with you," the larger boy said belligerently, obviously attempting to regain both his bravado and his standing among his fellows.

The ranking officer, Justin thought in amusement, allowing nothing of what he was thinking to show on his face. His expression was as stern as if he were dealing with an enemy.

"Since you're doing it on my land, I beg to think *whatever* happens here has something to do with me." He paused a moment to let that information sink in, before he added, "I'm Wynfield."

The leader's eyes widened. This time they examined his face and then ran with undisguised admiration over Star's gleaming hide before focusing on Justin's right boot, the one that hid the artificial foot.

"Whoever you are," the boy said, his mouth arranged in a sneer, "it's for certain you *ain't* the earl."

Justin hesitated only a second or two before he reversed his crop and tapped its thick handle against the toe of his shining Hessian. The sound the stick made was as solid as that of a knocker applied to a door. Distinctly not flesh and bone.

Hearing it, there were gasps and a muttered oath or two from the surrounding urchins, and even a softly breathed "Cor" from the sneering lad before him. After Justin had offered that indisputable proof of his identity, his gaze returned to challenge the boy who had doubted him.

"Guess again," he suggested softly.

" 'e ain't doin' nothin' wrong," the boy claimed.

Apparently the ringleader had decided that not only was Justin exactly who he had claimed to be, but that, as the earl of Wynfield and owner of this wood, he had the right to question their actions. Even to demand an accounting for them.

Wynfield studied the boy's face, its skin as grimy as his thin knuckles, which were bunched into fists. The pale, pinched features reminded Justin of the village urchins he'd played with nearly a quarter of a century earlier. For the most part they had been overly respectful of his and Robert's exalted positions. Occasionally there had been one this bold. Usually that had been the most intelligent of the lot, so maybe it would be worth the effort to try to change the dynamics of this situation, which he was beginning to suspect wasn't a new one.

"Any time you don't fight fairly you are doing wrong," Justin said. "The odds here seemed a trifle one-sided."

He deliberately allowed his eyes to fall to the smaller child. Justin had kept his voice low, but he made sure his words carried across the clearing, where dirt-smeared faces peered around the trunks of the circling trees. Despite their initial flurry to get out of the way of Star's advance, no one had left, more intrigued than frightened by his intervention.

"Little bastard," the boy Justin had pegged as the leader said dismissively. Then he spat on the ground, the spittle landing near the other boy's boots. The gesture, as well as his voice, indicated total contempt. Too much contempt, it seemed, for a child this young to have earned.

Justin's gaze moved to the face of the outcast. He was looking up at his rescuer, ignoring the others. The places where he'd been struck were reddened against his pale, fine-grained skin. He wasn't crying, however. And he hadn't been, Justin realized, not even when he had been getting far worse than he'd been able to give back.

The eyes of the child held his a long moment, and then the boy raised his arm and wiped at the blood trickling from one nostril with the back of his thin wrist. He succeeded in smearing the gore around a bit, but not in removing it. He sniffed, that gesture as ineffectual as the first at getting rid of the trickle of blood.

"They won't hurt you anymore," Wynfield said reassuringly.

"They didn't hurt me," the child said.

His voice still held defiance, and that emotion was evident even in the contours of the childishly rounded cheeks and the uptilted chin. It was only then that Justin noticed something he should certainly have observed before. This child's clothing was very different from that worn by the other boys.

Not one of the tenant children. Nor was he from the nearby village, Justin judged, assessing the short jacket buttoned to matching linsey-woolsey trousers. His boots were both well-polished and well-made. Which meant...

Justin took a breath, the sudden rush of blood loud in his ears because he knew exactly what it meant—this child in this particular location. And he had only to look more closely at the boy's face and dark blue eyes to have no doubt that he was right.

"Go home," he ordered, without raising his voice or removing his gaze from the child's face. "It's time for you to go home."

The child he had just rescued started forward, obviously intending to leave with the others.

"Not you," Justin told him. Surprised, the little boy ꓘked up, eyes questioning.

"ᵔir?" the boy said.

''Your name?'' Wynfield asked. An urge to masochism, he supposed. Like dressing for dinner. He was vaguely aware that the other children were following his command, slinking back into the forest around them.

''My name is Andrew,'' the boy said.

And the rest of it? Justin wanted to demand, but he restrained himself. What could it possibly matter whom Sarah had chosen as his replacement? That wound was old and should be well-healed by now. He had had years to recover from Sarah Spenser's jilting. Years in which he had certainly not been celibate, nor had he worn his wounded heart on his sleeve. He had recovered long ago from that youthful heartbreak, so he could not imagine why the realization that this must be Sarah's child should have this effect.

''But everyone calls me Drew,'' the boy added, blue eyes still focused on Wynfield's face.

He was obviously a Spenser. The features were too familiar for Justin to be in any doubt about that. After all, he had grown up next door to Sarah and Amelia, and had watched them change, almost unnoticed, from children into young women.

Then, one May night, he had encountered this same alignment of features across a crowded ballroom and had known them instantly. And surprisingly, within the course of Sarah Spenser's first London Season, he had fallen head-over-heels in love with a girl he had known all his life.

A girl who had, despite all the promises they'd exchanged and the plans they had made, fallen in love with someone else less than a year after he had been posted to Spain. Sarah's letter had been quite unequivocal on that score, and there had been little he could do from the Iberian Peninsula, of course, to change her decision. Even had he been in England, Justin admitted, his pride might have prevented him from begging Sarah not to break their engagement, despite how much he had loved her.

Loved her. The words reverberated in his head. He *had* loved her, he acknowledged, as much as he was capable of loving anyone at that time. And had he not gone to Spain, he realized, this child might very well have been his son.

"I'm Wynfield," he said softly, wondering as he did if the boy had ever heard his name in connection with his mother.

"You said that," Andrew said.

"So I did. My apologies." Justin allowed the smile he had resisted earlier. Its effect was an immediate and visible relaxation of the boy's shoulders, which had been tightened as if he expected another blow.

"Did you really do all the things they say?" the child asked, his eyes alight, alive in a way they had not been throughout the encounter with the village boys.

"Since I don't have any idea what 'they say,'" Justin said, "I couldn't tell you if I did them or not."

"Killed a thousand Frenchies. Rode like the devil right over their positions. Broke the squares so Wellington could win. Is that your charger?"

Justin laughed at the barrage of words. "Soldiers' exploits are usually exaggerated in the retelling," he said. "They make better stories that way."

"But they *did* cut off your leg," the child said, his eyes locking on the high riding boot that hid the defect. "I heard Sarah and Mrs. Simkins talking."

When the silence that followed his comment stretched, child's blue eyes lifted again to Justin's. Wynfield had what his face might reveal, but he knew that those simple words had had more of an effect than they should have had.

The thought of Sarah discussing his amputation with her housekeeper was for some reason as raw and painful as the stump itself. It took a moment for the import of the rest of that statement to register. The child had referred to her as Sarah.

Could he possibly have been mistaken? Justin wondered, again studying the familiar Spenser features presented perfectly in miniature. Amelia had died shortly after he had left for the Peninsula, so...if this were *not* Sarah's child, Justin thought, studying the small face, then who the hell was he?

"Sarah?" he asked carefully.

"My *maman*." Suddenly the boy's eyes widened. "I shall be late," he said, apparently only now realizing the danger of that. "And if I am, I shall be in a great deal of trouble."

Justin remembered the number of times he had hurried home from these woods, knowing that his tutor would call him to account for every minute of his tardiness. And that his accounting would be painful in the extreme. Although Justin couldn't imagine Sarah applying the birch, the anxiety in the boy's eyes was enough to encourage him to offer another rescue.

"I can take you to the ford," he said.

He reached down, holding out his hand to the boy. There was only a moment's hesitation before the child laid small fingers within the sunburned darkness of his. Justin pulled, lifting him easily into the saddle before him.

Then he directed Star toward the narrow stream that separated the two properties. He knew exactly where the child would cross. He and Robert had chased the village boys back across that rock-strewn ford innumerable times.

From there the path diverged, one fork going to the nearby village, the other winding through the Spenser half of the woods to Longford.

Feeling the child relax as he became accustomed to the height of the gelding, Justin urged Star into a canter, picking his way through the sun-dappled shade of the huge oaks. There was something satisfying about the small, warm body he held, seated securely in the saddle before him.

Sarah's son, he thought. And was again surprised by the sense of loss that realization engendered.

Chapter Two

"And then he tapped the handle of his crop on his wooden leg," Andrew said, his excited narrative only occasionally interrupted by a gasp or a twist of his head as Sarah attempted to apply liniment to his scrapes and bruises. "Like this," he said, demonstrating the sound the earl's crop had made by rapping his fist against the trestle table over which Sarah had spread out her medicinals.

"Andrew," she admonished, feeling a faint sickness stir in the pit of her stomach, which had nothing to do with the battle scars she was treating. She was thankful his scrapes were no worse, of course, and very glad Andrew had told her the truth this time about how he'd acquired them. Although she had long suspected he was the butt of the village boys' cruelty, he had never before admitted to being their target. Today, the news of Wynfield's intervention had apparently outweighed his reticence to tell her what they had been going on.

Sarah wasn't sure if Drew were mature enough to wish to spare her the knowledge of what they said to him or if he had been afraid that she might try to interfere on his behalf and make things worse. In either case, she supposed she had reason to be grateful to Justin for more than his timely rescue.

Wynfield, she amended. She had decided that using his title rather than the name by which she had known him from childhood would help her begin to put his return into perspective. Even if she had occasion to use it only in her mind.

Come home only long enough to sell the place, Lady Fortley had surmised, and she was probably right. Why would Justin, or anyone, for that matter, wish to remain in a place where children were tormented for the sins of their elders? she thought bitterly, dabbing too vigorously with her lint at a small cut over Andrew's brow.

"Ow!" he howled, pulling away.

"Sorry," she whispered, dropping a kiss on his golden curls.

He nodded forgiveness and then trustingly submitted himself again to her ministrations. He was very accustomed to Sarah fussing over him. After all, Drew had never had a nanny. It had been Sarah's deepest joy to care for him herself, which had led, she supposed, to their unusual closeness.

"You should have seen 'em scatter," Andrew said after enduring stoically in silence for a few minutes.

When she looked up, his eyes were full of remembered satisfaction over the routing of his enemies.

"They were afraid of his battle charger," he said, "but I wasn't. I wasn't at all afraid, Sarah. He even took me up for a ride. And I asked him about the war."

"Perhaps you shouldn't have," Sarah suggested quietly. *So grievously wounded* ran through her head.

"Why ever not?" Andrew asked. In his tone was a patent disbelief that anyone might be reluctant to talk about something as fascinating as His Majesty's war against the Corsican monster.

"Because the earl may not wish to discuss it. After all, he was gravely injured, Drew. And war is not a game."

"I know that," he said scornfully.

He thought she was being condescending, Sarah realized. Treating him like a baby. Which was, in Andrew's view, her most frequently committed and most heinous sin.

"They cut off his leg, after all," he added.

"Yes, they did," she said softly, thinking about what effect that mutilation might have had on the man she had known.

"Sarah?" Andrew questioned the silence that had fallen. Or perhaps he was questioning the fact that, hands unconsciously clenched together in her lap, she had ceased to dab at his cuts.

"I think you'll live," she said, looking up into blue eyes that were now full of a very adult concern.

"Does it make you sad?" he asked. "Thinking about the war?"

"Yes," she admitted. "And it may make the earl sad as well," she warned.

"He wasn't sad," Andrew asserted. "Bam, bam, bam," he said, eyes alight as he pounded his fist reminiscently against the table. "He wasn't at all sad about the war."

Sarah's lips quirked involuntarily. Whatever effect the loss of his leg had had on Justin, it had made him larger than life in the eyes of at least one small boy he had encountered today. Probably in the eyes of the others as well, she thought, judging by Andrew's unquenchable enthusiasm for the new earl.

"Did you thank him for intervening on your behalf?"

"I don't remember," Andrew confessed, his brow wrinkling as he tried to think.

"Then you must be sure to do so the next time you see him," Sarah said, beginning to gather up her materials.

"Will he come to service on Sunday, do you think?" Andrew asked, his eyes widened with hope.

"I don't know," she said. She had been wondering that since Lady Fortley had given her the news about the earl's homecoming. During the days that had followed that announcement, however, she had tried to push the anticipation of seeing Justin again from her mind. It was well enough for Andrew to idolize him, but it was quite a different story for her to do so.

Little boys needed someone to look up to. Someone worthy of their admiration. Someone brave and masculine. Suddenly Sarah's lips tilted, her eyes still on the medicines she was restoring to their chest. It was a smile full of self-mockery as she recognized an unmistakable portrait of Justin Tolbert in the glowing list of attributes she had just devised.

Andrew *had* missed knowing someone like that. And she supposed considering the earl of Wynfield as his personal hero was harmless enough. If only half the reports she had heard about Justin's military exploits were true, Sarah acknowledged, then Andrew's heroic image of Wynfield was highly accurate.

And after all, Andrew would probably not encounter their neighbor again during the short time he would spend in the district. Neither would she, of course. Which was just as well for her peace of mind.

Despite Andrew's hopes, the earl was not in church the following Sunday. The little boy's spirits had been momentarily crushed by the sight of the still-empty Wynfield pew. Although Sarah had had more practice at concealing disappointment, hers was just as powerful, she admitted, if not so open as Andrew's.

The following Monday morning, in an attempt to escape the pall of that disappointment, which had seemed to hang over her spirits all the rest of that quiet Sabbath, she determinedly undertook to complete all her accumulated errands. It was ironic that one of those would result in the very encounter she had told herself she was a fool to hope for.

She had set out very early on her rounds, starting with her father's aged or ailing tenants and ending up midmorning with a visit on the Wynfield estate. The Randolphs, one of the earl's crofter families, had been blessed with a new baby. Since it was their thirteenth child in less than ten years, Sarah wasn't sure how much of a blessing they considered the infant's arrival.

She had brought a beef roast, a large cheese, and two loaves of bread from this morning's baking for the new mother. She would leave it up to Meg Randolph to decide if the gifts were congratulatory or condoling.

As she drove her pony trap up to the front door, the sound of hammering coming from inside the cottage disturbed the country stillness far more than the squeals of the numerous Randolph children, most of whom seemed to be playing in the yard.

Sarah was naturally curious about that unmistakable noise of industry, since she had never known Jed Randolph to drive a nail in all the years he'd lived here. Of course, since the cottage seemed in danger of tumbling in on itself during the next stiff wind, perhaps Jed had decided that if he didn't make some repairs, no one else would. Or maybe he had been afraid that the new earl would turn him out for the shiftless lout he was.

As Sarah stepped over the threshold, invited shyly inside by the eldest daughter, her eyes rose to consider the repairs the shiftless Jed had finally undertaken. The hammerer, however, wasn't Randolph, she realized, her breathing suspended. Nor was he any of the neighbors, although the man who was pounding long nails into a brace affixed to a broken rafter overhead was as simply dressed as any one of them might have been.

His shirt had been turned back at the cuffs, revealing supple wrists, muscular forearms and finely shaped, sunbrowned hands. The garment itself, despite how casually it was worn, was made of linen and excellently cut. And, although he was wearing trousers rather than a gentleman's pantaloons, they, too, were undeniably elegant, slim enough to delineate strong horseman's thighs and narrow hips. They were worn over highly polished and obviously expensive, if worn, boots.

Definitely not a tenant, Sarah acknowledged, feeling her heart begin to race exactly as it had when Lady Fortley had given her warning of this on Sunday last. *Wynfield's home.*

"Lady Sarah!" Meg Randolph said, her voice full of genuine pleasure. She had stuck her head through the open doorway of the cottage's only bedroom. "You be *most* welcome, my lady," she added, her eyes taking in the basket over Sarah's arm.

At the sound of her name, Sarah glanced from that enticing view of the hammerer's back to her hostess's face. She smiled a greeting. Then, refusing to be denied, either by common sense or gentility, her eyes returned to the sight they had been feasting on. The earl of Wynfield, however, had already turned to face the doorway in which she was standing.

She could see him much better than he would be able to see her, she realized. The sunlight, coming from behind her, would make her little more than a silhouette. Fingering in through the open door, however, it served to illuminate his features clearly enough for her to realize how much Justin Tolbert had changed.

He was five years older, of course, but the maturity that had been etched into that handsome face went far beyond that span. His features were as darkly tanned as his hands, although it must have been some weeks since he had left the strong Iberian sun that had wrought that change. It had also lightened the chestnut hair, which, she noted in surprise, was already beginning to gray at the temples.

The small white lines that radiated from the corners of his eyes were new as well. Even the eyes themselves were changed, Sarah thought. Not in color, of course, but... Perhaps in what they had seen? she wondered. Or in what he had endured.

It had always been a very attractive face, charmingly boyish if a little unformed. There was nothing left there now of the boy she had known. The angles of the bones that underlay the weather-beaten skin were almost too harshly defined, the planes hardened by experience and deprivation. Whatever had happened to Justin Tolbert during the last five years, it had returned him home a man. Without any doubt, a man.

"Sarah?" he said, his eyes as questioning as his voice.

"Welcome home," she said simply.

To her own ears, the phrase sounded breathless, thready with emotion. The hazel eyes did not change, apparently finding nothing extraordinary about the commonplace she'd offered.

"Thank you," he said.

The corners of his mouth edged upward into an approximation of his once-familiar smile. And her rebellious heart, against all her strictures about how it should behave, turned over and then rose to crowd her throat.

"Time enough, I should think," he added, his smile widening.

"Time enough?" She floundered, wondering if he could possibly realize the effect he was having on her.

He turned, however, gesturing toward his handiwork. The brace he had added had not forced the beam totally straight, but the roof would have had to be lifted off and the cracked, sagging rafter replaced for that to be accomplished. So he had done the next best thing. At least the thatch wouldn't come tumbling in on the family with the next wind, and the rain and snow would be kept out through another winter.

"It's a start," he said, his eyes coming back to hers.

In his voice was an unmistakable pride in that simple accomplishment. Sarah wondered how many British earls personally repaired their tenants' cottages, and then decided that, whatever the number, it was probably not nearly as many as it should be.

"And all I can afford," Justin added, the white fan of lines around the corners of his eyes disappearing as he smiled again, openly mocking his predicament. "As I'm sure you've heard."

She wasn't certain how to respond to his honesty. He would know she was lying if she denied knowledge of the condition of his estate. She was, however, the last person in the world to condone gossip. She had endured more than enough about herself to consider listening to it a harmless pastime.

"I'm so sorry about Robert," she said, instead of commenting on his financial predicament. "I know how close you two were."

He nodded, his mouth tight. "Thank you," he said softly.

And then there seemed to be nothing else to say. In the suddenly awkward silence, Sarah heard for the first time the cries of the newborn she had come to visit.

"Have you seen the baby?" she asked. The Randolphs' new arrival should be a safe topic, even between the two of them.

"She doesn't care much for the hammering," he said, smiling.

"I can imagine she might not," Sarah agreed, returning the smile.

The encounter, after that first heart-stopping moment, was becoming far less difficult than she had feared. And less…less whatever else she had hoped for as well, she acknowledged. What had once been between the new earl of Wynfield and Lady Sarah Spenser was, at least as far as he was concerned, obviously over and done with. Justin might have been chatting with any member of the local gentry.

"How's your father?" he asked.

She wondered if he knew the truth of her father's condition and then decided that if he had, he would never have been unkind enough to ask that question. Almost no one inquired about the marquess of Brynmoor nowadays. Which meant that Wynfield hadn't yet encountered someone like Lady Fortley and been treated to the district's version of the Spenser family's recent history.

"He's very well," she said. That was the truth, of course. The disease that afflicted her father had not affected his health. Or his strength. *More's the pity*, she thought.

Meg Randolph bustled into the room at that moment, new babe in arms. Like all the Randolph offspring, this one was apparently topped by a fuzz of orange-red hair, which was peeking out under its white cap. She would soon acquire the matching freckles that adorned the others of Meg's brood. Right now, however, the baby's skin was pink and white, as delicate as porcelain. Without asking permission, Meg exchanged the baby, its cheeks still tear-stained, for the basket Sarah had brought.

"We do thank you, my lady," she said. "Lord knows we can use this." Realizing belatedly that her comment might imply criticism of the earl, Meg shot a quick glance in his direction, searching for some sign that she'd given offense. Apparently he had taken none, Sarah realized, also looking up from the baby.

Wynfield was smiling, long-lashed hazel eyes focused benignly on the baby she held. Her own gaze fell again, considering the endearingly blank face.

"A fine baby, Mrs. Randolph," the earl complimented. "But I don't believe she's had her christening gift."

Justin slipped his hand into the pocket of his trousers, flattening it to fit, and brought out a handful of small coins. Their total would amount to less than a guinea, Sarah guessed, but still, it was a nice gesture, and would make the approaching winter easier for his tenants.

Meg set Sarah's basket on the table and retrieved her daughter. "I could mention that ain't none of the rest of them had a christening gift from the Wynfields either," she whispered to Sarah, "but gift horses and all that."

She carried the baby across the room and held her out to the earl. Perhaps she had only intended to offer her daughter for his inspection, but if so, Wynfield misunderstood the gesture. He put the handful of coins on the narrow shelf above the fireplace and reached for the baby as he had seen Sarah do. Surprised, Meg made the exchange much more awkwardly than she had with Sarah. The baby began to cry as soon as the earl's hands replaced her mother's vastly more experienced ones.

"Don't you be offending your betters, lass," Meg said, patting her daughter's shoulder as she smiled at Justin. She guided the earl's left hand into place behind the baby's head.

He held the infant slightly away from him, her small bottom resting securely in the palm of his big right hand, his long tanned fingers spread behind her back. In that position he could look down into her face as he gently jiggled her up and down. Surprisingly, the baby's sobs lessened and then stopped altogether, replaced by the occasional hiccuping breath.

"She knows a handsome face when she sees one," Meg said.

"Maybe she's grateful the roof is fixed," Sarah suggested softly. She could no more have pulled her gaze away from the sight of Wynfield cradling that baby than she could have given Andrew to a passing Gypsy.

"Well, *I'm* grateful," Meg said. "And that's the truth, my lord. Jed's not very handy about the house."

"Neither am I," Justin admitted, smiling at her. "But I think this will hold through the winter. And as soon as I'm able, Mrs. Randolph…" He paused, his eyes making a survey of the dilapidated cottage.

"I know," Meg said softly. "We all know you'll be doing your best, my lord."

There was another awkward silence, which the earl broke by moving his right palm gingerly under the baby's bottom.

"I believe she's damp," he said, looking to Meg for rescue.

"I shouldn't be surprised," Meg said, laughing. "'Tis a frequent enough occurrence at her age, I assure you."

She reached for the baby, but just before she took her from the earl, she leaned forward and placed a kiss on the fingers of the sun-browned hand that was supporting the baby's head.

"You're a good man, my lord," she said softly.

Despite her attempt at a sotto voce delivery, Meg's words carried across the room, making Sarah wonder if Justin had heard her remark about the lack of any previous christening gifts from the Wynfields. But of course, if there were criticism in that statement, it had not been directed to the current earl. *Sins of the father,* Sarah thought, watching a quick rush of color sweep up Justin's lean cheeks.

"The Wheelers' well is fouled," he said, instead of answering Meg's compliment. "I've promised to see if I can discover why. You be sure to send me word," he said to Meg, "the next time something goes wrong here."

"We'll be fine now, my lord. I wouldn't have sent this time, but the last blowing rain we had wet the youngest ones' pallets. And I knew that, come fall..." Meg shrugged.

"You did exactly as you should have done," the earl said. "I'm only sorry you've had to wait so long for these repairs."

"Ah, well," Meg said, shrugging again. "You was away doing your duty for king and country. Things'll be very different, we all know that, my lord, now *you're* back." Again the silence was prolonged and a little uncomfortable.

"I'll walk you out," Sarah suggested, deliberately breaking it. She suspected that fouled well or not, Justin would be more than eager to escape babies and gratitude and any discussion about his plans for making changes on the bankrupt estate. Then she realized, belatedly, that he might be even more eager to escape her escort than any of those.

There was no way to rescind her invitation. So she waited for his response, her eyes held resolutely on his face. Whatever she had expected—or dreaded, perhaps—didn't come to pass.

Justin smiled again at Meg and then limped across the room toward the outer door. His gait was uneven, throwing his tall, straight body subtly out of alignment. It seemed painfully, even terribly awkward to Sarah, especially when compared to the grace of motion she had always associated with him.

Suddenly, too vividly, Sarah remembered the night he had first asked her to dance. The London ballroom had been overcrowded, its heat stifling. Justin had been wearing his uniform, the handsome regimentals setting off the perfection of his strong body and his still-boyish face. She had thought then that there was no man more handsome in the room. She had stepped willingly into his arms, and when the music began, she had drifted, following his lead. Their steps had melded perfectly, mindlessly. They had moved together without conscious thought. As if the two of them had been created to dance together…

And they would never do that again, she realized. Her eyes lifted, but she was forced to blink to clear the unexpected blur of tears. And when she had, she found that Justin was waiting for her beside the door, his eyes on her face, which was now as clearly illuminated as his had been when she was standing in that same position.

Then he turned toward the threshold, indicating with his hand that she should precede him. His profile was illuminated by the sunlight. She could see that his expression, which only a moment before had been filled with pleasure as he looked down into the wide, unfocused gaze of Meg Randolph's baby, was hard and set. A small muscle twitched beside his compressed lips.

Embarrassed by her tears, Sarah crossed the room, head down, and stepped outside, grateful for that small respite from those remarkable hazel eyes that saw far too much. She didn't slow until she reached the pony trap, forced to wait on Justin to hand her up and give her the reins. When he had, his long brown fingers perfectly steady under the trembling pressure of hers, she looked down on his face.

"I wanted to thank you for rescuing Andrew last week. I've suspected for some time that he was being bullied by the older boys, but he would never tell me the truth."

"He was giving almost as good as he got. He wasn't crying uncle," Justin said, smiling up at her.

Whatever she had read in his face a moment ago, when he had seen her so foolishly react to his injury, had now been cleared away, she realized. She had not been intended to see it, of course. That she had was something Justin would ignore, thereby demanding that she ignore it as well.

"I almost wish he would," Sarah said.

"Bullies delight in cowering victims, Sarah. Andrew had the right idea. Just the wrong technique," he said. "And a decided lack of size. Even that will probably come in time," he added.

There was another silence. Perhaps he was waiting for some comment about Andrew's father and what might be expected for the little boy's growth in the future. And she could make none.

"In any case," she said instead, "I'm very grateful for what you did. So is Andrew."

"I would have done the same for any child. I simply reacted to the one-sided nature of the chase."

"You didn't know..." She hesitated. Despite the fact that the district had long ago decided on the truth of Andrew's parentage, there seemed to be no way to ask that question.

"That he was yours?" he finished for her. "Not until I got a good look at his face. There wasn't much doubt after that." His smile was as natural as the one he had given Meg Randolph. And as impersonal.

"No," she said softly. "I don't suppose there was."

She held his eyes a moment longer, reading nothing more than an old friendship within them. Then she slapped the reins on the pony's broad rump and left the new earl of Wynfield standing alone in the lane.

"She's a good woman," Meg Randolph said to him as he retrieved the hammer he had brought out from the Park. "I don't care what anyone says."

Justin turned, looking down into that broad freckled face. "What anyone *says?*" he repeated, his tone quizzical.

Meg's eyes widened, and then she closed her lips, almost as if she intended to deny them the chance to let any other unfortunate words escape.

"Someone has been saying something about Lady Sarah?" he prodded, still holding her eyes.

"I didn't mean nothing by that, my lord. I swear I didn't."

Justin considered those words as carefully as he had the first ones, thinking about them in context with the rest. His eyes remained locked on Meg's. As he watched, a flush crept under her cheeks, making her face even ruddier than normal.

He knew there could be nothing more unseemly than to listen to his tenants' gossip, especially since he was so new to his position. However, the fact that, whatever this was, dealt with Sarah meant he couldn't let it alone. Seeing her today had aroused more memories, and more emotions, than he would want to admit, even to himself. And it had been their meeting, and their shared past, that had undoubtedly provoked Meg's comment.

"You must have meant something, Meg. I don't think you can say something like that and then just leave it."

"I'm sorry, my lord. I know that you and she…" Meg paused, apparently thinking better of pursuing that line as well. When she took a breath, fueling her halting explanation, her next sentence was not about his and Sarah's broken engagement.

"I didn't mean nothing bad about her, I swear," Meg said. "And it don't matter to me what the rest of them say. She's a good woman. She's had more to bear than most of us, and that's the God's truth. So…I don't want you to think I'm judging her, my lord, even if there's some around here who are more than willing to do that."

The red stain under her skin had deepened, and her lips were flattened again, her eyes determined, if wary. Justin knew he couldn't question her any further. If he did, he'd be no better than those gossipmongers Meg had referred to.

That didn't mean, however, that he didn't intend to get to the bottom of whatever she was talking about. Despite the fact Sarah's letter had made it very clear four years ago that she wanted nothing further to do with him, Justin found that he couldn't dismiss from his mind the strange notion that she needed his defense. Or his protection. Maybe Meg's phrase had been responsible for that feeling.

She's had more to bear than most of us. Justin had no idea what that comment referred to, but he intended to find out. He wouldn't do it, however, by questioning Meg Randolph. "You send word to the Park if you need anything else, Meg," he said.

"I will, my lord. And you forget what I said. My mouth runs away with me sometimes. Lady Sarah..." Again, Meg hesitated. "Whatever happened, a woman can understand it better than anyone, I guess. A woman that's part-ways human, at least."

Sarah didn't understand all the emotions that were cutting up her peace that night. Although she hadn't varied her day's routine in any way after her meeting with the new earl, in the back of her mind had lurked an unaccustomed dissatisfaction. A sense of deep unhappiness with her life that she hadn't openly acknowledged in years. *Because,* she thought, laying her needlework in her lap, *what would be the point of admitting it?*

Andrew had already had his supper and been put to bed. Even her father was sleeping. Or at least his manservant hadn't made an appearance, asking for her help in quieting the marquess. This was normally her favorite time of day, when the work was done and the whole house was silent and peaceful.

And Sarah could not quite decide why, suddenly, she herself was so...*unpeaceful.* So dissatisfied with her situation, she thought again. Which was futile, of course.

She picked up her sewing, determined to find gratification with the progress of the fire screen she was working. The pale, muted colors of the silks were still pleasing. This had been her own design, painstakingly created with her watercolors and then transferred to the canvas, but somehow tonight...

Disgusted with herself, she gave up, laying the piece on the table beside her chair. She stood, stretching out her back like a cat. Her eyes were drawn to the reflection of that movement in the mirror over the mantel. She walked across to it and looked at the woman in the glass. Only then did she realize how long it had been since she had really studied her own reflection.

There was nothing reassuring about doing so now. If she had found Justin changed by the long years that had intervened between their broken engagement and today, the same might very well be said for her. Her face was too thin, she acknowledged, touching her high cheekbones with the fingers of both hands. She looked tired. And there were faint lines across her forehead that she had never before noticed, she realized.

Those were almost certainly the result of frowning perplexedly as she tried to figure out what she should do next. She had had a lot of experience worrying about that since her father had grown increasingly unable to see to his own affairs. More and more of the responsibility for them, and for looking after his properties, had fallen onto her shoulders. Now the weight of that responsibility was evident in her face.

And my hair, she thought in dismay, putting up her hand to touch a curling tendril that had escaped the tight knot into which she had secured it. Dressing her hair this way was, of course, eminently suitable for her life in the country. Far more practical than soft curls clustered around her face, she told herself, although she knew that was the latest style. That was the way the Simonson girls had come back from London wearing their hair, after their Season.

This was far more practical, she told herself again, tucking in the wayward strand. But not nearly so becoming, she admitted. The style had even softened the Simonson sisters' long faces. As it would her thin one. She had thought when she saw those curls that she would like to try the effect.

And of course, neither Simonson sister had hair the color of sun-ripened wheat. That was the never-forgotten phrase Justin had used, more than five years ago, to describe hers. Now, with it pulled so tightly away from her face, its color seemed dull. Not nearly so vivid as the image those words had conveyed.

Dull, she thought, watching her lips compress into a line. *Dull and colorless.* She pinched both cheeks, giving them a series of sharp nips with her fingers, designed to induce some rose into them. That was a trick she had learned from her Aunt Fanny the year she had introduced Sarah to the London ton. The year she and Justin had fallen in love.

In love, she thought. Fallen in love. Whatever that meant. Thinking about her long-ago Season, she stared unseeingly into the mirror as the splotches of color along her cheekbones slowly faded, returning her face to the same paleness she had despised.

What it meant to be in love, she told herself fiercely, fighting again the unaccustomed burn of tears, was that she had cared for a man too much to allow him to be tarred with the same scandal that had blackened her name and made her an outcast from her own society. A scandal that had not been of her making, but one for which she could offer no defense. Not without destroying her dead sister's reputation and breaking the promise she had made to Amelia on her deathbed. So Justin Tolbert had been lost to her forever.

Soon someone in the district would be cruel enough to repeat to him the explanation for Andrew's birth they had long ago decided on. And then there would no longer be *anything* offered her in those beautiful hazel eyes. Not even friendship.

"I thought that we might open the house," the earl of Wynfield said to his butler at dinner that night. "I believe my mother had some kind of simple entertainment for the neighbors here at the end of every summer."

"Indeed she did, my lord," Blevins agreed, placing a bowl of soup before the new earl.

"I would wish the grounds to be in better shape, but people have been understanding. At least those to whom the estate owes no money have been," Justin added.

Blevins's face was carefully expressionless, as befitted his position. Justin's lips tilted, however. The spoonful of soup he lifted to his mouth hid that amusement.

The enormous debts, which everyone in the district knew about, of course, had seldom been mentioned publicly—at least not to him. It was almost as if they were a secret scandal. *A scandal,* he thought, remembering again the real purpose for which he had introduced this topic.

"I suppose there is a guest list of my mother's about somewhere," he said. "A list of those whom she always invited. Chattington and his wife, of course. Lord and Lady Fortley, I'm afraid. Brynmoor. And we must add Lady Sarah and whomever she married." Sarah, the daughter of a marquess, would have retained her own title, of course, no matter whom she had married.

Had Justin not been watching Blevins's face, he might have missed the reaction. The butler's lids flickered, the eyes themselves rising very quickly to Justin's face, and then falling again, just as rapidly.

"I'm not sure I've ever even heard the man's name,"

the earl prodded softly, openly watching the old man this time.

When the butler's eyes lifted again, there was no attempt to hide what was in them. They met Justin's and held a few seconds before he said, "Lady Sarah Spenser is unmarried, my lord."

His eyes fell again, and without any trace of haste in his studied movements, he replaced the lid on the tureen with a palsied hand and stepped back from the table.

"Widowed?" Justin asked, but he had already seen the answer in Blevins's face.

"No, my lord," the butler said, his tone without inflection. "Not widowed. Lady Sarah has, to my certain knowledge, never been married."

It was not until Justin was alone in his chamber that night that he allowed himself to consider what he had learned. By that time he had remembered the contempt with which the leader of the small gang of bullies had spat at the child called Andrew. And remembered the epithet he had used.

Little bastard. Justin had assumed at the time that the word had been chosen to indicate a verbal contempt to match the gesture, but it had, apparently, been a literal indictment.

Yet he could not understand how that could be. Gently reared young women of their class did not bear children out of wedlock. Knowing the hot-tempered marquess as he did, Justin felt the possibility that Brynmoor's daughter had given birth to a bastard was almost unimaginable. Whatever man had been responsible for seducing one of his daughters would have been forced to marry her as soon as that pregnancy was discovered.

There had always been well-born children who arrived

too quickly after their parents' hastily arranged marriages. But those marriages *had* taken place, and prior to the birth itself. And given the cloak of privacy that surrounded pregnancy and confinement, no one could be totally certain of the particulars of a birth, at least not until they were announced. There could be little doubt that such announcements were often delayed until the proper time.

But if he were not Sarah's son, then who the hell was the child who called her *Maman*, Justin wondered. A little boy whose face perfectly mirrored one that had been so beloved? A face Justin had once known better than his own, because it had been so often in his mind's eye. The face of the woman who had once been his betrothed.

And who had apparently, only a few short months after she had thrown him over, borne another man's child out of wedlock. *Little bastard* echoed again, along with Meg Randolph's far kinder words. *It don't matter to me what the rest of them say. She's a good woman. She's had more to bear than most of us, and that's the Lord's truth.*

Whatever the truth, Justin thought, easing the leather harness of his artificial foot off his aching leg, it was not his business. He had more than enough troubles of his own, without borrowing those of a woman who, more than four years ago, had made it extremely clear exactly how she felt about him.

Chapter Three

After that meeting at the Randolphs, Sarah saw the earl of Wynfield a number of times during the next few weeks. She was never again close enough to speak to him. Or to have him speak to her. Which was just as well, she had told herself resolutely.

Once he had been standing in the middle of the village green talking to Lord Fortley. He had been dressed that day in a manner befitting his station, and consequently, he had looked more like the Justin she remembered. He had not glanced up as she had been driven by in her father's closed carriage.

Sarah, however, had been unable to tear her eyes away, craning her neck in an attempt to prolong as long as possible that brief glimpse. And when she could no longer see him, she was beset by the same sense of loss and dissatisfaction that had haunted her after their previous meeting.

To make things even worse, everywhere she went there was talk of the new earl. Talk about what he intended to do to save the estate. About what he was trying to do for his tenants. It seemed that the Randolphs' cottage was not the only one to receive Wynfield's personal attention. He had told her that was all he could afford to give them—the labor of his own hands. Despite the high regard that his willingness to work to improve his tenants' lot was earning him in the district, it was surely, they all knew, too little and far too late.

That was something else that was being discussed everywhere—exactly how desperate Wynfield's plight really was. It was said he had tried to raise additional credit within the financial community. With the recession, however, there was little money to be had. And none of it would be made available to bail out an estate so deeply mired in mortgages and neglect that its future appeared hopeless.

It was also rumored that the earl's creditors were closing in, demanding payment of some kind for the long-standing debts. It was said, however, there was little left worth selling. His father and brother had seen to that, so it was only a matter of time until the lands that had belonged to the Wynfield family for more than two centuries would belong to someone else. Some outsider, the gossipers opined. Perhaps even one of the wealthy merchants the war had created.

It was hard to think of Wynfield Park falling into the hands of someone who did not belong to the family. Or even to the district, Sarah thought. And given the current tendency to enclosure, it was harder to think of what might happen to the homes of the earl's tenants if that dire forecast came to pass.

Like everyone else, however, she could see no way out for Justin. Apparently having served his country long and valiantly had no monetary value at all, not even enough to hold the creditors at bay for a decent interval after his brother's death.

Sarah would have liked to believe her anger over that

injustice had spawned the idea that grew in her head so quickly, once introduced, that it dominated almost her every waking moment. She knew, however, there was more to the recurrent thought than moral indignation. Especially when she heard the other whispers emanating from the ranks of the local gentry. There were heiresses aplenty in London, they said. Heiresses who were rich enough to save the Wynfield lands for the earl and who would be only too glad of the opportunity.

"Not of his class, you understand," Lady Fortley had said, one brow arched suggestively. Everyone understood that no member of the peerage would allow his daughter to wed a man in such desperate straits, at least none who had any hopes at all of arranging a decent marriage. Wynfield's only hope at this stage of the game, Lady Fortley had suggested, was to be found among the cits. They would be only too eager to align themselves with a nobleman, even a crippled and penniless one.

At those cruel words, Sarah had had to fight to maintain her composure, but she managed to sweep down the steps of the church without uttering a word in response to that outrageous suggestion. It was not until she was seated in the carriage, only half listening to Andrew's chatter, that she realized what Lady Fortley had said was not so outrageous, after all.

"Sarah," Andrew said plaintively, tugging on her elbow.

She focused her eyes obediently on his face, still mentally picturing Justin in the clutches of some social-climbing nouveau riche heiress who would make his life a complete misery.

"Is he *never* coming to church?" Andrew asked.

She didn't need to question whom he meant. Just as she was, Andrew seemed obsessed with the new earl. She would sometimes hear him at play, giving commands and strutting about the nursery in imitation of the kind of soldier he imagined his hero to be.

And, without permission, Drew had more than once cut through the woods to pay a visit at the Park. Sarah had sternly forbidden him to attempt to see the earl again in that manner. Thankfully, Wynfield had not been at home during any of Andrew's excursions. In his endless quest to find the means to save his inheritance, he was probably seldom at the estate, she realized.

"Perhaps not," she said.

"Then someone should tell him he shall go to hell," Andrew suggested with more than a hint of self-righteousness.

In spite of the seriousness of the little boy's expression, Sarah laughed. She wasn't completely sure of the purity of Andrew's motives in trying to save Wynfield from perdition.

Just as she could no longer be sure of her own, she admitted. She hadn't been, not since the moment the idea had first slipped into her consciousness.

"I don't think that should be you, however," Sarah said.

"I want to see him again. I have some things I wish to ask him," the child said, disappointment in his voice. "I thought I should see him often, since he is our neighbor, but..."

Sarah had wondered if Justin were deliberately avoiding them. If so, she believed she knew why. Andrew could thank the Lady Fortleys of the world for that maliciousness.

"I know," she said softly. "I'm sure you will see him soon," she said, catching the quivering chin with her thumb and her forefinger, and smiling determinedly at the little boy. "He would not like you to cry," she said softly.

"Soldiers don't cry," Andrew said, blinking hard.

"No, I don't suppose they do," Sarah agreed. "At least not where anyone else could see."

"He would never cry," Andrew vowed with conviction.

Andrew was right about that, Sarah thought. But given the situation Justin Tolbert faced, he might very well want to.

"Is this everything?" the earl of Wynfield asked, touching the stack of documents on the desk before him.

"All that have thus far been presented," Drayton Langley said. "There may be other creditors who have not yet learned of your brother's death. It is entirely possible that bills may be brought forward as much as six months from now, but we believe this to be the bulk of them. And when added to your father's debts..." He shrugged. "I did try to warn them, my lord."

"I'm sure you did," Wynfield said, running his thumb across the edge of the thick stack of notes Robert had signed. "And the estate is able to discharge what percentage of the combined total of these and my father's debts, Mr. Langley?"

"I would say...less than sixty percent, my lord."

"Bloody hell," Justin said softly.

"That is," the banker continued emotionlessly, "*if* you sell everything that is left. Horses, carriages, the plate, portraits and furnishings. The home farm and attachments. The Park and the land itself. And of course, all that is predicated on your being able to find a buyer, or buyers, for any of it. I'm afraid nothing will bring what it's worth, due both to the present economy and the rather advanced state of disrepair.''

''But that is what you advise? That I should sell it all?''

The banker lifted both hands, turning them slightly upward before they settled again on his ample belly. His eyes, almost sympathetic, rested on the earl's face.

Wynfield took a deep breath, thinking about what that would mean. He would still be deeply in debt, honorable debts that his family had legally incurred. And he would have nothing left, not even a roof over his head.

''If I may be so bold, my lord...'' Langley said.

Justin looked up, surprising a gleam of speculation in the cold, dark eyes. ''You know far too much about my business to stand on ceremony now, Langley. If you have any further advice, I should be very glad to hear it.''

The man's thick lips pursed, almost as if he were reluctant to speak. Justin wondered what news he thought might be worse than what he had already conveyed.

''There has been an offer,'' he said softly.

''An offer,'' Justin repeated, carefully controlling his voice despite the sickness knotting his stomach. He had come to this interview today expecting the worst. And that's exactly what he had gotten. So whatever this offer was, he knew he must consider it. ''To buy the properties?''

''No, my lord,'' Langley said.

''Then...what kind of offer?''

Again the banker hesitated, his eyes considering Justin's face. ''An offer of marriage, my lord.''

Justin examined the word, trying to understand exactly what had just been suggested. Gentlemen made offers of marriage. They did not receive them. ''Marriage?'' he repeated carefully.

And then, suddenly, he realized what the banker meant.

After all, Lord Fortley had already suggested this option to him. Find himself a rich heiress with a squint or an unfortunate propensity to spots or obesity, and marry her as quickly as possible. Marriage as a business deal. Which, even within the ton itself, was not uncommon.

Of course, given his situation, it would take more than a squint to lure a woman into such an arrangement, he thought. Apparently, from what Langley had just suggested, however, someone was willing to marry him simply for his title. Which would be all he would have left after he made an honorable attempt to pay his debts.

Accepting such an offer might be a solution. It was not, however, the way he had ever envisioned his marriage. The memory of how Sarah had looked on the summer night he had proposed to her was suddenly in his head. That long-ago evening seemed like a dream—distant and romantic. And impossible. But then, too much of what he had once anticipated about his future was turning out to be impossible. And very different from his expectations.

"It's a generous offer, my lord," Langley added. "One that includes the settlement of all your obligations."

"An offer to pay off my debts," Justin said bluntly.

Langley inclined his head, his fingers interlocked over his stomach and his hooded eyes considering Justin's face. "It is an honorable course," he said.

"Honorable for whom?" the earl asked bitterly.

"Both parties benefit from such an arrangement," Langley suggested. "It happens more frequently than people would guess."

"A bought title," Justin said.

"A bought husband in this case, I believe," Langley said.

Justin's eyes widened slightly in surprise. "Bought husband..." He hesitated, thinking about that wording.

"I don't believe this party is interested in your title, my lord. As old and respected as it may be."

Justin considered his man's face, knowing there was something here he wasn't being told. Something that Langley obviously believed might make a difference in his acceptance or refusal of this offer. And since Justin's acceptance would be in the bank's best interest... "Who?" Justin asked bluntly.

Again the banker's mouth pursed, and when he opened it to speak, the words that came out were the last the earl of Wynfield expected to hear. "Lady Sarah Spenser, my lord. The marquess of Brynmoor's only daughter. *And* his heir."

Proud, stupid ass, the earl of Wynfield repeated over and over again as the carriage wheels ate the distance that separated him from the estate he was about to lose forever, along with the long and honorable heritage of his family.

Whistled away on the wind by his father's and his brother's mismanagement. And by his own stupid pride. Because a woman he had once loved had chosen to love another. Someone who had been so unworthy of her gift that he had left her to bear a bastard child out of wedlock. And so Justin, in his arrogance, had chosen to hold on to his anger and bitterness against Sarah for her betrayal rather than to accept this offer, a solution to all his problems.

His refusal had not been made, he told himself, because she had borne an illegitimate child. No one of their world would blame him if it had been, but what had cut him to the heart four years ago—and still did, despite the fact that he was no longer twenty-seven years old and madly in love—was that Sarah had rejected him. And for some-one who obviously hadn't loved her.

Now he, who had always claimed that he had truly loved her, could reject *her* offer of marriage and have his long-delayed revenge. That was one of the uncomfortable prods his conscience had used to goad him since he'd left Langley's office. The other was that he had just thrown away whatever chance he might have had to redeem his inheritance. And to save it for his own sons.

His sons, he thought, remembering for some reason the wide unseeing eyes of the Randolph baby. And those of Sarah's little boy. His sons would probably never have been born, he told himself, no matter which choice he made. Because what Sarah had suggested was a marriage of convenience. Langley had been very clear on that point. This was no love match. Had Justin accepted her offer, the marriage would be strictly a business arrange-ment, of mutual benefit to them both.

"The marquess of Brynmoor is no longer able to see to his own affairs," Langley had said.

And with those words, Justin had remembered what he had seen in Sarah's face when he'd asked after her fa-ther's health.

"So the responsibility of those affairs has fallen on his daughter's shoulders, and despite quite good professional advice, she feels that Byrnmoor's interests are not being as well managed as he would wish. Or as she wishes. Since your two estates join, and since she is well able to offer the financial help you need..." The banker had paused, raising his brows in question.

Justin had listened to the rest, of course. A matter of courtesy toward both Sarah and his man of business, but there had been no question in his mind from the first moment what his answer would be. *Proud, stupid ass,* he thought again.

He knew, however, that he would not be able to live in the same house with Sarah Spenser and the son she had borne to another man. And that had been one of the few demands she had made in exchange for paying off his debts—that they all live together at Longford. That was something he could never do.

And in spite of his attempts to fathom her reasons for that requirement, Justin still didn't understand it. Perhaps she had made it merely for the sake of appearances. To make it seem to everyone that theirs was a normal marriage. *Her* pride, perhaps. However few Sarah's requirements for her monetary rescue of him had been, that was one he knew he could never carry out.

Sarah's child, he thought. He remembered the eagerness with which the little boy had responded to his casual attention. And he remembered the excited glow in the dark blue eyes, so much like Sarah's own, when Justin had held out his hand and offered to convey him back to his grandfather's property.

He had always liked Brynmoor, Justin admitted. More importantly, perhaps, the marquess had liked him, maybe because he hadn't fully understood the precarious financial condition of Justin's family. The marquess had readily given his permission for Justin and Sarah to wed, but apparently he had been unable to prevent his daughter's subsequent indiscretion.

Indiscretion, Justin mused bitterly. A charming euphemism for betrayal. For an illicit sexual liaison that he would never have dreamed Sarah might be capable of.

He remembered Meg Randolph's words about judging others. Which was exactly what he was doing, he realized. Judging Sarah. He couldn't know what had happened four years ago to drive her to that unbelievable act. Her father's growing madness. Her sister's death. His own departure for the Peninsula.

She's had more to bear than most of us, Meg had said. That was true, of course, but was it enough to earn his forgiveness? Not, he acknowledged bitterly, that Sarah had ever asked for that. Instead, she had made him an offer. A business deal that would benefit both of them.

He looked out on the dusk-shrouded countryside and realized he would soon be home. While his thoughts had circled, the matched team had been rocketing along. At least his father and brother had known good horseflesh. A pity they hadn't bought enough of it to make a dent in paying off the debts accrued in their other, less successful ventures.

Through the carriage window, the beloved fields and forests stretched like a panorama, unfolding before his eyes as the coach turned off the public thoroughfare and onto the private road that led to the estate. He knew every inch of this land, as he knew every corner of the old house. He and Robert had played in every nook and cranny from the attics to the vast underground passages. His home. His land. Which, unless he could come up with some viable solution to the problem he had been tirelessly working on since he'd been invalided out of service, he had just thrown away.

Proud, stupid ass, he thought again. This time it was Sarah's face that intruded in his mind's eye, blocking the sight of his estate. And Justin literally saw nothing else until the coachman drew up before the door of Wynfield Park.

"Refused," Sarah repeated faintly.

She sank down onto the chair behind the desk in the

estate office, her hands fastening too tightly over the carved wooden arms. Her eyes had never left Mr. Samuels's face.

She thought she had been braced for Justin's answer, but for some ridiculous reason, she had never expected a refusal. She had imagined many reactions from him, everything from gratitude to anger to a grudging acceptance. What she hadn't been prepared for was an outright rejection of the financial reprieve this marriage would provide him.

"The earl wishes me to express his gratitude, but I regret to inform you that...he is unable to accept your kind offer."

"I see," Sarah said, trying to gather the tattered shreds of her pride. "What will he do?" she asked, because, despite everything, she really wanted to know.

"Sell it all, I imagine. Pay off what he can and then live on the Continent, perhaps. There are many places where one may live more cheaply than in England."

She nodded, her disappointment so strong she could scarcely formulate the pleasantries needed to carry her through this painful interview.

"Was there anything else you wished to discuss, my lady?" her man of business asked finally, when she hadn't made any further response to his assessment of the earl's plans.

"Thank you, no, Mr. Samuels," she managed to reply. "I believe that will be all for this morning."

Samuels nodded his acceptance and had already turned toward the door when Sarah stopped him. She could not bear it, she had realized, if what she had offered Wynfield became common knowledge. And cause for jest.

Having been painfully burned once by the fire of gossip, Sarah said, "You should understand that I asked you to suggest a marriage of convenience to the earl because our families have been friends and neighbors for so long. And because, given his gallant service to our country and what it has cost him..." She hesitated, watching Mr. Samuels's eyes to judge if he believed her. "I had thought it would be a tragedy to see Wynfield lose everything," she continued, "but...I would ask that you not discuss what has occurred between us with anyone. It really is no one else's concern, as I'm sure you'll agree."

"You may rest easy on that score, my lady. Discretion is a necessity in my profession. You'll hear no talk of this. Unless the earl himself chooses to discuss it," he warned.

That caveat was in his eyes as well, and she nodded in dismissal. When her man of business had closed the door of the office behind him, Sarah didn't rise from her seat behind the desk. She thought about his warning and wondered if Justin *would* gossip about what she had done. If he did, she could imagine what they all would say. Automatically Sarah pressed cold fingers against the heat of the blush stealing into her cheeks.

And what did it matter *what* they said? she wondered. She could be no more an outcast from society than she already was. Besides, she knew Wynfield was too much a gentleman to betray her. He might not wish to marry her, and considering everything, she could understand his reasons, but Justin would never seek to humiliate her by making her marriage proposal public.

Only he would ever know she had made that offer. The only humiliation she would suffer from its rejection would be the one he had just dealt her. And that, she decided, was quite humiliation enough.

"I had hoped you would be at home," Andrew said, his voice full of undisguised joy.

Justin looked up in surprise and met the same dark blue eyes he had thought about far too often in the last five days. The child was sitting on the paddock fence, watching Wynfield evaluate the horses he was sending to Tattersall's next week.

The earl had been disturbed by his first encounter with Sarah's son. He had been jealous of the man who had won her heart. Jealous of this child, who should have been his. Now that he knew the truth, those emotions had been intensified. And, he acknowledged, they were even more despicable now.

"How is your wooden leg?" the child asked politely, his eyes falling to examine the line of the trousers the earl wore.

Despite his tangled emotions, Justin laughed. "Still wooden," he said easily.

"Do you tie it onto your other leg?" Andrew asked. "To make it stay on?"

Now that they had exchanged conversational tidbits, however bizarre, the child apparently felt that he had achieved the status of a legitimate guest. He began climbing down from his perch to join the earl in the paddock.

Justin watched until one small boot slipped from its hurried placement on a rail. Leading the mare, he walked over to the fence and, with one arm around the child's middle, lifted the boy down, setting him carefully on the ground.

"I could have gotten down by myself," Andrew said.

"And what if you had fallen and broken your head?" the earl asked, the ghost of his laughter still haunting his eyes.

He had had little enough to laugh about in the last few

weeks. For some reason, this child's interest in and investigation of the world around him amused him. And intrigued him. If what Justin had seen that day in the woods was any indication, this boy had few friends or playmates his own age. He was being raised in a household of adults, which probably explained the maturity of his speech as well.

"If I had, Sarah would have been angry," Drew confessed.

Stretching on tiptoe, he reached up to touch the mare's nose. Unaccustomed to children, she bobbed her head and snorted, provoking a childish thrill of laughter, but no evidence of fear.

"You like horses?" the earl asked, watching the eager fingers, undeterred, reach upward again.

"I like Sarah's pony," the child said.

"Do you ride him?"

"Sometimes," Drew said.

By now, the mare had decided the boy was harmless. She pushed her nose against Andrew's hand, and the child laughed again, more softly this time, but with a spontaneous and true delight.

"I ride the pony when Sarah has time to help me," he added.

"And your grandfather?" the earl asked gently.

The caressing fingers stilled. The child turned to slant a look over his shoulder. The blue eyes were no longer alight as they had been when he'd spoken from the top of the fence. Or even when he had approached the mare. Now they looked almost as they had in the clearing when, alone and friendless, Drew had been surrounded by a ring of catcalling enemies. Suddenly, at what was in the child's eyes, Justin would have given anything to be able to take back his question.

"Do you mean Brynmoor?" the boy asked.

Compelled by the darkly adult hauteur in that cold, blue stare, Justin nodded.

"He doesn't like me," Andrew said. "He doesn't want to teach me anything. I stay away from him."

And what hell that must be for a child like this, Justin thought. Living in the same household with a mad old man who disliked him. The same household, he remembered, into which Sarah had wanted to introduce his presence. And perhaps this was why, Justin realized. Because of this child. Her son. An outcast from his own society, just as his mother was. Despised by his grandfather for a sin that was not of his making.

"Did you cry when they cut off your leg?" the boy asked.

The bluntness of the question was startling, given everyone else's reticence to discuss that amputation. Almost no one had commented on the loss of his leg since he'd been home, Justin realized. Or at least no one had commented to his face, he amended, very well aware of how tongues in the district wagged. The obvious changes the war had wrought in the new earl would certainly have been discussed, simply not in his hearing. Not talking about it, however, didn't change the reality. A reality he had seen reflected in Sarah's eyes as she watched him limp across the Randolph cottage.

"I don't remember," he admitted, honestly trying to recall the operation. Those memories seemed hidden in a haze of conflicting and blurred images. "I had been well primed with brandy and laudanum," he said, looking down into eyes that hung on his every word. "I know I yelled a fair amount," he said, deliberately lightening his tone.

"Because it hurt you?"

Wynfield nodded, his throat tight.

"I yelled when Sarah dabbed my cuts with liniment," Drew said comfortingly.

"I think yelling is allowed," Justin said softly.

"*Especially* if they are cutting off your leg," Andrew said graciously, turning his attention back to the mare.

The subject had been settled to his satisfaction. And after all, Justin conceded, there wasn't a great deal more that might legitimately be said about it.

"But he didn't mind, Sarah," Andrew argued. "I promise you he didn't. He put me up on the mare he's selling at Tattersall's and let me ride her. He didn't mind me visiting him one bit."

"And neither did you mind," Sarah said, turning his argument against him. Her words were abrupt and more angry than was her wont in dealing with Andrew. The last time he had visited Wynfield Park without permission, however, she had warned him about what would happen if he disobeyed again. "You didn't mind what you have been told over and over."

"He is our neighbor," Drew said, his voice very small.

"You did *not* have permission to go there, Andrew, and nothing you say can change that."

The curly head hung. Not so much, Sarah suspected, in remorse as in anticipation of the punishment she had foolishly threatened. A punishment she would now have to administer. She realized, without knowing what to do about it, that this entire escapade had been blown out of proportion. After all, Drew had come home and confessed his transgression, too excited about the success of this particular trip across the ford to keep it from her. But then, he had always been an honest child.

"He didn't mind," Andrew said again, plaintively this time.

"Well, I minded," Sarah said. "You must learn that you can't continue to disobey because it suits your purposes. Soldiers who disobey orders are punished."

Given Drew's present fascination with anything of a military nature, especially his fascination with a certain ex-soldier, she thought this argument might carry more weight than the consideration that she had been worried when she couldn't find him. She didn't really believe her father would hurt Andrew, but his age-clouded mind had lately latched on to the idea that Drew didn't belong at Longford.

Sarah couldn't know how much Brynmoor remembered about Amelia's elopement or about David Osborne's role in it. Or even about the story she had told him when she had brought Andrew home. Her lie about fostering a dead relative's child had been paper thin, of course, and certainly no one else had believed it.

Despite the flimsiness of her explanation, however, her father had not forbidden her to bring the boy home. And it had been easy at first to keep the baby out of his way. Out of sight, out of mind. Especially out of the way of a mind that had begun to lose its battle against the encroaching darkness of senility, which tightened its grip with each passing month.

Now Andrew was no longer a baby or a toddler, but an active little boy... A little boy who needed a father's firm hand, she acknowledged. Or a grandfather's. And having neither, it had been left to Sarah to teach this child how to become a man—a gentleman, she amended—fit to take his proper place in society, which was a role she was scarcely suited for.

"Will you flog me?" he asked. "Like they flog sol-diers?"

Nausea climbed into Sarah's throat at the image, but it was not so far removed from what she had threatened. This particular threat had been the housekeeper's sugges-tion. Mrs. Simkins had raised five sturdy sons, and she had said this was the way other boys Andrew's age were punished.

Sarah looked at the cane lying on top of the scarred desk of the schoolroom. It had been left from her father's childhood, she supposed. It had certainly never been em-ployed to discipline either her or Amelia. A more docile pair of children it would have been difficult to find. One harsh word from their father, one glimpse of his purpled, enraged face, and they were almost too frightened to move.

Andrew was not that way. His temperament was very different from theirs. And of course, his father's blood as well as Amelia's ran through his veins. That was Sarah's greatest fear—that she would fail to subdue the tendencies in Andrew that he might have inherited from his wayward father. That was why Amelia had entrusted him to her. It was part of the responsibility Sarah had undertaken with the deathbed promise she had made her sister.

"It is a cane and not a whip," she said, sick at heart.

"I won't cry," Andrew said, his eyes suddenly flashing defiance. "You can't make me cry, Sarah. I may yell," he said, his voice for the first time touched with real fear, "but I won't cry. He didn't cry, not even when they cut off his leg."

Justin, she thought. Apparently this was something he and Andrew had discussed during their meeting today. And she had warned Drew not to talk to the earl about the war or his injury. It seemed that nothing she said had any effect on him anymore, she realized in despair. Just as her entreaties to David Osborne four years ago had had no effect on what he had done.

Somehow the image of amputation Andrew had introduced into the conversation lingered in her mind, along with the thought of Osborne's lack of responsibility. They had cut off Justin's leg to stop the spread of an infection that, if left untreated, might have cost him his life. The operation might have been brutally agonizing, but it had been necessary and undertaken for the patient's own good. *For the patient's own good...*

"You must lean over the desk," she said, her chest thick with self-loathing over what she had to do. She had never struck Andrew in his life, but Mrs. Simkins had warned her that she was making a baby of him. A spoiled baby too accustomed to having his own way. And when he went away to school, the housekeeper had said, or even when Sarah hired a tutor...

It will be the boy who suffers from your lack of mettle then, my lady. Better to discipline him firmly now and be done with it. Better for him. You'll see.

Trembling, Drew bent forward, exposing his small backside, which was still covered with the mud-stained trousers he had worn on his visit to Wynfield. Sarah couldn't stand the thought of using the slender birch to stripe the pale white skin of his bare buttocks. This would be hard enough.

Taking a deep breath, she drew back her hand and brought the birch down. And then again, steeling herself to complete this duty by keeping the maliciously smiling face of David Osborne in her mind's eye. When it was done, Andrew had made good on his promise. Like his hero, he, too, had refused to cry, even after the three strokes had been administered.

Alone in her room after the ordeal, however, Sarah found she was not so brave as Drew. Or as the earl. She also acknowledged that as much as she had hated disciplining her sister's son, some of the tears she shed afterward were the result of something else that had happened today. Something quite different from Andrew's punishment.

Part of what she cried about was an offer that had been bravely made, a desperate attempt to seize her last chance at happiness. An offer that had been just as quickly rejected, she remembered bitterly, forever destroying it.

Chapter Four

When Sarah awoke the following morning, it was not yet dawn. Her night had been restless, full of uneasy dreams. Nightmares, she admitted, remembering the images that had played so vividly through her sleep. Images of war. Of the military surgeons' bloodstained aprons and their ghastly instruments. And superimposed over them, Drew's face, fighting the tears that had glistened, unshed, in his eyes while she had punished him.

Even awake, she found the sense of despair those dreams had brought was not dissipated. It was joined instead by a deep regret and a foreboding that the events of yesterday marked a change in her relationship with Drew. He was growing up. That was undeniably true. But was he growing away from her as well?

She pushed back the covers and put her bare feet on the floor. Without bothering to pick up her wrapper from the foot of the bed, she walked across her bedroom and opened the door to the hallway. Andrew slept in the nursery, one floor above, of course. She had often made this silent journey, tiptoeing up the narrow flight of servants' stairs at the end of the hall to check on him.

When she reached the upper floor, she paused outside

Andrew's door. She put her ear against the thick wood, listening for any sound. Apparently he was still sleeping. She waited, hand on the knob. The door creaked when it opened, and she knew she might wake him if she looked in.

But if he woke, she thought, she could tell him good morning and begin repairing the chasm that seemed to have appeared in their previously close relationship. After all, she and Andrew really had no one else in the world but each other, and the sooner they mended the trauma of yesterday, the better it would be.

She eased the door open, cringing a little at the noise it made. The nursery was still dark, the curtains drawn over the high windows. She tiptoed to the bed, her eyes gradually adjusting to the room's dimness, and saw that it was empty. Her realization of what that might mean was slow in coming, however. It seemed impossible that Andrew should not be here. After all, there was nowhere else he could be.

Her eyes scanned the room, searching every corner, wondering if the little boy could be playing a game. Hide and seek, perhaps. Or maybe he had heard the door and was trying to punish her for what had happened yesterday.

"Andrew?" she called softly, holding her breath, listening for a stifled giggle. Drew had never been able to remain silent when she came close to discovering his hiding place. But there was nothing. No sound. The room was empty. It even *felt* empty, she thought. As cold and as lonely as this huge house would be without the dear presence of Andrew to lighten her days.

"Drew?" she called more loudly. "Answer me, Drew," she demanded, although her heart had already accepted what her mind denied. Andrew wasn't here.

She ran her hand across the tangled bedsheets and

found they were cold. Wherever Andrew was, he had been gone long enough for his body heat to fade, so he had not hidden when he heard the creaking door. Her searching eyes discovered his nightshirt lying across the foot of the bed. They then flew to the row of low pegs on the wall. As she had feared, the clothing he had worn yesterday was not there.

He had run away, she thought, her heart beginning to pound. Andrew had run away because of what she had done. She knew, of course, without any doubt in her mind, where he would have gone.

The earl of Wynfield opened the door to Star's stall and stepped inside. The gelding butted him gently in the chest, welcoming his master in a time-honored fashion.

After all, they had been companions for many years and through difficult circumstances. Despite that, the gelding's name had been added late last night to the bottom of the list Justin had dispatched to the great London horse market this morning. Star would bring a good price.

When this was all over and done, the estate sold, Justin had realized, he would have no way to provide for the animal. No way to provide for himself, either, he acknowledged, lips flattening. Although he was willing to do without a great many things in order to pay what he could of the debts his family had accumulated, he was not willing to let Star go hungry.

There had been few decisions in the last few weeks that had been more painful, but he knew he was doing what was best for Star. And nothing less than his long faithfulness deserved.

Justin lowered his head and, closing his eyes, laid his forehead against Star's nose, giving in again to the growing sense of loss he fought with each passing day. His hand automatically caressed the gelding's sleek and powerful neck.

"Are you crying?" a small voice asked.

Startled, the earl lifted his head and encountered the wide eyes of Andrew Spenser, peering up at him from the floor of Star's stall. The child was nestled in the straw, curled up comfortably in the darkness, almost under the gelding's hooves.

Still touching Star's nose with one hand to reassure him, Justin reached down and grabbed the child by the back of his jacket. He stepped back, lifting Andrew up by that fistful of fabric. As quickly as possible without startling the gelding, he carried the child out of the stall. Then he shut the half door to prevent Star from joining them. Inquisitively, the horse put his head over it and whickered in protest at the desertion.

Only when Drew was safely out of the way of those powerful hooves did Justin remember to breathe. More frightened than angry, he set the child on his feet with more force than was strictly necessary, still holding on to his jacket.

"What the hell were you doing in there?" he demanded.

"Sleeping," Drew said. His eyes had widened at the tone of the question or at its language.

"What are you doing here?" the earl persisted.

"I've run away."

"Run away?" Justin repeated disbelievingly. "Away from home?"

"I can help you take care of your horses," the little boy offered, his voice hopeful.

"Does Sarah know where you are?"

"No," Drew said, his eyes downcast.

"Do you realize that she will be very worried when

she finds you are gone?'' the earl asked, finally releasing his hold on Andrew's coat.

"I don't care if she *is* worried,'' the child said bitterly.

At his tone, Justin hesitated, his eyes examining the rumpled figure. Drew was wearing the same clothing he'd had worn yesterday, but the garments were wrinkled and covered with pieces of straw and dirt from the night he had spent in the stable.

The earl reached down and touched the boy's chin, forcing his face upward. He examined it in the growing light. The child's cheeks, too, were covered with a layer of grime, through which ran the clean, unmistakable streak of tears.

Justin began to bend, intending to get down on eye level with Andrew. He realized very quickly that would be impossible, given the inflexible nature of his right ankle. Instead, he put his hands under Drew's armpits and lifted him. He set the child astride a saddle that had been thrown across one of the railings. Delight flared in blue eyes that only a moment before had been full of anger and sadness.

"Why don't you care if your *maman*'s worried about you?'' Justin asked softly, watching grubby fingers run over the polished leather. Justin kept his hand on the child's waist in case he lost his balance, but Drew gripped the saddle with his thighs, just as he had been instructed yesterday.

"She doesn't want me to visit you,'' Andrew said.

His eyes fastened on the earl's face as if seeking an explanation for that ridiculous prohibition. There were several, Justin supposed, but none he could make to a four-year-old. Just as his own reasons for not wanting to further this relationship could certainly not be spelled out to the child.

"But you did, didn't you? Yesterday and last night. And you came without her permission," Justin said.

"I don't see why Sarah doesn't want me to visit you. I told her you didn't mind. You don't mind if I come to see you, do you?" Drew asked, his tone again hopeful.

"That isn't the point," Justin said. "The point is…"

He paused, wondering why Sarah had made that restriction. After all, if he had accepted her offer, he and Andrew would have been thrown in close proximity. Of course, since he had refused, maybe Sarah was simply trying to protect her son. It was obvious that the child had already formed an attachment to him. One that, given their circumstances, could not be allowed to grow.

And besides, he would be leaving as soon as everything was sold. If the child began to consider him as a permanent part of his life, then that departure would be wrenching. For both of them, he acknowledged, looking up at the small figure, whose eyes were still locked on his face, waiting for him to explain whatever the point was in Sarah's trying to keep them apart.

"The point is," Justin continued, carefully skirting the real issue, "that you must do whatever your mother tells you. Soldiers obey orders, even when they don't understand them."

"That's what she said," the boy admitted.

"She said it because it's true."

"I just wanted to talk to you," Drew avowed. "And to hear about your adventures in the war."

Justin smiled, reaching upward to ruffle the tangled curls. "Which were not nearly so exciting as you suppose them to be."

The child nodded, but his eyes were suspiciously bright.

"Would you like a ride home on Star?" Justin asked.

"I'm not going home," Drew said stubbornly. "I am not ever going home again." The small chin assumed a rebellious tilt.

"Boys belong at home. With their mothers," Justin said.

"Did your mother flog you?"

Justin laughed, and then realized he shouldn't have. The question had been serious. "Flog me?" he repeated.

"Well...beat you with a stick." The child carefully revised his version of Sarah's punishment.

At last Justin was beginning to understand what had occurred to drive Andrew to run away. Knowing Sarah as he did, he knew it was entirely possible this was the first time she had physically disciplined the child. And he hated to have been the cause of this rift. Hated that Drew had reacted as he had. The boy would certainly have his share of canings when he went away to school. Perhaps he needed to be made to understand that.

"Actually, my father caned me. Fairly often, as I remember," Justin admitted, almost amused by the memory of his easygoing father's inept attempts at punishment. "Not nearly so frequently, however, as my tutor and later my headmaster did." There had been nothing the least bit inept about those.

"I didn't cry," Andrew said. "Because you didn't. Soldiers don't cry." He repeated the words like a litany.

"Some of them do," the earl of Wynfield said, again studying the unmistakable stain of tears that marked the rounded cheeks. "Sometimes...we all cry."

The silence stretched. Slowly the little boy drew a breath, almost a sigh. It was certainly deep enough to be audible. Then, surprisingly, small, grubby fingers reached down to touch Justin's cheek, their caress as subtle as dawn. They remained there only a moment before they were again smoothing aimlessly over the leather of the saddle.

"If you don't ever plan to come home, Andrew," Sarah said softly, "I shall be very lonely."

Her voice had come from behind him, and Justin steeled himself to face her. He glanced up at the child before he did. Drew was looking at his mother as if he wanted to run to her and be safely encircled by her arms. His anger had been as ephemeral as the unspoken comfort he had just offered Justin.

"I know you're very angry with me," Sarah continued. She had moved nearer, and Justin knew he could no longer delay a response. He put his wrist on the bow of the saddle, lightly resting his fingers on one of the small legs that straddled it. He turned, his eyes finding Sarah's face.

The delicate skin under her eyes was dark, and the eyes themselves were full of anxiety. He briefly wondered if either of those might have anything to do with the answer he had instructed his banker to send to her man of business yesterday.

But of course, Sarah had her own problems, independent of those lurking in their shared past. Or in their present. And Justin was probably assuming that what he did or said had a far greater importance in her life than it really did.

At Andrew's continued silence, the earl's eyes left their contemplation of Sarah's face and again sought the child's. Drew's gaze was now on him, he realized, rather than on his mother. And Justin wasn't sure why.

"Your *maman* asked you a question," he admonished gently.

"Is she going to beat me again?" Drew asked.

Justin controlled the urge to smile.

"No, she is not," Sarah said decisively. "But she *is* going to take you home. I don't imagine you slept any better than I did last night."

"I slept with Star," Andrew said. His eyes glowed with excitement over having that remarkable event to report.

Sarah glanced at Justin as if for confirmation, and then at the big gelding, whose head was still extended over the half gate. She swallowed, the movement strong enough to be visible even in the dimness, and her lips tightened before she opened them to say calmly, "Then I expect you smell of horse."

Andrew sniffed at the sleeve of his jacket, which would probably never be the same, Justin thought.

"I do," he said proudly. "I smell just like a horse."

"Which is *not* something to brag about," Justin suggested. He lifted the child out of the saddle and set him on the floor. "Horse is not a fragrance gentlemen wear in the company of their ladies," he said, brushing straw and dirt from Drew's clothing with his hands. "Unless they are engaged in the hunt."

"Why not?" the child asked.

"Because it might offend them."

Small hands had joined his in attempting to remove the stains from his clothing.

"Why would it offend them?" Andrew asked, his eyes lifting to Justin's face. "Don't they like horses?"

"Only to ride," the earl said simply. "*Not* to smell."

Giving up on making the boy presentable, he placed his hand in the small of Andrew's back and propelled him toward his mother. At the same time, his eyes again found Sarah's face. It was no longer the smooth, girlish oval he remembered. She had changed almost as much as he had, he realized for the first time.

With the impetus of Justin's push, Andrew walked

slowly until he was within a few feet of his mother. Then he rushed forward all at once, throwing himself against her skirts and putting both arms tightly around her legs. She laid her hand on the back of his head, pulling him close.

"Thank you," she said softly, her gaze lifting from his disordered curls to Justin's face.

He shook his head slowly, denying her gratitude, but he didn't speak. He couldn't, because all at once the memories of what they had once been to one another were between them, as sharp and clear as the hint of fall in the morning air. And suddenly they were in her eyes as well.

Turning Andrew, Sarah put her hand around her son's shoulder and led him out of the stable. Behind them, the dust Justin had brushed from Andrew's coat danced, glittering in the shafts of sunlight. The stable was very quiet and, without them there, incredibly lonely as well.

"Lady Sarah Spenser has come to call, my lord," Blevins announced. There was not a trace of surprise or disapproval in the butler's voice. It was completely clear of inflection, his face perfectly composed.

Justin was sure the same could not be said, however, of his own features. "You may show her in, Blevins," he said finally.

It had taken him too long to get the words out, but when he had, he was pleased that his voice seemed steady. It reflected none of the turmoil his butler's announcement had generated.

"Very good, my lord. And shall I bring tea?" Blevins asked.

Somehow the idea of calmly having tea with Sarah seemed beyond him, so Justin shook his head. Even when the butler disappeared through the door of his father's study, the earl's eyes remained on the opening, his mind racing.

It had been three days since he had found Andrew asleep in his stables. And in the meantime, he had heard nothing from either of them. As he worked with the horses, getting them ready for the sale at Tattersall's, he had expected to look up at any moment and find Andrew watching him. He hadn't, however, so whatever Sarah had come here to say…

She was standing in the doorway, he realized. Her eyes seemed less shadowed than they had the last time he had seen her, but perhaps that was simply a trick of the light. "May I come in?" she asked.

Justin's chest was tight, a hard knot of disillusionment that seemed to interfere with the familiar process of breathing. There was nothing to divert attention today from what lay between them. No chattering Andrew to provide a welcome distraction from remembering how he had once felt about this woman. And no need to weigh every word he said in order to evaluate its possible effect on an impressionable child.

He inclined his head, granting permission without speaking. She hesitated a moment longer and then walked across the room to the chair that sat at an angle in front of his desk. Her hair, only a little darker than he remembered it, had been dressed today in very becoming curls that nestled against her cheeks. And there was more color in her face. He couldn't decide if that was from the outside air or from the strain of this meeting.

When Sarah reached the desk, she stopped, waiting for his invitation to be seated, perhaps. At his continued silence, eventually she sat down in the chair opposite his. She folded her hands in her lap and raised her eyes to his face.

"I don't believe there is any need between us to stand on ceremony," she began softly.

Deliberately, he allowed the upward tilt of his lips, the movement mocking. And she knew it. The knowledge that he was mocking her understated summary of all that stood between them was reflected in her blue eyes.

"I made you an offer," she continued doggedly, the color rising more strongly into her cheeks. "And you refused it."

Justin said nothing, but his eyes, relentlessly without expression, held their focus on her face.

"What will it take for you to accept it?" she asked.

Whatever he had expected, it was not this. Something about Andrew, perhaps. Or an offer to buy part of the land he was being forced to sell, which, after all, marched on Brynmoor's.

"Your offer was extremely generous," he said. "And explicit. My refusal had nothing to do with its terms."

"And everything to do with me," she suggested.

Since it was the truth, he didn't bother to deny it.

"And Andrew?" she asked.

He lifted an eyebrow, questioning.

"Everything or nothing to do with Andrew?" she repeated.

"Andrew has nothing to do with this."

"He needs…" She hesitated, seeming reluctant to state the obvious.

"A masculine influence other than Brynmoor's?" he finished.

"Yes," she agreed.

"Then may I suggest you apply to his father for assistance."

"His is not the kind of influence I would wish for Andrew," she said. "Nor is my father's. At least...not now."

"He frightens Drew," the earl said.

"I know, but...I don't think he would hurt him."

"You don't *think?*" Justin repeated incredulously.

"My father sometimes...gets ideas in his head that are difficult to dislodge. Right now, he's decided Andrew doesn't belong at Longford."

Most people would agree with the assessment Sarah's father had made, but however he felt about what Sarah had done, Justin could never condone the mistreatment of a child. And had Brynmoor been in his right mind, nor would he.

"I can't do anything to change that, Sarah. And I can't, of course, accept your offer," he said again, his voice deliberately decisive. As unequivocal as the letter she had once sent him.

"Why not?" she asked. Her eyes were level and unflinching.

"If you don't understand why I can't marry you, then there is probably nothing I can say to *make* you understand."

"I have a son who needs a man's guidance. He listens to you. He respects you."

"He's hungry for attention," Justin said dismissingly, despite the uncomfortable reaction in his stomach to her words.

"Hungry for masculine attention," she agreed. "Andrew probably isn't particular about the kind. I am," she added, her voice very low.

Justin's eyes came up at that. He laid the pen his fingers had found back on top of the painful listing of the estate's few remaining assets, which he had been in the process of composing when Blevins interrupted.

"No, Sarah," he said softly.

She took a breath, her eyes still holding on his face.

"Andrew needs to be taught how to behave as a gentleman. He needs to become one. And to be accepted as one."

Again she hesitated, and when she went on, her voice was very quiet. It was filled, however, with a conviction Justin couldn't doubt, despite his inclination to disregard both her words and their intent.

"There is no one who is more admired in this district than you are. No one more respected, especially now. If there is anyone who can do for Andrew what must be done, then it is you."

"What do you think *I* can do?" he asked. "Besides teach him civilized behavior. You can hire a tutor for that. Believe me, it will be much less expensive."

For some reason the pen was again in his fingers. Disgusted, he threw it down on the desk and pushed himself up, limping across to the window. When he turned, he was expecting that same pitying revulsion in Sarah's eyes he had surprised there before. Instead they were locked on his face, still hopeful.

"I can't be father to your son, Sarah," he said. "I may have nothing to leave to my own sons, but I want them," he acknowledged bitterly.

Her pupils widened, and it was not until they did that he realized the interpretation she had put on those words.

"I can't marry you," he said bitingly. "I can't change Andrew's situation. This is something you've dreamed up because you don't want to see him hurt."

She nodded, her eyes wide and dark, swimming with tears. "I don't want to see him hurt," she repeated in agreement. "None of this is his fault."

Or mine, Justin longed to say. *What happened four*

years ago was not my fault. I can't change it. I shouldn't be asked to.

"There is no going back," he said instead.

"I'm not asking for that. Whatever was between us…" Her voice faltered, and one slow tear slipped down the cheek that was now blanched and white. "Whatever happened, Andrew shouldn't be made to bear the brunt of it."

The sins of the father, Justin thought. They were inescapable. He had spent the last five years fighting honorably for his country. It had cost him more that he was willing to openly acknowledge. And now he was being forced to pay for his father's sins. That was simply the way of the world.

"You can keep all of this," she said. "Nothing has to change. Nothing lost. You can keep it exactly as it is."

It was enticing, especially given the contents of the list on the desk in front of him. Everything he owned was on it, from his grandmother's diamonds, which had been a bequest intended for his unborn daughter, to Star, the beloved gelding to whom he owed his life.

"Keep it for whom?" he asked softly, and watched the color rush in again under the alabaster skin.

They were silent a long time. Long enough that he was aware of the clock on the mantel ticking off the passage of the slow minutes. Exactly as it had in this room for more than a century.

"If…" she began, her voice little more than a whisper. She stopped, swallowing against the constriction in her throat, and then, strengthening her tone, she went on. "If that is what you want… If that is your condition…"

He laughed, realizing, even if she did not, that he was in no position to bargain or to set conditions. This marriage was simply something he knew he could not do. He could not live with Sarah and her son, not even to save a heritage he loved.

Until he saw her face change, he hadn't realized the unthinking cruelty of his laughter or how she would interpret it. Only when she stood and rushed blindly toward the door, bumping into the chair she had been sitting in, did he understand what she thought.

"Sarah," he called, knowing only then the scope of the mistake he had made. "It's too late, Sarah. Don't you know that? Don't you understand that it's all too late?"

She was already gone. The last word echoed in the room, which seemed as empty now as the stables had that morning when she and Andrew had left. *Too late. All of it, far too late.*

Chapter Five

"My lord! My lord!"

The shouts broke the peaceful stillness of the afternoon. The earl and his head groom had been engaged in a discussion about the horses that were to go up to London on the morrow. Justin wanted them to arrive a few days before the auction so that they would have fully recovered from the journey and be in prime condition at the time of the sale.

Both men looked up in response to the cry to see Meg Randolph's oldest son, Tom, running down the long, sloping hillside toward the stables. His face was white beneath its covering of freckles. "Come quick, my lord," he shouted, waving his arms over his head. "Mum says you must be quick."

Accustomed to reading men and their voices, even when they were distorted by stress, Justin had begun to run toward the shouting lad. He realized immediately, however, that whatever the emergency Meg Randolph believed required his attention, he would never arrive in time to do any good if he attempted to get to her cottage on foot.

"Saddle the gray," he ordered, throwing the words

over his shoulder as he limped as rapidly as possible, without risking a fall, to meet the approaching boy.

By the time he had, Meg's son seemed totally out of breath and near collapse. He bent over in front of the earl, his hands on his knees. He was, however, able to gasp out the plea for assistance he'd been sent to deliver.

"The Spenser boy," he managed to say, pulling enough breath into his starving lungs to push those words out.

"Andrew?" Justin questioned.

The boy nodded, lifting his head to look up into the earl's face. His breath was sawing in and out, his hands still on his knees, supporting him. It was more than two miles to the Randolph cottage, even if one cut across the hills and dales as Tom had. Apparently he had run at full speed all the way.

At the word *Spenser,* Justin had felt his breathing falter. He waited impatiently for the rest of the message. Finally, he grabbed Meg's son by the shoulders, forcing him upright. "What about the Spenser child?" he demanded, shaking Meg's son.

"They got him," Tom gasped out. "Them as is always chasing him. Mum said you was wanting to know."

"I wanted to know," Justin said, thanking providence that he had thought to send that message to Meg, whose cottage was nearest the path to the ford and the woods. "Where are they?"

"They caught him as he crossed the branch. Mum says he was probably heading here," Tom said.

Meg was undoubtedly right. After all, Justin had expected Drew's arrival almost daily, hoping for Sarah's sake that the child would not disobey again. As apparently he had today.

Even as Justin thought that, the groom ran up, leading

Star. Without hesitation, knowing enough from Meg's message and from what he had witnessed that day to fear what he would find in the woods, the earl swung into the saddle.

"Tell your mother I'm grateful," he shouted to the boy, before he touched his heels to his circling mount.

Leaning over the neck of the gelding, Justin gave Star his head across the open country, allowing him to run off his eagerness in a burst of speed that carried them over the hills and meadows that stretched between the Park and the woods.

Despite Meg's warning, he didn't know if he'd arrive in time to prevent the village boys from taking their revenge against the child he had already rescued once from their clutches. They had chosen Andrew as their victim, and then he had interfered. They had probably been biding their time, waiting for another chance. The inexplicable hatreds of childhood were often based on nothing more than someone being different. As Andrew certainly was.

And of course, in Drew's case... The earl remembered the leader's taunting sobriquet and the gesture that had accompanied it. That contempt had been taught, and it would not have been directed against an illegitimate child of their own class.

Drew had, however, in their eyes at least, been born with two stigmas he could never escape. First, he was not one of them. And secondly, he had been pointed out as the bastard son of one of their betters. Those differences set him irrevocably apart from the other children, and there was no more vulnerable position for a boy of that age to find himself in.

Justin was forced to slow his pace as he entered the woods, which were deceptively peaceful. He strained, listening for any sounds that would help him find the group of boys. However, he was almost at the clearing before he became aware of the noise they were making.

They were much quieter than they had been that first day. Their champion did not appear to need their cheers to urge him on. He was pounding at the head and shoulders of the smaller child with a rhythm that seemed dogged, almost mechanical. And this time, Justin realized, his heart lodged in his throat, there was no resistance. Andrew lay limp and unmoving on the ground.

The earl's approach was less cautious than it had been during the previous encounter. He deliberately spurred Star into the circle, which broke and scattered as quickly as before. This time, he was off his horse almost before the boys' frightened explosion of movement gave him room to dismount.

Just as he had clutched the back of Drew's jacket to pull him out of danger in the stables, he now grabbed the collar of the boy who was pummeling him. Fighting to control his own fury, Justin pulled the larger boy up and flung him away from the unconscious child. The boy stumbled backward, almost falling.

Justin let him go, his attention focused completely on the motionless figure on the ground. He dropped to his knees beside Andrew, his fingers quickly finding the reassuringly strong pulse in the delicate throat.

He remembered to breathe then, knowing, at least intellectually, that his terror had been out of proportion to the danger the child was in. He had, however, knelt over too many fallen comrades during the last five years to have felt any hope when he had seen the lifeless body on the ground. Realizing that his wartime experiences had obviously led him far astray from reality brought a relief so profound as to make him light-headed.

The earl of Wynfield closed his eyes, his quick, word-less prayer of thanksgiving as fervent as any he had ever uttered. He was uncaring, almost unaware, that the boys who had taken part in this attack were disappearing into the woods as quickly as they possibly could in an attempt to avoid being called to task for what they had done. Or for what they had witnessed.

"Andrew," the earl said softly, cupping his thumb and fingers gently around the white face. The child's skin was as fair as his mother's, he thought irrelevantly, and the line of his jaw as fragile as the bones of a bird. Too fragile.

"Drew," he whispered, running his thumb across the opened mouth. The lips were slack and pale, but even as he watched, the blue eyes opened. Then, almost in won-der, the pupils widened as the little boy looked up into his face.

"You haven't gone," Andrew said.

"I haven't gone," Justin agreed, his throat aching at what was in those eyes.

"They said you were going to London."

"Not to stay. Only to sell the horses."

The child's eyes shifted to the spent gelding, standing patiently where he had been left by the earl's precipitous leap from the saddle.

"Not Star," Drew pleaded. "Not your very own charger Star."

There was nothing Justin could say to relieve the gen-uine horror of that thought, clearly reflected in the child's eyes. After all, his own almost matched it. He was an adult, however, and he had made his choice. Not only about Star, but about Sarah and this child. And his refusal had been made with his eyes wide open as to its inevitable consequences.

"Can you sit up if I help you?" the earl asked, instead of admitting, at this point at least, that Star's name was indeed on the list of horses bound for Tattersall's.

"I think I broke my head," Andrew said, struggling to sit and rubbing his fingers against the back of his skull at the same time. It was tender enough, apparently, to provoke a grimace.

"You hit it on a rock," the earl said.

He pushed the offending stone aside, his thundering heart rate beginning to return to normal as he realized the child was relatively unscathed. There were certainly bumps and bruises and even a cut on his chin, in addition to the blow to the head that had rendered him briefly unconscious.

"My lord!"

Both Justin and Andrew looked up at the sound of Meg Randolph's voice. She came hurrying through the woods, a broom clutched in one hand. Her skirts and apron were held up by the other, revealing thick white legs thrust into half boots. Her fat face was red with exertion. Jed hurried behind her, carrying a hoe. Assorted Randolph children trailed their parents.

"Is the lad all right?" Meg called.

It was obvious now that, thanks to her warning, Andrew *would* be all right. Of course, Justin realized, there was no guarantee that what had occurred this morning wouldn't happen again. For the first time since he'd dismounted, he looked around the clearing. The boys who had participated in the attack had disappeared, but they wouldn't be hard to track down and punish.

He would be well within his rights to do so, especially since he had warned them off his land and this kind of behavior once. Justin wasn't sure, however, exactly what punishing them would accomplish. Maybe simply more trouble for Sarah's son.

Meg huffed to a stop beside them, sweat gleaming on her red, freckled face. "You poor, dear lamb," she said.

"I broke my head," Andrew offered. With the resilience of childhood, he was beginning to bask in the attention.

"What was you doing with them ruffians, dear?" Meg asked. She lifted her skirts and sank to her knees with a sigh beside the earl. The aroma of fresh baked bread and dried lavender surrounded her, along with a less pleasant miasma composed of perspiration and lye soap.

"I was coming to see the earl," Andrew said, his voice touched with self-importance. "I had heard he was going away."

"Going away?" Meg repeated, her eyes lifting to Justin's. "Why, he's just come home. And he's got things to see to around here," she said. "Why ever would you think he'd be going away?"

There was silence as two pairs of eyes regarded Wynfield, awaiting the denial he could not, in all honor, give them. Not to Andrew, who desperately needed his attention and his friendship. Or to Meg, who wanted what was her due, and what had been denied his tenants far too long—an earl who would put the good of his people and his lands above his own selfish concerns.

"You aren't going away, are you, my lord?" Meg asked as the waiting silence expanded. "You've only just come home," she said again. "You can't be thinking about going away already."

"To London," Justin said, looking not at Meg but into a pair of dark blue eyes that had suddenly filled with hope at her reassuring words. "Just for a few days."

"And you wouldn't ever go away without saying goodbye,'' Andrew suggested. The marks of the older boy's fists were more obvious than they had been before. They were already beginning to discolor the pale, fine-grained skin. ''Promise me you won't,'' the boy said. ''Promise you won't ever do that.''

''I'll never go away without saying goodbye,'' the earl of Wynfield vowed softly. ''I promise you that, Andrew.'' It was simply another commitment, he acknowledged, another duty and responsibility to add to those he had already shouldered.

''Of course, he won't,'' Meg said brusquely. ''Now let's get you up on your feet and see to the damages.''

Using the support of the earl's shoulder, she struggled to her feet. Then she held out her hand to help Justin up. Her eyes expressed surprise when he took it, but he had no doubt that after she witnessed his awkward climb to his feet, she understood. Once he was standing, Justin was made painfully aware of how great a price he would pay for that precipitous leap off Star's back into the middle of the group of boys. Of course, that was unimportant now, but it was something he would have to deal with in due time.

With Mrs. Randolph's help, he got Andrew to his feet. Meg felt the lump on the back of the little boy's head with gentle, but experienced fingers.

''Big as a goose's egg,'' she said, smiling at the child when she had finished, knowing full well he would consider that knot a badge of honor. ''You tell Lady Sarah to make you a nice vinegar poultice, and it will take the ache right away,'' she promised.

Then, perhaps thinking of Sarah's likely reaction to what had happened, she began straightening the child's clothing, attempting to remove the signs of his contact with the ground.

"Mrs. Simkins will brush them up," Andrew assured her, gingerly touching the back of his head again as if to ascertain that it still hurt. Judging by the face he made, there was no doubt it did.

"Of course she will," Meg agreed, picking bits of grass and a few leaves off the back of his jacket. "She'll have them right as rain in no time. I would take you home with me and do it myself, but I suspect Lady Sarah will be wanting you home. Did she know you were coming to see the earl, love?" she asked, her eyes skating quickly up to meet Wynfield's before they returned to the little boy's face.

"I wasn't running away," Drew said. "I was just wanting to say goodbye. If you were leaving," he added, his eyes finding Justin's. "But you aren't leaving, are you?" he asked again.

"Of course he's not," Meg said, giving up her efforts at cleaning Drew's clothing. Her own brood had crept ever closer to the drama and were now standing around the three of them, wide-eyed with interest in the goings-on of their betters.

When Meg realized that, she lifted her apron and brought it down in a shooing motion, sending them scattering as effectively as Star's arrival had scattered the village boys. "What are you all gawking at?" she asked. "There's chores to be done. Get home with you," she ordered.

Since Jed turned away with the children and began to trudge back in the direction of the cottage, it was clear who ruled the Randolph household, Justin thought. Of course, there had never been much doubt about that.

"Shall I take him home, my lord?" Meg asked.

Andrew moved closer to Wynfield, pushing his fingers into his hand. Despite Justin's quite rational decision discouraging any closer relationship between them would be for Andrew's own good, he couldn't prevent his own fingers from closing around the warmth of the small hand.

"Star could carry us both," Drew said softly.

Justin looked down on the battered face, raised so hopefully to his. There would have to be an accounting, he knew, but perhaps this was not the time for truth. Or for rationality.

"I supposed he could," he agreed, instead of saying any of the things he knew he should say.

The blue eyes glowed, and the boy's mouth moved into a smile. A smile that was too much like Sarah's, the earl thought. He tore his gaze away and focused instead on Meg's freckled face.

"Thank you," he said.

"That's a bad lot, my lord. Make no mistake," she said seriously. "I told my boys to look out for this one, but..." She hesitated, her eyes touching on Andrew's face before they came back up to his. "But there's no saying someone will be around the next time to see what's going on," she warned.

The earl nodded.

"You'd best explain the situation to Lady Sarah," she added. "So she can be on her guard."

Again the earl nodded, but he knew how difficult that would be. *Your son is in danger, real danger, because of something you did more than four years ago. He is taunted and abused because he is a bastard, so you must guard him more carefully.* That was not a warning any mother would wish to receive, and in this case Justin was the worst possible messenger to bring it.

Still holding Andrew's hand, he limped heavily over to the gelding, who was somewhat recovered from the run they had made. They would both be better for a rest, but

Meg was right, of course. The child must be conveyed home and Sarah informed of what had gone on here today.

And since Drew had already chosen his preferred method of conveyance, he might as well get it over with, Wynfield thought, determinedly disregarding the growing pain in the stump of his right leg. There would be time enough to deal with that when this distasteful task had been completed. Too soon, he knew, he would have nothing left but time.

Andrew led the way up the broad front steps after the earl had handed him down into the arms of the waiting footman. Justin followed more slowly in his wake, each step an increasing agony.

He knew, of course, what he had done. Too much of his weight had landed on the newly healed incision when he had unthinkingly thrown himself off his horse to break up the fight. That action had been taken with a complete and total disregard for his injury. He had literally not even remembered it, had not once thought of his leg. Not as long as he had been on Star. Not when he'd seen Andrew's seemingly lifeless body. Now, however, every step he took was a brutal reminder.

"Who are you?"

At the question, Justin looked up from his careful negotiation of the low steps to find the marquess of Brynmoor standing in the doorway to his estate. The old man was squinting at Justin's face, trying to bring it into better focus, perhaps. His hair, which had gone completely white, floated in wildly disordered wisps about his face.

Surprisingly, however, given the changes that same span had wrought in Sarah and in himself, other than the whitening of his too-long hair, Brynmoor seemed to have aged very little. Though his once-trim waistline had expanded, and the sartorial perfection that had always marked his appearance was now sadly lacking.

The clothes he wore were as fine and as costly, perhaps, as his wardrobe had been then, but they were worn with a carelessness that was uncharacteristic of the former dandy. There was even a spot of food on the cravat, and the coat was not cut to fit perfectly over the thickened torso.

"I'm Wynfield," Justin said simply, wondering if the old man would remember him. He was almost grateful for the delay the marquess was causing. Justin did not anticipate the coming interview. He waited, his weight resting on his sound leg, and let Sarah's father examine his features.

"You ain't Wynfield," the marquess said finally. "You got the look of him, all right, but I know the earl well. You might be his by-blow, I guess. Is that what you're claiming?"

Andrew had been edging away from the old man, although so far the child had been ignored in Byrnmoor's rude commentary. At last, moving slowly backward, Andrew had reached the earl. He leaned against Justin's leg, his eyes locked warily on his grandfather's face.

"You knew my father, I think," Justin explained, putting his hands on Andrew's shoulders. He squeezed gently, trying to give the little boy courage.

"Your boy?" the marquess asked. His faded eyes, which had once been the same dark Spenser blue as the child's, had obviously observed the protective gesture.

"Lady Sarah's son," the earl said.

"Sarah's got no son."

Justin said nothing, but he felt the child shrink more

closely against him. "Is Lady Sarah at home?" Justin
asked.

The marquess's eyebrows, which were much darker
than the hair that framed his florid face, lifted. His mouth
assumed a smirk that was almost lascivious. "A suitor?"
he said, somehow imbuing the word with a sexual con-
notation it did not normally have within their class.

"A caller," the earl corrected softly. Unconsciously,
the tone of his voice had grown politely distant, as his
father's sometimes would when he was confronted with
someone he disapproved of.

"My daughter's dead," the marquess said abruptly.

Suddenly he stepped back into the hallway and closed
the front door in the earl's face. Stunned by the bizarre
behavior and the abruptness of Brynmoor's departure,
Justin hesitated. He felt Andrew's head turn against his
thigh, and knew Drew was looking up at him. Smiling,
he lowered his own gaze from the door that seemed to be
still vibrating with the force of its closure, to meet the
boy's.

"He'll be gone soon and then we can go in. You
mustn't be afraid," Drew said. "He won't hurt you. He's
just confused."

The observation was certainly an echo of something
the boy had been told. Justin could almost hear Sarah's
calm voice underlying the childish one. "I know," he
said. "I knew him once. A long time ago."

"His daughter died, and his mind's unbalanced," Andrew said.

Again the adult phrases had obviously been learned by
rote. Justin wondered if the child understood half of what
he'd been told. What he had just parroted was in such
direct contrast to his physical reaction to his grandfather.

"Shall we go in?" Justin asked.

"I think Sarah will be angry with me," Drew said softly.

"I think you may safely assume that."

"But you're coming, too?" Andrew asked.

A difficult interview all around, the earl thought. But in for a penny, in for a pound, he supposed. It was too late to desert Andrew now. They would see this through together, and when he was sure Sarah understood what was going on, he'd begin the process of disengaging the hold her son's small fingers had already taken around his heart.

She had simply humiliated herself, Sarah acknowledged for the hundredth time. And in doing so, she had accomplished nothing. Nothing that would help Andrew. Or Justin. And certainly nothing that could possibly be of any benefit to herself. The earl of Wynfield had made it quite clear that he had no intention of accepting her proposal, no matter in what terms it was couched.

Couched. What an appropriate image, she thought bitterly. She had offered her inheritance *and* her body to Justin Tolbert and both had been summarily turned down. Not just turned down, she remembered. He had laughed at the idea of allowing her to bear his sons.

She had made a fool of herself. First by her offer of financial assistance, presented in terms that anyone with half a brain might have seen through. As Justin certainly had.

She didn't need a factor for her father's estates. She needed a mentor for Andrew. Someone who would teach him all the things he would have to know if he were ever to become an accepted member of society. Someone whose regard in that society was so high it might carry poor Drew to acceptance there as well.

But it had taken her the last two days to acknowledge that her own needs, as urgent and as basic as breathing, had really been what had sent her to Wynfield to embellish her original offer. And two days to admit that she had gotten exactly what she deserved—Justin's scorn of her maneuvering. He had seen through her "generosity" as if she had been made of glass.

"I have broke my head," Andrew said.

She looked up from the estate books she had been pretending to peruse as those endless recriminations circled through her mind. Whatever the truth of Drew's statement, she realized, her eyes resting with dismay on his face, he had certainly suffered injury. "Andrew," she whispered.

She rose and hurried around her father's desk. She had almost reached the little boy when she realized he was not alone. The earl of Wynfield stood in the doorway behind him. The shadows of the hallway had hidden him until he stepped forward into the light. Although his face was not marked, it seemed as white and stiff as the child's.

"I believe the hurt is not so severe as that," Justin said.

His tone was deliberately light, probably for Andrew's benefit, but she didn't like the strain in his face or what was in his eyes. She studied them a long moment, but he said nothing else. And offered no other explanation.

Finally she followed her first instinct and dropped to her knees on the thick Oriental rug in front of the little boy. She touched the cut on Andrew's chin and ran trembling fingers over the discoloration under his eye. "What happened?" she asked.

"I hit my head on a rock," Drew said.

He captured her fingers in his own and carried them to

the back of his head, placing them carefully over the lump.

"Is it as big as a goose's egg?" he asked.

It was obvious he was hoping for an affirmation, so she obliged. "I think it might be," she said. "And you hit it on a rock?" she asked carefully, knowing that didn't begin to explain the injuries to his face.

"When I fell," he said. "The nice lady said for you to put a vinegar…" He hesitated, searching for the missing word, before he looked up at the earl for aid.

"A vinegar poultice," Wynfield supplied, his eyes on Sarah's, whose gaze had followed the child's to his face.

"It will take out all the ache," Andrew said decisively. "Do we have a vinegar one of those?"

"I expect we have," Sarah said, her eyes still on Justin.

The earl's mouth was tightly compressed. She had seen that expression before, and it had portended bad news. This was how he had looked when he told her his regiment had been posted to Spain. There was more here than either of them had explained.

"But you haven't told me about your face," she said, her eyes coming back to Andrew even as her mind tried to fathom why Justin looked so stern. So coldly controlled.

Andrew glanced up at the earl and some silent masculine communication took place between them. Drew took a breath, the depth of it lifting his small shoulders, almost in surrender.

"Those boys," he said. "The ones from the village."

"They hit you?" she asked.

"The big one. He doesn't like me."

Sarah's eyes again found Justin's, but his expression gave her no clue as to what had really happened.

"Have you done something to him, Drew?" she asked.

The child shook his head.

"Called him names?"

Again, the slow negative motion.

"Then perhaps he's jealous that you have more than he. More advantages. Sometimes people who have little feel that way about others who are more fortunate," she suggested.

Drew nodded.

"Do you suppose Mrs. Simkins might manage the poultice?" the earl said.

Surprised, Sarah looked up at him.

"We need to talk," he advised her bluntly.

Without Andrew, she realized.

"I'll take him to the kitchen," she said.

Justin nodded, his face still set in the same grim lines it had held since the beginning of this interview. Obviously, something had happened that he believed she should know about. Something Andrew had said or done to precipitate the boy's attack? she wondered.

Of course, speculation accomplished nothing. It seemed Justin would be more than willing to tell her the bad news. He had brought Andrew home, apparently for that very purpose. And the sooner she got this over with, the better. Sarah rose from her knees and put a guiding hand on the back of Andrew's head.

"Ow," he said, dodging the touch of her fingers. "You forgot my head is broken," he accused.

"I'm sorry, Drew. We'll ask Mrs. Simkins to see to it. Will you wait here?" she asked the earl, already directing Andrew around him and into the hall.

He nodded, but he didn't move as they passed him, Andrew skipping ahead of her, obviously little the worse for wear after his ordeal. She could only hope she would endure half so well the one that would be awaiting her when she returned.

The earl of Wynfield leaned tiredly against the frame of the doorway in which he was standing. His eyes examined the office where Sarah had been working. It seemed strange to think of her in this setting. He had always associated Sarah with sprigged muslin dresses and dance cards. Not with ledgers and ink-stained fingers. Of course, if she really managed her father's properties, then those were a necessary part of her life now.

And Longford seemed to be prospering under her supervision. Everything he had seen as he'd brought Andrew home appeared prosperous and well cared for. In direct, and painful, contrast to his own holdings, he acknowledged. Judging by his encounter with poor Brynmoor, that was all due to Sarah's direction.

"You wanted to talk to me?" she said.

She had stopped behind him in the hall, he realized, maybe waiting for him to go into the office. He found himself resistant to that idea. For one thing, he didn't want to move. The agony in his leg had subsided to a grinding ache and he didn't want to exacerbate it. He needed all his wits about him in order to make Sarah understand what was going on without totally insulting her. He also didn't want to sit across the desk from her. That proximity would be painful as well, but for other reasons entirely.

"About Andrew," he said, turning to face her. "It might be better if we talk inside."

Her eyes seemed very blue, almost luminous in the dimness of the hall. "All right," she said.

He stepped aside, and she slipped through the doorway.

She didn't touch him as she brushed by, but suddenly there was an evocative hint of rose water in the air.

She walked over to the desk and stood behind it. Justin remained where he was. She waited a moment, obviously expecting him to come inside the office, but when he didn't move, finally she spoke. "There was more to what happened today than he told me," she suggested.

"I'm afraid so."

She sat down, her eyes meeting his. "Then why don't you tell me," she said. "That's obviously why you came."

He wondered if it were. Meg would have brought Andrew home. And he hadn't been forced to respond to the child's wishes in the matter of his conveyance.

"I believe your son is in danger," he said.

She didn't answer at once, her chin lifting minutely as Drew's did when he was being challenged.

"From the village boys?" she asked, but then she spoke again before he could answer her question. "They're children. They don't understand."

"They understand too well. That seems to be the problem," Justin said. "Someone has taken the trouble to give them a very clear understanding of the circumstances of Drew's birth."

Her eyes widened, and then they fell. However, that was only for a moment. When she raised them again, they seemed to be calm and assured. "You believe he is being victimized because of the circumstances of his birth?" she asked.

"Because he's not of their class," Justin said. "Because of his size, perhaps. The difference in his clothing and theirs. But certainly, primarily, because of what they have been told about his parentage."

Her lips, which had been tightly held together through

that listing, moved, almost loosening before they tight-ened again.

"Being different in childhood is an incredible burden," Justin continued. "Drew's is heavier than most."

She said nothing in response to that, either, but her eyes didn't falter again.

"Meg Randolph says those boys are dangerous. She's in a better position to know that than I am, of course, but from what I have seen…" He paused, not wanting to cause her to overreact.

"You think they'll do him serious harm."

"I think it's possible."

"What do you suggest I do?" she said. "Send for the magistrate? Pack Drew off to school? Keep him prisoner? Flog him if he leaves the house again?"

There was an edge of bitterness to the questions. And Justin had no answers, of course, so he didn't attempt to make any.

"Andrew is an outcast," she said deliberately. "He will never be anything other than an outcast unless some-one…unless someone other than I or my father takes a hand in the matter. I can physically protect him, perhaps, but it isn't in my power to change his situation."

It *was* in his. Justin fully understood what she was try-ing to tell him. He had the power, she believed, to change Drew's life. To protect him not only from those children, but from the rest of the world, which would certainly always look askance at who, and what, Drew was. And even the power to strengthen him against Brynmoor's contempt. To mold this child, who so obviously longed to be molded, into a man.

And, at the same time, he had the power to put an end to his own painful situation. All he had to do was to say he would live here at Longford. Agree to exist under the same roof with the woman he had once loved. *And* her bastard son. A son she had borne to another man. A man she had fallen in love with so quickly it was obvious that what Justin felt about her had made no impact on her own emotions.

A simple choice. Save Drew. Save his own heritage. Restore his family's name. And all Justin must give up in order to achieve those things was his pride. And a long-ago summer dream of what his life would be. His life with this woman.

But of course, his life had already changed so greatly as to be unrecognizable. He was no longer—and never would be again—the man who had sailed to Iberia five years ago. He was forced daily to acknowledge how very different he was from that man. His awkwardness reminded him. The debilitating pain. His inability to push his body beyond certain boundaries.

The old dreams were ashes. There were, however, some things that could be salvaged from what the flames of war had devoured. His land and its people, who were, like Meg Randolph, depending on him to make things right again. And the life of an innocent child, who had slipped small, trusting fingers into his.

He would never have Sarah. There had been nothing in her manner to indicate that there was anything left of what she might once have felt for him. If, indeed, she had ever felt anything at all. Granted, she had indicated she would sleep with him if he demanded it. Sacrifice or duty—and done for Andrew's sake, rather than her own. Or for his. And of course, knowing that, it was a demand he would never make.

Thoughts and images moved through Justin's head as rapidly as summer lightning. Star. The differences between his neglected and abused lands and the richness of these. Meg Randolph's earnest face assuring Andrew that the new earl didn't intend to leave because he still had things to make right here.

And overshadowing all the others, Drew's hand sliding into his. The small, warm body riding trustfully in the saddle before him and shrinking back fearfully against his leg when confronted by his own grandfather. Drew's eyes, looking up to assure Justin that Brynmoor wouldn't hurt him.

"Have them draw up the necessary papers," he said harshly. "You'd better do it quickly before your bridegroom is clapped in Newgate. And don't let Drew out of your sight," he ordered, his tone more suited to the battlefield than to an agreement about marriage settlements.

"Then…" Sarah's voice faltered, her eyes stunned.

"You've made yourself a bad bargain, Sarah, but if you need to hear it, then yes. I shall leave it to you to tell Drew."

Without another word, the earl of Wynfield turned away from the doorway and disappeared into the shadows of the hallway, leaving Lady Sarah Spenser alone and openmouthed with shock.

Be careful what you pray for, they warned, *because you might get it.* And, Sarah thought, despite everything, even the harsh terms in which the response to her prayers had been expressed, she just had.

Chapter Six

"Keep your left up," the earl of Wynfield instructed, his voice carrying through the crisp, late-November air. "And keep your chin down."

Obediently, Andrew ducked his chin and raised his left. His feet danced and his miniature fists stabbed the air as his small body circled the earl, who was moving far more slowly.

"That's it," Justin declared.

He put his hand on Drew's shoulder, seeming to lean some of his weight on the child. Contentedly, the boy slowed his pace, matching it to the limping one of the man he clearly adored.

They were coming up from the stables. Sarah had heard their voices through the office window, which, despite the cold, she had opened earlier in anticipation of their arrival. At the sound, she had risen from her desk to look out on them.

Justin had forbidden Andrew to leave Longford without his permission, a restriction that, as far as she knew, the child had obeyed. Of course, there was no longer any reason for him to travel through the woods where he had been attacked. After all, the object of Drew's previous quests was no longer there, but was installed now at Longford instead.

Sarah looked down at the gold band on her left hand. She wondered how many people knew what a sham this marriage was. Her abigail, certainly. Peters, the earl's valet. If they did, then eventually all of the servants would. And there was nothing she could do about that below-stairs gossip, as humiliating as it was.

When her gaze came back to the window, the two of them had disappeared from sight. Andrew would almost certainly stop by the office for a visit, but the glimpse she had caught of her husband was probably the only time she would see him today. The only sight of him she would have, if the normal pattern of their relationship was followed.

As soon as their vows had been exchanged, she had authorized Mr. Samuels to write drafts for whatever sums the earl requested. She didn't want Justin to have to come to her for money. Not for what was needed to pay off his debts or for what he had begun infusing into his long-neglected estate.

Although he slept at Longford, as per the terms of their agreement, most of Justin's days were spent at Wynfield Park, where he worked from dawn until dusk. The improvements he had made were remarkable, and it was only because he was willing to devote so many hours and so much energy to the task, of course, that he had achieved such a turnaround in so short a time. And again, his name was on the tip of every tongue in the district.

Lately, more than one of those wagging tongues had expressed concern to Sarah that her husband might be working too hard, given the fact that he had been invalided out of service only a few short months before. She had been unable to comment on those avowals of dismay for the simple reason that she seldom saw Justin in order to form any opinion on the state of his health.

They didn't share meals. Or conversation. Or anything else, she thought. Nothing but a mutual love for Andrew. She supposed she should be grateful they had that in common. It had, after all, been the purpose of this arrangement. Whatever Justin felt about her, he had not let it influence his attitude toward the little boy whom he mistakenly believed was her son.

When she had given her oath to Amelia to keep the details of Andrew's birth a secret, it had seemed such a simple promise. She had not thought twice about making it. And now, no matter how much she might regret it, she was bound by that vow.

So stupidly bound, but bound all the same, she thought, taking a deep breath. She had struggled with her conscience, wanting desperately to tell Justin the truth. She had told herself that Mellie had not meant she should keep the secret from her own husband. That was against every moral precept she had ever been taught.

Of course, so was breaking an oath, she admitted. Especially one made on her mother's grave—to her dying sister. Besides, why should Justin believe her, even if she told him the truth? As far as he knew, as far as anyone knew, Amelia had been dead and buried months before Andrew's birth. Would Justin not despise Sarah even more for seeming to try to push her own sin off on her dead sister?

She shook her head, the movement very slight. She was overwhelmed again by the moral dilemma her circumstances had created. She was Justin's wife, something she had wanted to be for as long as she could remember. As long as she had known what being a wife entailed. Yet she was not. Not in any way that truly mattered. And unless he somehow discovered the truth about Andrew, she knew that she never would be.

"I've been learning to mill 'em down," Andrew announced as he rushed into the room, bringing the freshness of the outside air in with him. "Wynfield is teaching me."

The use of Justin's title was a compromise they had come to together, Sarah supposed. They had certainly not discussed with her what Drew should call the earl.

"I was watching you through the window," she confessed.

"Did you see my left?" Andrew asked.

He had stopped at the desk and picked up the magnifying glass she kept there to decipher the former steward's nearly illegible handwriting. She frequently checked the progress of the estate against past records, which had been meticulously inscribed in his crabbed hand. As she had learned more about estate management, she had had just reasons to be pleased with the comparison. At least until the sudden and severe drain on its resources caused by her marriage.

"It's a fine left," she said, smiling. "And on whom do you plan to use it?"

"I used it on the groom," Andrew said. "When we were sparring."

"Sparring?" Sarah questioned, unfamiliar with the term.

"Pretending to box," Andrew explained. "It's what Wynfield did at Gentleman Jackson's in London."

After all, she thought, reading his tone, she was only a girl and could not be expected to know about such important things. She hid her smile, watching him lower the glass over a variety of objects on the desk.

"Wynfield milled 'em down," Andrew said, enamored of the colorful phrase he had obviously heard only today.

"And was more frequently milled down himself."

At the sound of that deep voice, Sarah glanced up in surprise. And exactly as it had the first time she had seen him at Meg's, her heart reacted in a highly inappropriate manner. After all, this was her husband. Of almost two months. Whom she had seen perhaps a dozen times in that span. And from whom she could not have pulled her gaze away had her life depended on it.

He *was* thin, she thought. Far too thin. Of course, as hard as he was working, perhaps that should not be so surprising. Since he had spent many of those hours outdoors, his skin had not lost the bronze it had acquired in Spain. There was now, however, a grayness in the slight hollows in his cheeks, despite the tinge of red that seemed to heighten his cheekbones.

Cheekbones that were too prominent, she decided. If she had believed his skin stretched too tightly over the underlying bone when he had first come home, what should she think now?

"That's a whisker," Andrew accused, his eyes glowing as they did whenever he even talked of his hero, much less when he was confronted with the reality.

"Andrew," Sarah admonished.

"But it isn't true, Sarah. You were a good boxer, weren't you?" Andrew demanded. "Before they cut off your leg, I mean."

This time, Sarah didn't dare open her mouth.

"Not nearly so good as Jackson," the earl said easily. "Or as some of the others who practiced there."

He looked up at Sarah, and she wondered what he could read in her face. Shock at Andrew's openness about the loss of his leg? Concern for his health? From a wife who had no right to express that concern. They had simply made a bargain, a business arrangement. She had only to look at and listen to the ecstatic Drew to know that Justin was carrying out his part of it.

The child accompanied the earl almost everywhere, even occasionally allowed to tag along during the long days he spent at Wynfield. And Justin was careful to take Drew along when he visited his tenants and hers. They both knew that would eventually lead to what she had wanted for her son: acceptance by the district, however grudgingly given, because its beloved earl accepted him.

She had also fulfilled her part of their agreement, of course. The sums of money that had been withdrawn from her accounts in the last two months were staggering. More than once Mr. Samuels had spoken to her about it, but she had told him that the earl was to have what he needed. And whatever it cost, she thought again, looking down at Andrew's face, it was well worth it. More than worth it. Besides, Justin had very honestly warned her of the expense of what she'd proposed.

They had both kept to the terms of their agreement. Their bargain had not, however, included any provision for friendship. Or anything else.

"I'm going to London tomorrow," Justin said. "I have some business with my bankers that can no longer be delayed."

She nodded, understanding that he was not seeking her permission, but rather informing her.

"I could go with you and keep you company," Andrew offered. "So you won't be lonely. I have never been to London."

The earl smiled at him. "We've already discussed this, Drew. Another time. Another trip."

"Have you ever been to London, Sarah?" the child asked.

"Yes," she said softly.

Images of the last time she'd been in London were suddenly in her head. Justin, incredibly handsome in his regimentals. A crowded ballroom. A proposal of marriage. How different from those memories was the painful situation between them now.

"I was there a very long time ago," she said.

Her eyes rose to her husband's, but as soon as they had, holding on his face for only a second, he turned from the doorway and stepped into the hall. Sarah thought there was a small, but rather sharp intake of breath when he moved. The sound was gone so quickly she could not be certain—not even when she thought about it later, reliving the scene in her head countless times—that that was what she had heard. Or certain it had any significance. She listened as his uneven footsteps faded away.

She looked back at Andrew, who was again applying her magnifying glass to the papers on the desk. At least Justin's absence would give her some time with Drew. She didn't begrudge the boy the obvious joy he felt in the hours he spent with the earl, of course, but she had missed him. Perhaps she missed being the center of his world as well. What had once been their small world. Which was now shared by a man who seemed an enigma. And far more distant, even living under the same roof, than he had ever been before.

The days of the earl's absence passed slowly. In the week since Justin had been gone, she and Andrew reestablished their old camaraderie. There was no doubt, however, how much the little boy missed him.

Drew chattered about Wynfield constantly, recounting

every moment they had spent together and devising things that he planned to suggest they might undertake together on his hero's return. Since they had been given no estimation as to when that might be, the days stretched long and empty for both of them. Sarah had not realized how much she looked forward to those occasional glimpses she had had of her husband. Or how much she had cherished them when they occurred.

"When is he coming back?" Andrew asked plaintively after the tenth day without any communication from the earl.

"When he completes his business, I suppose," Sarah said, looking out on the rain-swept vista of the cold December day. She wondered if Justin would even consider traveling in these conditions. And if he did, whether he would be warm enough. And if he were working as hard in the capital as he had here.

She knew that he had put into effect a great number of projects at Wynfield before he had left, despite the inclement weather. Of course, if you were willing to spend enough money, there were quite enough workers in the district who were willing to brave the elements to earn it.

The improvements the earl was instituting at the Park were resulting in a boost for the entire local economy. Probably another reason for his popularity, Sarah thought. Her lips curved into a slight smile over the irony that although it was her money being spent at Wynfield, it was doing nothing for her own acceptance in the district. And truthfully, she didn't care.

"We could write to him," Andrew suggested. "I am not entirely sure that I told him what I wanted for Christmas."

"I should hope you did *not*," Sarah said. "Little boys

who demand Christmas treats frequently don't receive them."

"But how should he know what I truly want if I don't tell him?" Andrew asked.

"Whatever you receive from the earl you should be very grateful for," Sarah admonished.

"Of course, I will," said Andrew, "but I cannot see how it should hurt if I give him a hint about what I really want."

"You could give me a hint," she suggested, smiling at his undeniable logic.

"And you will tell him? You will write to him in London?"

"Perhaps," she said.

"You only want to know what *you* should give me," he said.

Sarah laughed. "What's wrong with that?"

"But this is a special thing. And only Wynfield can give it to me," Andrew said.

"I see," said Sarah.

"I hope you are not…" Andrew paused, searching for the proper word.

"Disappointed?" she suggested.

"Jealous," he supplied.

"Jealous?" she repeated in astonishment. And then she realized that there was some part of her that *was* envious of the closeness of Andrew's relationship with the earl. But not, she admitted, on the grounds Andrew feared.

"Because I like him so very much," Andrew explained. "I love you just as well, Sarah. You need not be afraid of that."

"No, dearest," Sarah said, looking down into earnest blue eyes, "I'm not afraid of that."

"It's just that I am growing up, you know."

She nodded, not trusting her voice.

"And...I have never before had a papa."

"He isn't your father, Drew," she said softly, her heart contracting with how much she loved him.

"I know. We have talked about that," he said.

Sarah wondered what that conversation had been like, considering Andrew's tendency to speak whatever was on his mind.

"But..." Again he hesitated, his small face still serious. "He is very close to one," he finished wistfully. "As close as I shall ever have to a father, I expect."

There was nothing she could say to that. After all, this was part of what she had hoped for when she had made her offer. She put her hand behind Drew's head and drew him close enough to press her lips against his curls. He allowed the caress, and then, straightening, he pulled away from her.

"I'm not a baby anymore, Sarah," he said.

"I know," she agreed.

Her eyes again sought the chilled and desolate landscape outside and wondered, as longingly as Andrew, when the earl would be coming home.

"Why, Sarah," a pleasant voice admonished. "So early at work. And so industrious."

It was a voice and an accent Sarah would have recognized anywhere. Her eyes lifted, widened in disbelief. A smiling David Osborne stood in the open door of the estate office.

He was wearing a caped greatcoat unbuttoned to reveal a coat of bottle-green superfine and a striped waistcoat that elegantly spanned a still slender waist. His cravat was high and heavily starched, reaching almost to his smoothly shaved chin. Even his eyes smiled at her, as if he were truly delighted to see her again.

"What are you doing here?" she asked, a frisson of fear flickering through her body. All the memories of that terrible time in Ireland were suddenly in her head.

"Is that any way to greet your dear brother?" he chided, amusement lurking in his eyes.

"You are *not* my brother, dear or otherwise," Sarah said.

"But I am the father of your…foster son, is it?"

Sarah knew the uncertainty in his voice was as false as his smile. As false as everything about him. Unconsciously, she contrasted it to another masculine smile, and as she had from the moment of her introduction to Osborne, found it wanting.

"An inconvenient foster son. Especially now," he added softly. Despite the softness, there was a hint of malice in his tone. It did not match the smile that lingered about his lips.

"I don't know what you mean," Sarah said. She wondered if he had somehow heard of her marriage and meant to make mischief. "What are you doing here?" she asked again.

"Times are hard, Sarah. If one can't count on family in difficult economic situations, then who can one depend on?"

"You have no family here," she said coldly.

"I have a son," he said. "Or have you conveniently managed to forget that truth in the midst of all your other lies?"

"Rather the reverse, I should think," Sarah said, but now she knew what this was about. Just what it had always been about with Osborne. He was single-minded in pursuit of his objectives, and one of them had always been the Spenser money. That was the reason for his original courtship of her. And of Amelia.

But he had very rightly come to fear Brynmoor's rage, which was why he hadn't made any demands on the marquess, even after successfully stealing his daughter. That original plan had been destroyed by her father's announcement of Mellie's death. Perhaps there had been some method in his madness after all.

"You have so much, Sarah, and I so little. Only the dear memories of your sister's love. A son I never see. A child who doesn't even know me. That's precious little to show for my life. And not of much…practical worth," he added, smiling. "So I find I must throw myself on your mercy."

"No," Sarah said.

"You haven't managed to spend it all, have you, Sister?" he said, smiling again, obviously not at all dismayed by her refusal. "But of course, you have a new husband. An expensive one, I understand. Is that what's behind your hesitation?"

"My husband," Sarah said, feeling her anger rise, "and his affairs are none of your concern."

"As long as the estate can afford him."

She clamped her lips over the rejoinder she longed to make. It had nothing to do with him if her husband had need of her inheritance. Or if she were spending it a little prematurely.

"Does your father know what you're doing with his money?" Osborne asked. "Buying yourself a husband, I mean. I promise you, my dear, I could have been had much more cheaply."

"I'm sure you could have been," she said. And then she realized that she had just acknowledged he was right:

her marriage had been very expensive. "Only I wasn't interested in that arrangement, of course."

"As long as your husband doesn't take away from what is due to my son," the Irishman said, still smiling, "I don't suppose I can complain about your…self-indulgence."

There was so much blatantly wrong with the conclusions inherent in that statement that Sarah was momentarily rendered speechless. "My self-indulgence?" she repeated incredulously.

That was the accusation that hurt most, of course. But Osborne's suggestion that she was buying herself a husband at Drew's expense was equally ridiculous. As was the implication that David was the least bit concerned about his son.

"Forgive me if I'm wrong, but this *is* the same man you were so enamored of when we first met, isn't it? Of course, now he has a title as well. Much better than a lowly soldier's rank. Congratulations, Sarah. You've gotten what you wanted."

This time Sarah held her tongue. Nothing she had said had been to her advantage. She didn't know where David had acquired his knowledge of her affairs, but if he had spent any time in the district before he'd made his appearance here this morning, then she could be sure he had been given an earful.

"My primary concern, in addition to my own financial situation, is that my son is being taken care of. I have always had the utmost confidence in your love for Andrew. But now…now I suppose, as his father, I must ask the question, no matter how uncongenial it seems. Is your new husband good to the boy?" Osborne asked. "We both know that sometimes stepparents are indifferent to the welfare of their stepchildren."

"You may rest assured that is not the case here," Sarah said.

Her distaste was growing the longer she looked at that still-handsome face. In contrast to Justin, Osborne seemed unmarked by the passage of the years. He looked exactly the same as when he had courted her. Of course, his experiences had not been those Wynfield had endured. David Osborne did not believe in enduring. Not for love or duty.

"Then he's fond of the child," David said.

"Very fond," Sarah said challengingly. "You need have no concern on that score. Or on any other."

As if you had ever been concerned for Drew, she thought, but she was trying to say as little as possible. The quicker this was over, the better. She was only thankful David had chosen to make his appearance while Justin was away.

And then, thinking how convenient that was, she wondered if he had known the earl was in London. After all, the David Osbornes of the world seldom relished dealing with someone like Wynfield, who seemed incapable of being cajoled or intimidated.

"The boy isn't...in the way?" David asked.

"In the way?"

"New marriage and all," he said. "I thought that perhaps you might wish me to take him off your hands."

The words were casual. Almost offhand. And hearing them, Sarah felt the blood in her veins freeze, her entire body chilling with their threat. "What do you mean?" she whispered.

"Why, simply that you have had the burden of raising my son for more than four years. And now, considering the very changed circumstances of your own life..."

He let the words hang in the air between them. Sarah

tried to decide what might have brought this on. David had never before professed the slightest interest in Andrew's welfare, much less a desire to assume responsibility for raising his son.

"No," she said softly.

"And if I insist?" he said, his voice just as quiet, his smile lingering about the corners of his mouth as he held her eyes.

"You have no right to insist. You don't care about Andrew," she accused. "You never have."

"Every father cares for his child. At least you'd find it difficult to convince people otherwise. And Andrew is, as far as I am aware," he said, his voice almost amused, "my only son."

"No one knows he's your son," she said.

"That's because you never told them," he suggested. "Instead you fabricated some cock-and-bull fable about fostering him for a dying Spenser relative. I suppose you *could* provide the name of that relative, Sarah. *If* anyone should ask. Or perhaps some proof that the arrangement was indeed entered into?"

She couldn't, of course, but Sarah was still trying to fathom David's purposes in making this threat. He didn't want Drew. It didn't fit into his character to wish to be saddled with a small boy. And he didn't care if Justin was good to Andrew or not. So what was this all about?

What was David Osborne about? she thought, answering her own question. "You want me to pay you money so you won't take Drew away from me?"

He smiled at her again. "I'm simply telling you that I'm now willing to assume the responsibility for my son."

"You can't prove he's your son."

"Ah, Sarah, you are so astute. It *would* be very difficult to establish whose child this is after all this time. Especially considering what has been suggested through the years to explain his birth. Or should I say to explain why a spinster such as yourself would, after a prolonged absence, bring a baby home. There were so many rumors, I understand.''

''None of them concerned you,'' she said. ''Or Amelia.''

That was the one thought that had comforted her through the maelstrom of gossip. Rumor had pointed its finger at her as the sinner and not at her sister, who was, of course, supposed to have died and been buried months before the baby was born.

''But you and I know the truth,'' Osborne said.

''A truth you can never prove.''

''You mean prove it, for example, in a court of law?'' he asked innocently. ''I suppose to do that would require documentation of some kind,'' he suggested.

He was right, Sarah realized in relief. To claim Drew legally David would have to have some kind of documentation. Otherwise, she would fight him every step of the way, using the old gossip to her own advantage. Her heart, which had faltered when he'd mentioned the courts, began to beat steadily again.

''But I have that, of course,'' David added. He reached into the inside pocket of his greatcoat and removed a paper. ''The priest who attended to the baby's baptism and Amelia's death was kind enough to supply it. Don't you remember? As next of kin, *and* as a witness to both, you even signed this.''

Sickness washed over her in a great wave. She *had* signed a document. David had told her it was necessary to have Amelia buried. Sarah had been distraught over her sister's death and far more concerned about keeping the baby alive than she had been about any legal or even religious requirements. She had signed whatever David pushed across the table to her. Signed it, so relieved that he had finally seen to something.

"It's all here," he said. "If you want to read it. Or perhaps your husband sees to your affairs now."

She stood up, knees trembling, and held out her hand for the paper he held. Again Osborne laughed.

"I said *read* it, my dear. Not have it. I'm very much afraid I don't trust you to treat it with the care it deserves."

She hesitated, not wanting to be any closer to him than she already was, but she'd be a fool if she took his word for what was written on that paper. She might have let David trick her into signing this thing years ago, but she was a very different person now than she had been then. More knowledgeable about how one carried out business, for one thing. There were certain men whose word was their bond. Then there were others....

David Osborne very definitely fell into the second category. Trembling with fury, she walked around the desk and to the doorway where he stood. Exactly where Justin had stood when he had told her he was embarking on his trip to London.

"All right," she said, her eyes demanding.

Osborne unfolded the paper he'd taken from his pocket and held it up for her inspection. It was exactly what he had said. A document verifying the baptism of an infant boy. Andrew David Osborne. Son of...

She took a breath. The names written on the paper were quite clear. Son of Amelia Spenser and David Osborne. And beneath them, equally clear, was her own signature, as carefully inscribed as for a schoolroom exercise.

"You don't want Andrew," she said.

"That isn't the point, my dear. The point is that you

do. That's what makes a bargain, Sarah. If one party wants something badly enough to pay the price.''

"And what *is* the price?"

Whatever it was, she knew she would have to pay it. And then, remembering the enormous withdrawals that had been made from the estate's accounts in the last few weeks, she wondered suddenly if she would be able to.

"I haven't quite decided," he said, his manner almost teasing. "But I will very soon, I promise. And I shall certainly be in touch, Sarah."

Without another word, he turned and disappeared into the shadowed hallway where she had last seen her husband. And where David's words still seemed to echo. *I shall certainly be in touch.*

Chapter Seven

"Are we almost there?" Andrew asked. He had been asking the same question at quarter hour intervals since they left Longford.

He could be no more eager to reach London than she, Sarah thought. After the confrontation with Osborne, she had wanted to get Andrew as far away from Longford as possible. Somewhere his father could never find him.

That had been her first instinct. Her second had been to seek Wynfield's protection. This journey they had undertaken satisfied both. She hadn't questioned why she felt so certain Justin could keep Drew safe when she could not. Simply because he was Justin, she supposed. And because she knew he was more than a match for her sister's lover.

Sarah had come to the ironic realization that if Osborne *did* go through with his threat to go to court, Justin would finally know she had not betrayed him. Perhaps then the cold indifference that was in his eyes when he looked at her would disappear. And she wanted that more than she had ever wanted anything in her life. Anything other than Andrew.

And she could really lose Andrew if Osborne went to

court. She had now had time to think about what he
threatened. He didn't want Andrew, not unless taking the
boy was the only way he could get what he *did* want—
what he had wanted from the beginning. As much of
Brynmoor's wealth as he could possibly manage to acquire. If Sarah didn't pay whatever he demanded, he
might very well take his document to court to try to recover anything that might be due to Drew as Brynmoor's
grandson.

She took a deep breath and smiled at the little boy,
despite her anxiety. He couldn't be allowed to know that
she was so full of foreboding. She pulled him against her
side and tucked the lap rug more securely around him.

"We'll be there soon," she said. "Are you tired?"

"I just want to see him," Drew said.

"I know," Sarah whispered, putting her lips against
the small head that was leaning on her shoulder. "I know
you do."

So did she. She wanted to tell Justin the whole sordid
tale. To confess the lie her letter to him four years ago
had contained. To tell him about the promise she had
given her sister that had compelled her to write it.

*Don't tell anyone. Not even Papa. I could not bear for
them to know what I've done.* Poor Amelia. If David did
what he'd threatened, then it would all come out. In the
worst possible way. It would ruin Amelia's name, and the
very public scandal of a court case would haunt Drew the
rest of his life.

And Sarah had no idea how the courts would view the
claims of an illegitimate grandson. The rights of male
descendents were always considered to be of more weight
than those of females. The only reason she and Amelia
were to inherit her father's properties was because there
was not a single living male relative to lay claim to it.

Perhaps Andrew's claim, in the eyes of the law, was as good as hers.

It was not, of course, that she would begrudge Drew that inheritance, but if her father died before Andrew reached his majority, as seemed very likely, then David Osborne would have complete control of his son's money. And, more importantly, in order to get it, he would take control of the child himself.

Sarah didn't care about the money, even though she knew what would happen to it in Osborne's hands. But she cared very deeply about losing the little boy who had belonged to her since he was only a few hours old.

All the possible outcomes of David's threat circled maddeningly in her brain. If Osborne told the truth in court about Drew's birth, she might win back the love Justin had once felt for her. But she might lose Drew, she thought in despair.

Either way, Andrew would certainly lose whatever opportunity he might have had to escape the scandal. Indeed, it would be spread far and wide if it became a battle in the King's courts. And if David won, Drew would also lose Justin, of course, who was, in his eyes, already his father. A far better father than the man who actually held that position.

"How much farther?" Drew asked.

"At least another hour, I think. Shall I tell you a story?"

"A military one," he requested.

"I don't know any military stories," she said truthfully.

"He does," Drew said.

There was only one "he" in Andrew's small world. The man who was at the center of his universe. Sarah herself had arranged to put him there, so how could she allow him to be torn away? But if the truth came out...

Deliberately, she forced herself not to think about any of it anymore. Instead, she squeezed the small body closer to her side, resting her chin on his head and looking out on the desolate landscape, revealed through the windows of the coach.

They had been lucky that the roads were frozen, but not covered with snow. That had been a distinct possibility, and her coachman had quite wisely advised her against making this journey. But she had wanted to be near Justin if this storm broke over their heads. Not the snowstorm, of course, which had not entered into her decision at all. She was far more worried about the storm Osborne threatened to bring down on them.

"Then you may tell another kind of story," Andrew conceded. "But make it exciting, Sarah. I'm not a baby any longer."

When he had been, she thought, he had been *her* baby, given into her keeping by her dying sister. A trust and a promise.

"All right," she agreed, trying to think of any tale she knew that would be bloodthirsty enough to keep him occupied until they arrived at her father's town house, yet not give him nightmares.

"Once upon a time," she began, and her voice didn't fade until his head lolled, relaxed in sleep, against her breast. Then, again, all the permutations of what might happen if Osborne did what he had threatened ran endlessly through her head.

She had intended to go to her father's house. And of course, she didn't expect Justin to be there. He would be staying at his own residence in town. By the time they reached London, however, she knew that neither she nor Drew would be satisfied until they had seen him. That was why she had made this hastily planned and perhaps foolishly executed journey.

She had not warned Justin she was coming and could not be certain of her reception. But after all, she told herself, she was the earl of Wynfield's wife. She had every right to present herself at his door and seek shelter for the night. She had not taken time to send ahead and warn the staff of her father's London house that she would be arriving, so no one there was expecting her, either. It simply made more sense to go to Justin's, where the staff was already in attendance on the earl.

When the coach pulled up to the front entrance, however, it didn't appear that anyone was in residence. It took an inordinate amount of time to get someone to the door, despite her coachman's determined knocking. Whatever transpired between her servant and the footman who answered those knocks, the coachman eventually returned to hand her down.

Once she stepped inside the town house, she quickly realized that although the earl had been in London for almost two weeks, he had done no entertaining, despite the holiday season. The furnishings of the formal rooms were all shrouded with their winter holland covers, and the house was so cold she could see her breath before her.

Drew huddled for warmth against her skirts as they stood in the wide front hall, waiting for Wynfield's majordomo to appear. Her coachman assured her he had been sent for, but as the slow minutes slipped away, she began to wonder if she had made a terrible mistake in coming here.

Sarah heard distant, hurrying footsteps, and finally the earl's London butler appeared at the other end of the hall where she and Andrew were waiting. It was obvious his clothing had been quickly donned, since he was still in the process of adjusting it. And it was in need of refurbishing, Sarah realized, as he came close enough for the lamp he carried to reveal the condition of his rather rusty black coat.

Of course, given the fortunes of the Wynfield family in the last few years, that should not be surprising. Her husband's recent projects had, apparently, all focused on his country properties and their tenants.

"I am the countess of Wynfield," she announced, and realized this was the first time she had had occasion to use her title.

"My lady." The butler almost stammered his response.

"The earl is in residence, I believe?"

The man seemed uncertain about how to answer, and for a long time he didn't.

"Is he dining out tonight?" she questioned finally.

"And is the earl expecting you, my lady?"

Sarah knew, of course, that Justin's father and his brother had let their properties go to rack and ruin, but it seemed they had also failed to train their servants. "I'm sure that is none of your concern," she said softly, her voice holding exactly the proper amount of censure.

She could feel Drew shivering. And after all, she was, as she had just claimed, the countess of Wynfield. However ill-run this household might be, it *and* its inhabitants were now her responsibility.

"If the earl *is* here," she continued, "I wish to be taken to him at once. Then you are to prepare adjoining rooms for my foster son and myself. Be sure there are good fires burning in them and that the sheets on the bed are fresh and thoroughly warmed," she added, watching the butler's eyes widen. "You may direct our luggage to those rooms when they are ready. Then have someone see to the horses, please. We've had a long journey."

Apparently, this was a tone the majordomo had at one time been accustomed to. His eyes moved quickly to her coachman, who was standing near the entrance watching the proceedings. Intending to insure she was treated with the proper respect due the marquess of Brynmoor's daughter, Sarah realized in amusement.

The butler's gaze came back to her. He looked as if he wanted to say something, to make some excuse for his behavior, perhaps, but he wisely decided it might be better to simply do as he had been told. ''If you'll follow me, my lady,'' he said.

Sarah put her hand on Andrew's shoulder, directing the exhausted child. The lamp the earl's butler carried wavered before them, almost the only light in the house. The central staircase, beautifully designed, was dimly revealed as they followed him. It was not quite dark enough, however, to hide the stains and signs of wear on its faded carpet.

There was no noise but their footsteps. Not even the subtle whispers of sound produced by a large below-stairs population. Such sounds were so familiar to the inhabitants of a great house like this that they usually went unnoticed. Unless one listened for some indication of the servants' activity, as Sarah did now.

There was nothing of that evident here. No cheerful blaze of wax tapers. No warmth from the enormous fireplaces that would be found in almost every room. No rushing maids and footmen called to see to the needs of the earl's guests. Sarah decided very quickly that a more dismal dwelling it had never been her misfortune to enter.

Still the lamp ahead of them climbed. One flight and then a second before he led them down a dark hall. There could be nothing on this floor but bedchambers, Sarah thought. Surely the man had not misunderstood her instructions, deliberately or otherwise. She had clearly asked to be conveyed to the earl.

Just as she was about to protest, he raised his hand to knock on a door. It moved backward before he could carry out that action, exposing the figure of Justin's valet. Peters had obviously been about to leave the chamber, but confronting the earl's unexpected guests, he stopped in the doorway, mouth dropping open at the sight of Sarah.

The butler's fist, raised to knock, slowly lowered and then fell back to his side. After a heartbeat or two, the valet pulled the door closed behind him. He stood in front of it, the gesture almost protective.

"My lady," Peters said. It didn't seem to be as much a greeting as an expression of shock. Or a question, perhaps.

"I should like to see the earl," Sarah said calmly, determined to keep her composure, despite this united masculine display of near hostility. Then, for the first time, she began to think about why they should be so shocked to find her here and why the valet had stationed himself in front of Justin's bedchamber. A reason that had never occurred to her before now.

Had Justin come up to London expressly to visit his…? To visit a…? Her thoughts faltered, because she was unsure of the terms she should use. She knew her father had had a mistress. Brynmoor had even mentioned her name to Sarah once in one of his disjointed and rambling discourses.

Justin, who had been out of the country for years, had spent some days, maybe even some weeks, in London before he had come home. Perhaps he had renewed an old…acquaintance in the capital. Or made a new one. If either were the case, he would certainly not welcome

Sarah's unannounced presence in this house tonight. Nor would his loyal servants.

The agony of the image of Justin and some other woman together behind this door was far more powerful than the sick embarrassment that had begun roiling in her stomach. No wonder they were blocking the entrance to his bedchamber.

She had made a fool of herself in coming here. In running to Justin at the first sign of trouble. Despite how she felt about him, he had made her no promises about his private behavior. And, of course, she had asked him for none, because she had never even thought about this. Naively, she had never considered the possibility that Justin might seek his carnal pleasures outside the marriage bed.

"Is the earl expecting you, my lady?" the valet finally found composure to ask.

"No," she whispered, without correcting his impertinence.

"What's wrong?" Andrew asked.

She looked down at him, grateful for the excuse not to have to face the two men guarding the earl's privacy. In his tiredness, or perhaps in response to the cold darkness that surrounded them, Drew had been clinging to her skirts in a manner he had outgrown, at least since Wynfield had entered their lives.

Now he was looking up at her, anxiety in the depths of his eyes. His face blurred in the sudden, unexpected burn of her tears. She blinked them away, clearing her vision and then taking a deep breath. "We have to go on to my father's," she said. "We are not expected here." *Or welcome.*

Drew's eyes widened as they searched her face. "Isn't Wynfield here?" he asked. "You said he was." His voice had risen. Tears stood in his eyes, a product of fatigue and this terrible disappointment after their long journey. "You promised me, Sarah," he accused. "You promised I should see Wynfield."

"What the hell is going on out here?"

The angry voice unmistakably belonged to Justin. As with David Osborne's, Sarah would have recognized its distinctive timbre anytime. Anyplace. Pulling her gaze from Drew's face, she looked up in time to see the door behind the valet flung open, so that the small room itself was revealed.

At least there was light, she thought. And warmth. She could feel the welcome heat of the fire that burned on its hearth seeping out into the cold hall where she and Drew stood.

The valet had turned at his master's voice, and then, bowing slightly, he moved aside, revealing the man who had opened that door. Shockingly, Justin was leaning on a crutch, and the blaze from the fireplace behind him cruelly highlighted the reason. The right leg of his trousers hung straight, obviously empty below the knee. And Sarah felt the hot sting of tears again.

"Wynfield," Drew said excitedly.

At the sight of Sarah and Andrew outside his door, Justin's eyes widened, just as his valet's had. The effect was far more pleasant, however. At least more pleasant to her sensibilities. Of course, it had been so long since she had seen him. So many days that she had been deprived of those secret glimpses of her husband that she cherished.

"Sarah?" he said, his voice filled with the same questioning disbelief it had held that first day at Meg Randolph's cottage. And her heart again lodged in her throat.

She was aware that Drew broke away to run through the open doorway and fling himself against his beloved

Wynfield. The earl staggered when the hurtling body hit him, but using the crutch and a quick backward hop, he managed to regain his balance. He put his free hand on the back of the little boy's head and squeezed him close against his good leg.

His eyes, however, never left Sarah's face. They hadn't, not since the valet had moved away from the door, revealing her presence. They held on hers, through a long breathless silence, before he asked softly, "What's wrong?"

Dear God, how much she wanted to tell him. The words trembled on her tongue, demanding release. She had come to him for protection, the instinct to do that so strong, in the face of David Osborne's threat, that her usually reliable common sense had not been able to overcome it.

But of course, she could tell him nothing of what had occurred. There was no explanation of what Osborne had said that would not reveal the Irishman's relationship to Drew. And the details of the boy's birth that she had guarded so long.

"Andrew missed you," she said instead. *And I missed you. I need so much to be with you. I need to know that you are nearby.*

Those words, as true as the others, were left unspoken. She stood in the doorway, watching him. His eyes, luminous in the dimness, continued to assess hers. Once he had known her well enough to know whether or not she was telling him the truth.

Now he must be uncertain of her motives. She was as well. Uncertain of everything except the instinct telling her that as long as they were with Justin, nothing very bad could happen. He wouldn't allow anything to happen. Not to either of them.

Into the considering silence that stretched between them, Andrew's voice intruded. "It's almost Christmas," he said.

Justin's eyes fell, thankfully focusing on the child's face rather than on hers. "And you came all this way to wish me happy Christmas?" the earl said, smiling at Drew, his tone deliberately lightened from his worried question to Sarah.

"No," Andrew said, laughing.

"To bring me presents?" Justin teased, ruffling the little boys's hair with one big, dark hand.

Andrew turned to look at Sarah, his brows raised in inquiry.

"We came to shop," she said.

It might have been the perfect excuse for their unheralded arrival, with Christmas little more than two weeks away, had it not been for the length of the journey and the difficulties of travel this time of year. The earl's gaze followed Drew's back to her face, and at the puzzlement in his eyes, she felt her color rise.

"To shop?" he repeated carefully.

"The shops here are so much better than the ones in the village," she said.

"Of course," Justin concurred.

There was another silence. Thankfully Andrew, who seemed unaware of the unease between the two adults in his life, broke it again. "It's warm in your room," he said.

"Would you like to come in?" the earl invited.

He smiled down at the child. Then, turning awkwardly, he used the crutch to make his way back to the desk, which had been placed near the fire. It was obvious he had been sitting there before their arrival. As he sat down in the chair behind it, he leaned the crutch against the edge of the desk.

"What are these?" Andrew asked.

He had followed his hero, and was looking down at the papers spread out across the expanse of the desk. Even from where Sarah was standing, she could see that they were drawings. Not letters. And not business papers.

"Plans," the earl said softly.

"For what?" Drew asked.

"For things that may never come about," Justin said, smiling.

He lifted the boy onto his lap. Then he pulled the top drawing closer and together they examined what he had been working on. The earl's servants had disappeared into the darkness behind her. Still Sarah hovered by the door, feeling out of place. Left out of the bond the two of them had formed. A bond she had wanted for Andrew, but still…

"It's warmer *inside*, Sarah," Justin said. "It will be more likely to stay that way if you close the door."

She looked up from her unseeing contemplation of his drawings to find that his eyes were on her. And in them was something she had not thought to see there again. Not welcome, perhaps. That was too much to ask. But…acceptance. Acceptance of her right to be here.

It's warmer inside. That had been an invitation. And Sarah, who had stood outside this new-made bond, drawn like a lonely moth to the flame of the growing affection between Justin and Drew, stepped inside her husband's bedroom.

Justin knew there was more to this unexpected arrival than a shopping expedition. He was almost certain Sarah had thought up that excuse as she hovered uncertainly in the door to his room. And uncertainty was not something he associated with the woman she had become.

He had been amazed at what she had accomplished at Longford. In contrast to his, everything on her father's estate, from the dairy to the farm, ran smoothly. And profitably. Her tenants were well cared for, and her books probably balanced. He wouldn't dare ask if they still did, not with the amounts he had taken out of her accounts in the last few months.

Far more than he had really needed to withdraw all at once, he admitted. He had warned her that their bargain would be expensive, and he supposed he had been determined to prove the truth of that.

She had never complained, although, as the sums had grown, he had certainly expected her to. He had almost hoped she would, so that he could throw her protest back in her face, but she hadn't reneged on their agreement. He would give her that. She had kept to the terms of their bargain, allowing him to institute the necessary repairs to both the Park and the cottages that surrounded it. And his father's and brother's debts had all been paid in full.

Despite the enormous drain all of that must have been, even on a fortune as large as Brynmoor's, Sarah had not uttered one word of protest. Neither had Mr. Samuels, of course, but Justin had seen his shock on more than one occasion at the sums he'd requested. And in the beginning, he had intended those to shock.

He had also been determined, of course, that winter would not again find his tenants in need of either food or adequate shelter. And some of the projects he had ordered at Wynfield Park had been necessary to keep it literally from falling down. But come spring...

"What are those?" Sarah asked.

He glanced up and found that instead of approaching

the warmth of the fire as he had expected, she was standing beside his chair, looking down on his drawings.

The days and nights he had spent in London had been long. And very empty. Empty for more reasons than one, he acknowledged, as the faint, feminine fragrance of rose water permeated the very masculine atmosphere of his room. A scent that was too evocative of a long-ago summer in this same city.

"Things I hope to implement in the spring," he said. "Some new methods of husbandry I've been reading about."

The books he had read were scattered around the perimeter of his desk and stacked on the floor beside it. That had been something else he had been allowed to rediscover. The joys of reading, of studying a problem and finding a solution.

His situation the last five years had not allowed time for the intellectual. Or the academic. But during the two weeks of enforced inactivity he had endured in these rooms, he had again found joy in those pursuits. Of course, that was something else he would probably never explain to Sarah.

"You haven't opened the town house," she said.

"No," he admitted.

"Because you're going to sell it immediately?" she asked.

"Not unless you are calling due my notes," he said. An ill-advised jest, he realized, seeing the color drain from her face.

It had been hard having to take Sarah's money, which was another reason, perverse as it might be, that he had been determined to spend as much of it as he could. Being forced into this marriage had been a blow to his pride, already almost as badly damaged as his body. That wasn't

Sarah's fault, of course, and he regretted the gibe as soon as he'd uttered it.

"Call due your notes?" she repeated.

He couldn't read her voice. Once he had been so good at that. At knowing what she was thinking. And feeling. At knowing what she wanted. She was so changed now that he was lost in how to deal with her, especially in their situation.

"Forgive me," he said with real contrition. "Too much time in my own uninteresting company."

"I hold no notes of yours," she said softly.

"I know."

Her eyes held a moment longer, very dark in the firelight, and then they shifted back to the endless and highly detailed drawings he had made. There had not been much else he could do. Nothing, the surgeon he consulted had ordered, but sit and give his leg a chance to heal. And that forced inactivity, when there was so much he needed to be doing, had been almost unbearable.

So he had begun to plan for what he would do when the wound he had broken open two months ago by leaping off Star's back had finally healed enough to allow him to use the artificial foot again. Then he was determined to resume the schedule he had adhered to before he had come to London. Determined to return Wynfield Park to what it had once been. Determined to repair his family's fortune and good name. And determined to repay Sarah.

"This is Wynfield," she said, looking down on the diagrams for terraced fields and windmills and irrigation ditches.

Of course, Sarah knew every mile of these properties, just as he did. She had walked them or driven across them all her life. Far more years than he had, he realized, given his long absences on duty. "Yes," he agreed softly.

"And these are improvements you want to make there."

"Eventually," he said. "I want not only to restore the Park, but to make it more than it was. To make it what it should be. All that it can be."

Her eyes were on his face now, watching as he talked. And Justin realized that he probably sounded mad to her. Gentlemen, especially impoverished ones, did not worry about planning drainage ditches for their meadows.

"But you are not restoring *this* house?" Sarah asked.

He wasn't sure what she meant. Or why she should be concerned. After all, if she wanted to come to London, there was always her father's house, far more elegant than this. Even its location in the heart of Mayfair was more desirable.

"I don't think we should need two London residences. And the market is very good for property here, despite the economy."

For the first time since he had opened the door and found her and Andrew huddled together in the hall, her mouth relaxed, the taut lines giving way to what was almost a smile.

"It might be even better for a little…refurbishing."

"A great deal of refurbishing, I should think," he said. Of course, that would require more money. By now, his initial anger over having been "bought" had subsided, and he had already decided to sell the house just as it was, and to apply whatever it would bring to his debt to Sarah.

"As long as I'm here…" she said hesitantly.

"I beg your pardon?" he said.

"Unless you have an interest in choosing fabric and carpets."

"You are offering…" He paused, unsure exactly what she might be offering.

"To see to the house. I think that putting it back to something like it must once have been can only increase its value when you put it on the market. It's just good business."

"What about your shopping?"

"I don't think that will occupy all my time," she said, really smiling at him for the first time.

It was almost the smile he remembered. Almost Sarah's smile, and something shifted in his chest in response. And then he realized that whatever was in Sarah's smile or in her eyes, it could never be the same. Neither of them was the same.

He was a cripple, dependent on Sarah's charity. And she was the woman who had rejected him when he had been neither of those things. There was nothing left of the relationship they had once shared. All that was between them now was a business arrangement.

That's all this offer was. Sarah was astute enough to know that with a few minor expenditures for cosmetic purposes, the house would bring much more than if he put it on the market as it was now. The sooner it sold, the sooner she would get her money back. He should read nothing more into her offer. And nothing into her arrival on his doorstep looking as if something had frightened her.

Frightened her. That was what he had seen in her eyes—fear. But if Sarah were running away from something, he would be the last person she would come to. Why would he think she might want his protection? Or believe he could protect her? He couldn't, of course. Not anymore.

"I think he's asleep," she said softly.

She bent, stooping by his chair to look at the face of the child he held on his lap. Justin hadn't been aware that while they talked, the little boy's head had drooped lower and lower, until it was resting unmoving against his shoulder.

Sarah looked up from that small relaxed countenance to smile into his eyes. And he fought the pull of it. Fought the emotion that tender smile engendered, forcing himself not to return it.

No romantic fantasies about what Sarah might be doing here were allowed. No fantasies about what he thought her eyes were saying. He couldn't afford them. He had enough to deal with without imagining that a woman who hadn't wanted him when he was strong and whole could possibly be interested in him now.

"You'll have to take him," he said brusquely.

Her eyes widened. At the sharpness of his tone? Or at her realization that he could not carry the boy to bed?

"Of course," she said, but she didn't move. Instead her eyes held his. "Are you all right, Justin?" she asked softly.

The question pierced whatever armor his pride had managed to strap into place as he had stood in the open doorway, exposed to Sarah for the first time as what he now was. Half a man.

And bloody maudlin about it, he chastized himself angrily, as soon as that forbidden thought had formed. From the first, he had been determined that he would never allow himself to wallow in self-pity. "Of course," he said.

His tone was again too sharp. Hard and cold. Although he recognized that in her slight recoil, he said nothing to soften its effect. Let her think him a bastard rather than a coward.

Still she didn't move. Not until he roughly put his hands under Drew's armpits and held him out to her. She gathered the child close. Then, putting her hand on the arm of his chair to help her up, she rose to her feet.

She stood beside him a moment, still holding his eyes. Then, without another word, she turned and walked across his bedroom and opened the door into the hall, closing it behind her.

Justin's mouth tightened, fighting the urge to call her back and apologize. She had been concerned about his health—a very natural concern—and in response, he had been rude.

He pushed up from the desk and fitted the crutch under his right arm. He swung over to the fire and, laying his left arm along the mantel, leaned his forehead against it, looking down into the flames. There was more to Sarah's unexpected arrival than she had told him. But if he continued to treat her as he just had, she would never confide in him. Of course, considering his present situation, he wasn't sure what he could do about whatever had sent her hurrying up to London.

At least they were here where he could watch over them. And as long as there was breath in his body, no matter how inadequate that body might now be, he would do that. He would protect either of them with his dying breath, he vowed fiercely. And he denied the urge to examine exactly why he was so sure of that. And so damned passionate about it.

Chapter Eight

There was little Justin could do during the next two weeks but watch as Sarah transformed his household. The most immediate change was in the deportment of his staff. And amazingly, despite the fact that Sarah had them working harder than they had in years, the servants seemed to think highly of their new countess.

Due to his stubborn determination not to parade his disability more than he had to, Justin was still taking his meals in his rooms. However, the temptation to join Drew and Sarah at dinner was almost enough to lure him out of his self-imposed exile. Especially when he sat by his lonely fire, the agricultural plans that had occupied him for weeks almost forgotten as he pictured the two of them downstairs together.

He didn't lack for company during the day, however. Andrew spent most of his time in Justin's rooms, except when he went shopping with Sarah. He came back from those expeditions bubbling over with excitement, his cheeks reddened from the cold and his eyes sparkling.

It was after one of these trips that Justin realized how rapidly the holidays were approaching and that Drew would almost certainly expect a present of some kind from him. He could dispatch one of the servants to shop for the child, but that seemed impersonal. And highly unsatisfactory.

The one person who would know what Andrew really wanted would be Sarah, of course, but Justin hadn't talked to her since the night she and Drew arrived. Remembering his terse response to her concern that evening, he shouldn't be surprised she was avoiding him. He knew it was up to him to make the next move. And to make what amends he could for his boorishness.

He could legitimately ask her to come to his rooms, but that was nothing less than an act of cowardice. And even if he was an ungrateful bastard, Justin had decided, he was not yet a coward. So girding himself mentally, just as he had once done before battle, he determined to seek Sarah out and make his request.

He took more pains over his appearance than he had in months. After the first glance in the mirror in his room, however, he didn't look at it again. Vanity, he acknowledged, but he didn't allow his eyes to focus again on his reflection.

He made his careful way down the grand staircase. As he stood at the bottom of them, he could see into most of the formal rooms. And for the first time became aware of how much Sarah had accomplished in the time she'd been here. Accustomed to the deprivations of campaigning, Justin supposed he hadn't realized how much needed to be done to bring the town house back to the standard of elegance it had once enjoyed. Not until he saw it now, almost exactly as he remembered it from his childhood.

Such a miraculous change could have been accomplished only by throwing an enormous amount of energy at a problem. Sarah had obviously done that. The old house gleamed. Wood and brass had been highly polished, so that every table carried a fresh coating of bees-wax, and the scent of lemon oil permeated the air. The rooms were warmed by cheerful fires, and each crystal in the massive Venetian glass chandeliers glittered.

Sarah had even seen to it that there was some touch of greenery in every room. That had surely been done with Andrew in mind. Although his family had never spent the Christmas season in London, it seemed right to Justin that the rooms should be filled now with its scents.

He was overwhelmed by Sarah's generosity, especially in light of the sums he had spent on the Park and his tenants. Now, he realized, he was even more indebted to his wife. On a personal as well as a financial level.

"Justin?" Sarah questioned.

She was standing in the doorway to the grand salon. Behind her, a bevy of maids were working. She had obviously been directing their activities when she had heard his distinctive footsteps in the hall.

The gown she wore was a plain gray merino, very suitable for housekeeping. Her fair hair, except for the curls that touched her cheeks and forehead, was covered with a lace cap. It was the first time he had seen her in this mode, Justin realized. Unconsciously, he smiled at Sarah's attempt to assume a proper matronly air.

An attempt was all it was, he thought. Somehow she looked younger in the mob cap than she had in her bonnets, although it should have had the opposite effect, of course. Perhaps it had more to do with the blush of color in her cheeks and the gleam of excitement in her eyes, a gleam almost matching that in Drew's.

This was the Sarah he remembered, he realized. Just as he had pictured her through those first lonely months in Spain. Before he had received her letter, which had shattered his dreams of the life they had planned together.

Deliberately, Justin pulled his gaze away from her face, pretending to contemplate the changes around him instead.

"A remarkable accomplishment, Sarah," he said finally. "I should never have believed the house could be like this again."

He looked back in time to see the sweep of color intensify across her cheekbones. The result of his compliment, he realized. And there had been far too few compliments, after all that she had done for him.

He supposed he had been too concerned with his own pain. Not just the physical one, although when he had left Longford to come here that had been real enough. He had been too proud to acknowledge what this marriage had meant to him financially. And, he admitted, bitter over the fact that five years ago Sarah had so quickly and completely fallen in love with someone else.

"It's a lovely house," she said.

"It is now," Justin said softly. "Thanks to you."

"I had thought..." she began, her eyes on his face. "That is, I had hoped—if you don't mind, of course— that Drew and I might spend all of Christmas here. The roads are very likely to become impassable this time of year. We were fortunate in our journey to town, but we might not be so lucky on the return."

"This is your home, Sarah. Especially now..."

He paused, again fascinated by the effect of his words. She took a breath, high breasts lifting under the tight wool bodice. Incredibly, his own body reacted to that small movement, his arousal sudden, and obvious, he feared.

Again he pulled his eyes away, fastening them instead on the kissing bough someone had hung over the doors where Sarah was standing. It was gay with streamers and fruit. Among the greenery were candles that would be lit on Christmas Day. And traditionally, of course…

Justin's lips tightened, remembering other Christmases, long-ago holidays when he and Sarah were growing up. Their families had often entertained one another during the season. Until Sarah and Drew arrived here, however, he had almost forgotten the holiday, which had once been one of his favorite times of the year. A time full of wishes come true, especially for children.

"I have a favor to ask," he said, remembering his mission.

"I wondered what had drawn the lion from his den."

His eyes came back to her face. She was teasing him, he realized, seeing the small tilt of her lips. It was too close to the truth, however. He had taken to his rooms like some elderly invalid. And he wasn't. His movements might be awkward, but he was no longer ill. The inflammation was subsiding, and he felt better than he had in weeks. Strong enough not to put the servants to the trouble of climbing the stairs with his meals.

"More apt a bear with a sore paw, I should think," he said. "Can you forgive my behavior the night of your arrival?"

"Forgive you?"

"I was rude. And unwelcoming."

"You were *invaded*," Sarah said. "If anyone needs forgiveness…" Her voice faded over the apology.

"Will you tell me now the real reason you came?" he asked.

Her eyes widened slightly, but then she hid them with the downward sweep of her lashes. He knew by her reaction that he hadn't been wrong. There was certainly more to Sarah's flight from Longford than she had told him.

''I don't know what you mean,'' she said. Her chin had risen minutely when she looked up again.

''Did your father do something to hurt Drew?''

''No,'' she denied quickly. ''Of course not. Brynmoor would never hurt Drew.''

''Andrew isn't sure of that.''

''I know,'' she admitted. ''But...''

She took another breath, and resolutely he kept his eyes on her face, remembering the effect that subtle movement of her breasts had had. Falling in love again with Sarah Spenser wasn't something he could afford. Or anything she would welcome.

''There was nothing like that,'' she said.

''Still not ready to confide in me, Sarah?'' he asked quietly. ''I promise I can keep a confidence.''

''I'm sure you can,'' she said. And then after a moment, she added, ''But I haven't any to make. You mentioned a favor?''

It seemed pointless to pursue it, considering her determination. She would trust him with the truth or she would not. He couldn't force her to tell him why she was running away.

''It's Andrew,'' he said. ''He's certain to expect some sort of present, but I haven't any idea what he'd like. I'm afraid that shopping for it...'' He hesitated, envisioning the streets at this time of year, teeming with shoppers, despite the cold.

''Would be difficult,'' Sarah finished for him.

Her eyes were as calm as her voice. There wasn't a trace of pity for the acknowledged impossibility of his venturing out to the shops. That had been a simple statement of fact.

''Yes,'' he said.

"And you would like me to make that purchase for you."

"Would you mind?"

"Of course not," she said. "Tell me what you have in mind."

Almost reluctantly, his mouth relaxed into a smile. "I had hoped you might have a suggestion," he admitted.

"There was something…" she began, and then she shook her head. "Drew never told me what, I'm afraid. Something that only Wynfield could give him. I believe that's what he said."

"Something only I could give him?"

Sarah nodded. "Maybe he mentioned it to you? Something he has been wishing for?"

"Nothing," Justin said, trying to remember any hints Drew had dropped.

"Subtlety isn't Drew's forte," Sarah suggested. "I suspect that if you give him an opening…"

"He won't be able to resist the opportunity to tell me."

"Probably not," Sarah agreed.

"I haven't had much experience with children, I'm afraid."

She said nothing, and her smile had faded.

"That's obvious, I suppose," he added.

"Drew adores you. You must know that," she said.

"Drew had a need for masculine attention that we both recognized," he said. "And a gruesome fascination with the bits and pieces of me that are missing, along with a natural curiosity about how that came about."

She said nothing for a moment, her eyes dark, her mouth unmoving. "I'm sorry," she said finally. "I'll speak to him."

"No, Sarah. Good God, I didn't mean that. Andrew's openness is far easier than the other."

Justin hadn't meant to suggest she should chastise Drew for his natural curiosity, but despite his attempt at control, there was a trace of bitterness in the words.

"The other?" she repeated, and waited through the silence.

"The pretense that nothing has changed," he said finally. "That it's...unnoticeable."

"Or unimportant," she said.

Again the silence grew. He had revealed too much. Said too much. Sarah was more astute than he had expected.

"It *is* unimportant, of course," he said, lightening his tone, hating the self-pity he had heard there. "After all, I survived. Believe me, I'm very grateful."

"Believe *me*," she said softly, "I'm very grateful as well."

She held his eyes only a second longer, and then she turned and disappeared into the salon. He could hear her voice raised to direct whatever the maids were doing, its tone so different from the soft agreement she had just made. *I'm very grateful as well.*

Perhaps she was grateful for Drew's sake? he thought. But later, alone in his room, remembering what had so briefly been in her eyes, he had to wonder if concern for Drew had anything at all to do with what she had said.

Neither Andrew or Sarah urged him to join them for Christmas Eve, but he had asked his valet to find out what time dinner would be served, even before he made his decision. When he had, he dressed as carefully as he had the morning he sought Sarah out to ask about a present for Andrew. And this time he resisted looking into the cheval glass at all.

Despite providing plenty of opportunities for Drew to

make his request, he still had no idea what the little boy had been referring to when he had mentioned something only Wynfield could give him. Having run out of time, Justin had reluctantly dispatched his man to the shops. The comfits and the mechanical toy he'd brought back seemed very little, but unless he wished to ask his wife for a loan, Justin thought, they would have to do.

As he descended the stairs, he could hear Andrew's laughter. He and Sarah were probably playing games before dinner, a Christmas Eve tradition. This was one of the few times during the year when children were encouraged to take part in entertainments usually reserved for adults.

Drawn by the sound of Drew's giggles, Justin swung across the hall and stopped in the doorway to the parlor. He hadn't been mistaken. They were engaged in a spirited game of spillikins, fair heads close together. As he watched them, Sarah's laughter joined her son's, filling the room with a gaiety that had long been missing from this house.

As if sensing his presence, Sarah lifted her eyes suddenly to the doorway, finding his face. Her laughter died as her eyes dilated in shock. What he saw in them, however, was not unwelcoming.

Before he could fully analyze it, Drew shouted, "Wynfield!"

He ran toward the doorway, and Justin braced himself. This time, however, the little boy skidded to a stop and took Justin's hand, pulling him toward the game table where he and Sarah had been sitting.

"I hope I'm not intruding," Justin said to her.

"In your own house?" she questioned, smiling at him. "I should think not. We are very glad to have you join us. Merry Christmas."

"Thank you," he said softly.

"I have beaten Sarah soundly," Drew announced.

"Without any mercy at all," Sarah acknowledged cheerfully. "Would you like to try your skill?"

"I am acquitted to be a fair hand," the earl said to Andrew, as he eased down in one of the chairs that had been placed around the gaming table. "Lead on, Mac-Duff."

"Who is MacDuff?" Drew asked with interest, preparing the jackstraws for the next game.

"A character in a play by Mr. Shakespeare," Sarah explained.

"Can we act it out after dinner?" Andrew asked.

Sarah laughed. "MacDuff is from a play that is, I believe, unsuitable for holiday masquerading."

"Was he a soldier?" Drew asked.

Sarah's eyes, filled with amusement over his obsession with the military, lifted over Drew's tousled curls to find Justin's.

"I believe he was," she said. "At least, when he was called upon to be. The rest of the time, I think he was simply a very good man."

The evening passed in a blur of rich food and games and laughter. A company of mummers came by, offering a spirited performance in the street outside. Although he was country-bred, Andrew had never seen a troop of mummers before, and his excitement was infectious. Despite the cold, Justin found himself standing beside Sarah in the entrance to the town house, both of them laughing along with Drew at their antics.

As the hours passed, the constraints that had been between Sarah and himself seemed to lessen. It was too easy to remember other evenings they had spent like this, her eyes smiling into his. Too easy to forget what had happened to push them apart.

It shouldn't have been. Not with Drew as a constant reminder. The child, however, had won his own place in Justin's heart, no longer simply a symbol of his mother's infidelity.

"What shall we do next?" Drew asked after they had finished a lively game of snapdragon, in which Andrew, by design of course, had acquired most of the raisins.

"Perhaps we should think about bed," Sarah said. "Or at least you should," she amended, glancing up at the earl.

The flush that suddenly marked her cheeks had nothing to do with the cold. The laughter, however, seemed still caught in the midnight blue of her eyes. Perhaps that was simply a trick of the candlelight, Justin thought. Or a reflection of the sapphire satin of her gown.

Sarah had left off her cap tonight, he noted with amusement. She had adorned her hair instead with a simple diamond-and-sapphire band that caught the candlelight whenever she turned her head. And she had never been more beautiful.

Realizing he was still holding her gaze, he turned his head as if searching for the decanter of port that stood on the wine tray the butler had brought in. He had not yet indulged, but if Sarah was going to go to his head, then it might be safer to clear it with strong drink.

After all, he had made this same mistake once before. The mistake of believing that what he saw in Sarah Spenser's eyes matched what he felt for her. His emotions tonight were nothing more than the product of his loneliness and long isolation.

It wasn't surprising he had had such a strong physical response to Sarah's beauty. It had been months since he had been with a woman. Since before he was wounded, of course.

Despite his injury, despite his natural reluctance to expose his mutilated body to anyone, much less to the delicate sensibilities of a woman, his physical needs and desires had not disappeared. With the long denial, they had sharpened instead. And they would continue to do so, he thought, taking a deep swallow of the wine, if he spent more time around his wife.

His wife. A wife whom he had not touched in the long weeks of their marriage. He had not even touched her fingertips, he realized, except perhaps accidentally. Nor had she touched him.

He watched her hands now as she cut the Christmas pudding, putting a slice on a plate for Andrew and another for him, he supposed. They moved over that simple task with the same grace and economy of motion as they did over all others, whether ink stained from writing in the estate books or gently smoothing Andrew's hair.

He had watched their easy interaction tonight. Drew leaning against her knee, listening to every word she said. Sarah's hand cupped around the child's cheek. And Justin was ashamed to admit he had been jealous of their open affection. The same jealousy that had drawn him down here tonight—out of his lonely room and into the light of their acceptance.

An acceptance of who and what he now was. Sarah's seemed as genuine as Drew's. She had not once by word or deed reminded him of the debt he owed her. Or indicated that she found him to be less than the same man she had known five years ago.

"Good night, dear Wynfield," Drew said. "Happy Christmas."

He looked up from his empty glass to find the little boy

standing by his chair. Without thinking, he leaned forward and pulled the child to him, holding him close.

"Happy Christmas, Drew," he whispered.

The child rested contentedly against his chest a moment before he leaned back to look up into his face. "I have a present for you," he said. "It is something I made myself."

"Did you?" Justin said, smiling.

"Have you…?" Drew paused, glancing nervously over his shoulder to where Sarah was watching, knowing full well that to ask the question he wanted to ask was forbidden. "That is…" he began anew, his voice much softer. Again he hesitated, his eyes probing Justin's.

"Have I a present for you?" the earl asked for him.

Drew nodded.

"A small one," Justin confessed. "I wasn't sure exactly what you wanted."

"Sarah says you aren't supposed to tell people what you want, but I don't know how they should know if you don't tell them," Drew said reasonably.

"Nor do I," Justin agreed, smiling.

"I have made you a marker for your books," Drew whispered, "but I can't give it to you until tomorrow."

"I'm sure it's very fine," the earl said, almost as softly.

"It's so you will always know where you have left off reading."

Justin nodded, his throat thick.

"Sarah suggested it," Andrew confessed, "but I made it myself. And I have drawn Star on it. I thought you would like that because I'm sure you miss him."

"I will like that above all things," Justin said.

"Did you make my present yourself?"

"Not…all of them," he admitted, remembering the toy and the sweets his man had chosen. Justin had known in his heart they weren't right, but he hadn't known why. Now, of course, he did.

Drew nodded. "I'm sure they are very fine, all the same," he said comfortingly. "And have you something for Sarah? Brynmoor doesn't remember Christmas, you know. She has only what I give her. And the servants' Christmas wishes, of course."

Justin realized he had never thought about a present for Sarah. They were adults. And too much lay between them. Too much that was painful. Too many things Drew could never understand, of course.

"It will mean more if you have made it yourself," Drew advised. "Sarah loves presents you make yourself because they have some part of you in them."

Justin nodded, wondering as he did at his willingness to lie to this child. Somehow the little boy's words, obviously an echo of what Sarah had told him, struck a blow to his conscience.

Sarah really did have no one. A mad father who didn't know the year, much less the day. A child too young to understand all the intricacies of the adult relationships that surrounded him. And a husband who had not considered that he should offer her a Christmas gift, not even after all she had done for him.

"Bedtime, Drew," Sarah said softly.

They both looked up, startled by her voice, to find her standing near Justin's chair.

"I'll take you up and tuck you in tight," she said. "And when you wake, it will be Christmas Day."

She was smiling at the little boy, her eyes carefully avoiding his, Justin thought.

"Good night," he said to Drew.

Unable to resist, he touched his fingers against the fullness of the child's cheeks, provoking a smile. Then Andrew took his mother's hand and followed her out of the room. Justin could hear Drew chattering as they made their way up the stairs.

He poured another glass of port from the decanter the butler had thoughtfully left near his chair. Strong drink and a restless sleep, or thoughts of Sarah circling in his head all night. Given those options, he raised the glass to his lips and drank the wine down in one draught, almost like a dose of medicine. Maybe it was. At least a preventative.

Justin couldn't get Drew's words out of his head. Nor could he destroy the images they had produced. Sarah alone. Rationally, he didn't know why he should feel sorry for Sarah Spenser. She was one of the wealthiest heiresses in England. She could certainly afford to buy whatever she wanted or needed.

And knowing his circumstances better than anyone other than his man of business, she would not be expecting presents from him. *She* wouldn't be disappointed. *She* understood the boundaries of their relationship as clearly as he did. Drew, however…

Drew *would* be disappointed, he admitted. On Sarah's behalf, of course. And disappointed in him. Justin knew that, and it troubled him even more than the thought of the years when Sarah had had no one to give her a Christmas present.

Which had been by her choice, he told himself bitterly. But after the evening that had just passed, the reminder of her infidelity rang hollow. Without force. And it seemed, somehow, not a good enough excuse for what he had not thought to do. It was too late, however, to correct his oversight tonight.

Sarah loves presents you make yourself because they

have some part of you in them. It was too late for that as well, he realized, glancing at the clock on the mantel, which indicated it was well after midnight. Too late, even if he knew of something he could make for her. Or for Drew.

His eyes found the trinkets Peters had bought. The shop had wrapped them in a small piece of colored silk and tied the bundle with a ribbon. They weren't good enough, of course. They never had been, but until Andrew had explained it to him, Justin hadn't really understood why.

Some part of you in them... The phrase seemed to haunt him. There was nothing he could make, but perhaps there was still something he could do. There were things here, in this house, that had some "part of him" within them. At least some part of what he had once been. A little boy just like Drew.

Standing, he fitted his crutch under his arm and crossed the room. When he opened the door, the hallway outside was dark. Even the servants had gone to bed, and what he sought was on the top floor. The night nursery and the schoolroom were both there. Those rooms were where he and Robert had spent most of their time when his family had been in residence here. They were the places, therefore, where he was most likely to find something of his own childhood that Drew would like to have.

He began to move toward the back stairs. They were narrow and steep, far more difficult for him to negotiate, but there was also less chance he would encounter anyone. He had gone only a few feet down the hall toward them when he realized he was beside the door to his mother's room. A room he hadn't entered since her death, more than ten years ago.

Acting on the same impulse that had driven him out of his room, he put his hand on the knob and turned it. For

some reason, he expected the door to be locked. It wasn't.
It swung inward, revealing his mother's boudoir, which
appeared unchanged.

It even smelled of her, the faint scents evoking memories of his childhood. Sometimes he had been allowed
to sit here and watch her dress for a ball. He would visit
with her as her maid powdered her hair and helped her
choose a patch from the ornate box in which they were
kept. Once she had allowed him to choose the one she
would wear. He could even remember it—a small black
heart, which, smiling at him in the mirror, she had pressed
at the corner of her mouth.

And when she had turned around for his inspection, he
had thought she was the most beautiful creature in existence. He took a deep breath and could almost sense her
presence in the faint, lingering essences of hair powder
and lavender. Almost as if her ghost were still here.

He smiled at his foolishness. *Too much port,* he
thought, moving across to her dressing table. There would
be nothing here but baubles, he knew. Robert or his father
would have sold whatever was of value long ago.

He lit the candles that stood beside the mirror and then
opened the drawer of the table, his long fingers pushing
through the gewgaws. A paste broach she had once worn
to a masquerade. A pair of ivory hairpins, which had been
lovely in his mother's dark hair, but would not serve for
Sarah's. A ring of twisted dolphins he did not remember
at all, its base metal green with time. And a strand of
small, misshapen pearls.

His hand hesitated, and then he fingered them out of
the heap, pulling them up so that they gleamed softly in
the candlelight, more gray than white. He had bought
these for his mother's birthday, he remembered, a little
surprised at the clarity of his recollection.

He had been older than Drew, he imagined, but not much. And he had purchased them from a street vendor using his own pocket money. He had thought the necklace was the most beautiful thing he had ever seen, especially when his mother had worn it looped loosely about her slender, white throat when she had come into the nursery the next night. She was already dressed for a dinner party, and she had been wearing his pearls.

He knew now that she had almost certainly taken them off as soon as she stepped out of the nursery. At the time, however, he was certain she valued them as much as she did the diamond-and-ruby set his father had had made up for that same birthday. Certain she had worn them proudly to the party. And that she had been the most beautiful woman in attendance.

Smiling at the memory, Justin began to allow the strand to coil back into the drawer. Then his fingers hesitated again, before they caught the rest of the small uneven beads with a quick upward toss. He held the necklace out on his palm a moment before he dropped it into the pocket of his waistcoat. He had left his coat in his room. At this hour, of course, there was no one about to be shocked by his shirtsleeves.

He swung back across the room, closing the door carefully behind him. Shutting out memories that were not unhappy, but were simply faded, like a beloved fabric, well used and well loved. Whatever troubles his father had faced financially, and he knew now that there had been many even then, he and Robert had been insulated from their effects by their mother's love.

Just as Sarah tried to protect Drew. From the gossip. From learning the truth of his parentage. Now Justin had become a member of that conspiracy. And he couldn't begrudge Drew what he himself had enjoyed. A child-

hood as free from worry as the adults in his life could
manage.

With the thought of Drew, he remembered why he had
begun this journey. Surely there would be something suitable to give the child in the rooms upstairs. A book he
had loved, if nothing else. Soon Drew would be old
enough for a tutor. Until that time, he might enjoy being
read to aloud. He wondered if Sarah did that. And if Drew
would like for him to.

Whether it was the darkness, or the fact that in his
hurry to make his search, he was paying too little attention
to the placement of his crutch on the stairs, he could never
be sure. There was no railing, of course, given the nar-
rowness of the steep steps, and when the tip of the crutch
slipped off the edge of the one he had carelessly placed
it on, there was nothing he could do to stop his fall. He
had only climbed about a third of the way up, so there
was no danger of injury, at least none beyond some bruis-
ing. And a massive blow to his pride.

When his quick downward passage had stopped, he
was sprawled at the foot of the staircase, his upper body
propped on the steps themselves. His crutch had clattered
noisily past him, out of his reach, onto the wooden floor.

"Bloody hell," he breathed, more angry than hurt.

He automatically took stock of the aches and pains. All
of them seemed minor. At least not a setback to what had
already been his frustratingly slow convalescence. He
would never have forgiven himself if he had delayed his
recovery.

"Are you hurt?"

The whisper was so unexpected he pushed his upper
body up, his hands on the step behind him before he answered.

"Only my pride," he said truthfully.

Sarah walked across the hall and set the candelabra she was carrying down on the hall table. Then she stooped down beside him. In the wavering candlelight, he could barely see the contours of her face. He hoped she could see him no better.

He pushed up again, lifting his hips onto the bottom step and then onto the next, so that at least he was sitting up and not lying in a heap at her feet.

"What happened?" she asked.

Her gaze moved up the narrow staircase and then came back to his. He could see her now. Her face was calm, and she hadn't offered to help him up. For which he was eternally grateful.

"I finished the port," he said. And watched her lips tilt.

"Foxed," she offered, smiling at him.

There was a touch of relief in her voice as well as in her smile. Either because he was unhurt or because he hadn't retreated behind the same boorishness with which he had responded to her initial concerns about his health.

"Properly," he lied.

"But what were you doing out here?" she asked, her eyes again moving up the narrow stairs.

"Looking for more port?" he suggested.

This time she laughed, and the hard knot of mortification that had been aching in his chest since he had recognized her voice eased. At least he could still make Sarah laugh. And if she did, she might never suspect how humiliating it was to have her find him like this.

"It's customary to ring for your servants if you need something," she said. "You *are* the earl, you know. And I think that now they would probably even respond."

Her tone was light. She put her hands together in her lap, sitting back on her heels. Not before he had noticed they were shaking. Apparently, if he could pretend, so could Sarah.

"I prefer tippling in secret," he said. "Much less gossip, you know." And realized from her quick intake of breath that was the wrong word. Wrong at least for this woman. Gossip was a cruel and hurtful subject to her. Not something for jest.

"Your servants are too well trained to gossip," she said.

She rose, her movements graceful in spite of the voluminous nightgown she was wearing. Because of the cold, it was high necked and long sleeved. It was thin enough, however, that since she was now standing between him and the candles, Justin could clearly see the outline of her body. Still as slender as a girl's, despite the fact that she had borne a child.

Again, his body reacted, his arousal immediate. Disgusted with his lack of control, he also stood, finding his balance carefully, one hand on the wall beside him.

Sarah bent down and retrieved his crutch from where it had fallen. She stepped nearer, holding it out to him. He hesitated a moment, searching her eyes for any sign of disgust. Finding none, he took the crutch, fitting it under his arm before he removed his hand from the support of the wall. Then, almost of its own volition, that same hand reached out and fastened around her upper arm.

Sarah looked down on his fingers, their darkness a contrast to the white of her night rail. Slowly, her eyes lifted to his. They were wide and dark, but still there was no revulsion in them. No pity. Nothing of what he had expected if he ever dared touch a woman again.

He pulled her toward him, and she took the step that was required to bring her near enough to allow his mouth to lower over hers. And there was no hesitation in her response.

It seemed to him he had always known he would kiss Sarah again. And that it would be the same. That it would send this scalding rush of heat through his body, just as it had the first time he had kissed her. A kiss just as stolen, and almost as frightening, as this one.

. Her mouth trembled under his. So soft. Unexplored. Before, with the constraints of her age and position, this brush of lips had been enough. It had had to be. Now, however...

He pushed his tongue against their frail barrier, demanding entrance. Demanding response. And finally he was answered. Her mouth opened, breath sighing out in a sweet release, even as his tongue invaded. And conquered. Unwilling to be denied. Sarah was a woman now, his wife, and no longer an uninitiated girl.

His hand released her arm, slipping to her back and pulling her more firmly against him. Her body was pliant, seeming to melt into his. Welcoming his touch. Realizing that, he deepened the kiss, plundering the sweetness of her mouth. Using every bit of the expertise he had acquired in the long years that had passed since he had first kissed Sarah Spenser.

She had trembled in his arms then, just as she was now. Responding to him. Her mouth moving hungrily against his. As hungry for this, it seemed, as he had been.

He could feel her breasts, their small peaks hardened with the cold or with desire, pressed into his chest. His hand slipped lower, cupping under the softness of her buttocks, lifting her up into his erection. Wanting her so badly he was almost mindless with need. With love—

Her mouth opened with a gasp. She jerked away, pushing against his chest and almost unbalancing him. When he opened his eyes, hers were on his face. Too wide and dark, as if dilated with shock. The tips of her fingers were pressed to her lips, which looked swollen. As if they had been well kissed. And they had been, he acknowledged. Damnably well kissed.

''What's wrong?'' he asked softly.

She had been enjoying this. He was certainly experienced enough to know that. He hadn't been celibate so long that he couldn't recognize the nature of her reaction. Her body had responded as strongly to that kiss and their nearness as his had. And then suddenly…

''No,'' she said.

Her arms crossed protectively over her breasts, hands rubbing up and down the long sleeves of her nightgown as if she were cold. She was shivering, he realized, her body vibrating as strongly as if she were in fever.

''Sarah?'' he questioned. He took a step toward her, his crutch echoing on the wooden floor. Intrusive. Too loud among the sibilance of their whispers.

She didn't answer him. Instead, she turned and ran, slender ankles flashing beneath the white of her night rail. Her bedroom door banged closed behind her, the sound sharp in the quietness of the sleeping house.

And he was alone again in the hallway. It was almost as if it hadn't happened. Almost as if Sarah had not been here. As if he had dreamed the encounter.

He had not, of course. The hard, painful ache in his groin assured him that the woman he'd held had been no figment of his imagination. She had been real and warm and responsive. And then…

He released the breath he had been holding. And then she was gone. Almost as if he had frightened her. Almost as if she had been shocked by what he was doing.

He stood a moment, trying to understand what had happened. And he didn't. Finally he turned and, taking more care this time, he climbed the narrow steps of the servants' stairs, moving out of the light of the candles Sarah had brought and back into the cold, lonely darkness.

Chapter Nine

"I have to go back to Longford," Sarah said.

Her face was composed, the lines in which it was set too tight, almost pained. And her blue eyes were shuttered.

"On Christmas Day?" Justin asked disbelievingly.

Despite the lecture he had given himself last night, disappointment knotted his stomach. He still didn't understand what had happened to make Sarah run away, but he hadn't been able to forget how she had responded to his kiss before she did. He had been looking forward to spending the day with both of them. Now it was apparent her flight hadn't ended last night when she had slammed her bedroom door against him.

"My father..." Sarah's voice faltered, almost as if her throat had closed against the words. She put her lips together, her teeth catching the bottom one briefly before she opened them again and went on. "He has episodes where he's even more confused than is now normal for him. Sometimes he even becomes violent."

"Surely you can wait until—"

"No," she interrupted. "They can't manage him. They

never can when he's like this. They sent for me yesterday, but I received the message only this morning.''

"If you can wait a few days—'' he began.

''Not even a few hours, I'm afraid,'' she said. ''I have to start for home now if I'm to arrive before nightfall.''

He couldn't tell if she regretted that need for haste or not. She had already turned toward the door of his room when he asked, ''What about Drew?''

The question stopped her, and she didn't answer for a long moment, even after she had turned to face him again. Her hesitation reinforced his suspicion that the reason she had traveled to London in the dead of winter with a snowstorm threatening had something to do with the child. Had Andrew had another, more dangerous, encounter with the village boys? If so, he had said nothing about it in the days they'd spent together.

''It *is* Christmas,'' he reminded her, hoping that he was seeing a wavering of her determination.

''Are you suggesting I leave Drew here?''

He hadn't been, but there was no reason why she couldn't, he realized. Drew wouldn't mind. He was afraid of the marquess, although he had tried very hard not to admit that. And it *was* Christmas. ''Why not?'' Justin asked.

Her eyes examined his face as if she were trying to decide.

''I'll bring him home when I come. Or…'' Now *he* hesitated, wondering if everything would go back to the way it had been between them at Longford. To that distance and sense of estrangement, which, he acknowledged, had been by his choice. ''Or you can come back here when you've seen to your father.''

He didn't know what had prompted him to make that suggestion. A tendency to masochism, maybe. Of course, after last night, living under the same roof with Sarah, no matter which roof they were under, was going to be much more difficult.

"Are you coming back to Longford soon?" she asked.

As soon as the surgeon gives me permission, he thought. That was an admission he didn't articulate. A reminder of things he didn't want to have to think about right now. And didn't particularly want Sarah to think about. Not after last night.

"As soon as I can," he promised. "Until then...why *not* let Andrew stay here with me?"

"Are you sure?" she asked.

"I think it would be better for everyone concerned."

Reluctantly, she nodded. She knew he was right, but he understood how much she would miss Drew. Just as he would miss him if Sarah carried the boy home with her. The huge house would seem as cold and lonely as it had before their arrival.

"Then...I won't plan to come back to London." she said. "There's really no reason to do that. The house is ready to be put on the market whenever you wish. And at Longford there's always so much that needs to be done...." Her words trailed away, her eyes still on his face.

"I'll take care of Andrew," he promised, knowing somehow that's what she wanted him to do. That it was the reason she had brought the boy to London in the first place.

Finally, she nodded. He tried to find something in her eyes of the woman she had become—so briefly—in his arms. There was only anxiety there instead.

He slipped his hand into his coat pocket and brought out the present he had wrapped after he returned to his room last night. It wasn't enclosed in silk like Andrew's or tied with ribbon. Instead, he had put the strand of worthless freshwater pearls, which would probably be even more obvious trumpery when viewed in the sobriety of daylight, into the middle of a sheet of plain paper and twisted the ends. Then he had written Sarah's name across the front. It looked ridiculous held out on his palm. Sarah's eyes considered it a moment before they lifted to his.

"Happy Christmas, Sarah," he said softly.

Even as he watched, her eyes glazed with moisture.

"It isn't much," he warned, realizing with a flood of regret how little it really was. He must have drunk more of the port than he'd realized to have imagined that Sarah, or any woman, could want this. "These were my mother's," he said, trying to think of some logical explanation for his gift, which he was suddenly afraid she might even view as insulting. "I bought them for her when I was about Drew's age. I thought…"

He stopped, because he couldn't really explain to her any of the things he had been thinking when he selected these from among the remnants of his mother's possessions. Nor could he tell her anything of what Andrew had said to him.

Sarah's eyes again fell to the package. Slowly her fingers removed it from his palm. She made no attempt to untwist the ends and reveal what he had given her. She held it enclosed in her hand, which fell slowly back to her side. When she looked up at him, her eyes were more open than they had been before. And no longer touched with tears.

"I don't have anything for you," she said.

He smiled, thinking of how much she had already given him, and knowing instinctively that neither of them wanted to be reminded of that debt. "I didn't expect anything," he said.

She nodded again, and then, almost as she had last night, she turned away from him and left his room, closing the door softly behind her.

"Your very own first whip?" Drew said.

His eyes had been shining since he had been invited into Justin's room. His thin childish voice had piped out almost the entire first verse of a carol before the earl had gotten to the door to open it. Andrew had finished the song, although a few of the unfamiliar words had been slightly mangled in his rendition.

Justin managed not to smile until it was done, and then he had invited Drew in. He knew that in many families presents were exchanged on New Year's or more frequently on Twelfth Night. He and Robert, however, had received their presents on Christmas Day, and those had always been something more than the traditional shillings and sweets.

He wasn't sure what Andrew was accustomed to, but since he had decided last night on an appropriate present for the child, he wasn't going to delay in giving it to him. And he knew now that his choice had been exactly right.

Drew had told him that he was sometimes allowed to ride Sarah's pony. He himself had seen from the child's interaction with Star that he liked horses. And Drew was certainly old enough to learn to ride. Justin couldn't remember when he and Robert hadn't had a couple of fat ponies, contentedly plodding around the paddock with them bouncing along on their backs.

"And you will teach me to use it?" Drew said.

That had been part of his present, of course. The promise to teach Andrew to ride. Something he was looking forward to, Justin realized, as much as the child seemed to be.

"Or how *not* to use it," he corrected. "When you understand your mount, and he understands you, you will have less occasion to use the crop. It is simply something gentlemen carry."

Drew nodded, his eyes falling again to the miniature whip. Justin had forgotten its existence, but when he had seen it last night on a shelf above his old bed in the night nursery, he had known that it was perfect for his purposes. The perfect gift for Drew. This and the promise of riding lessons.

"Thank you," Andrew said, looking up at him again.

"You're very welcome," the earl said softly.

"I shall go get your present," the little boy announced.

He carried the crop with him, of course, transferring it carefully to his left hand as he turned the doorknob and slipped out of the room. Behind him, Justin's mouth relaxed into a smile. At least he had gotten one of them right, he thought, remembering Sarah's eyes as they looked up from that ridiculous package he had held out to her.

"I'll make it up to you, Sarah," he whispered, staring into the fire. "Someday, I swear, I'll make it up to you."

All the way back to Longford, Sarah thought about Justin. Just as it seemed they had been on the verge of recapturing something of what had once been between them—their friendship, if nothing else—she had been forced to leave.

And he had doubted her reasons. She had read that quite clearly in his eyes this morning. Of course, after last night, why should he not believe she was running away from him?

She had dreamed about reawakening Justin's feelings for her since he had come home. Indeed, she was honest enough to admit that her marriage proposal had been as much about that hope as about Andrew. And then, just as it seemed she might have succeeded, she had bolted.

Justin had kissed her, and her reaction had been panic. And she couldn't even begin to explain why. The feel of his body against hers, so incredibly hard? Or his hand on her hip, pulling her into an even more intimate contact with him?

Sarah had known what was happening. Virgin she might be, but she was no fool. And she had spent too many years in the country to be totally innocent about what transpired between a man and a woman.

Justin obviously believed she was far less innocent, however, than she really was. Knowing something intellectually, in the abstract, was far different from knowing it physically. What had happened last night had been very physical. And frightening, like anything that was truly unknown.

Still, she didn't understand why she would ever be afraid of Justin. He had never hurt her. He *wouldn't* hurt her, but as exciting as it had been, there had been something missing from last night's interaction. It had been so sudden. Too demanding. As if he expected too much too quickly.

That wasn't Justin's fault, she acknowledged. She was his wife. She had given him no reason to believe she would not welcome his attentions. She would. Oh, dear God she would. But…obviously he expected her to know far more than she did about what would happen between them.

If their marriage were consummated—and now that seemed almost inevitable, she admitted, given their en-

forced proximity and Justin's obvious desire for a physical relationship—then the truth about Andrew's birth
would be revealed. Which was something she would welcome, of course. And it would happen in a way that could
surely not be considered breaking her oath.

So why had she run away last night? Her eyes fell again
to the strand of pearls. They lay in her lap, the paper on
which he had written her name beneath them. They had
been there throughout the whole of this long journey.

With her finger, she touched one of the small, irregular
beads. Her lips curved, remembering what he had said.
He had been Drew's age when he had picked these out.
For his mother. And now he had given them to her.

She wasn't sure of the significance of them. Maybe
nothing more than the fact that Justin had been foxed last
night. He had openly confessed that, and she had tasted
the wine on his lips.

Had that been the explanation for his kiss, and not the
growing closeness that she had imagined during the evening? Not forgiveness for what he believed she had done.
Not…love. Or even affection. Or friendship. Had that kiss
been simply the effects of too much Christmas spirits?

She lifted her eyes from the pearls and looked out the
window of the coach, gauging its location. She would be
home in less than an hour. Back to the same problems
that had occupied her thoughts and her energies in the
years since she had broken off her engagement to Justin
Tolbert. Worries about her father. About Longford. Drew.
And now about David Osborne.

She had almost been able to block that threat from her
mind while she had been in London. Andrew was safe
with Justin, who would never let anything happen to him.
Nor would she, she vowed. If money was all it would
take to prevent David from going to court to try to take

Drew away from her, then she would give him money. Whatever he asked for, she thought fiercely. She would give him whatever he demanded, but she would never, ever give him Drew.

"Oh, my lady," Mrs. Simkins cried almost as soon as Sarah had entered the house. She came hurrying down the hallway, her black bombazine skirt rustling. The housekeeper, probably the entire staff as well, had obviously been anxiously awaiting her arrival. "It's that glad I am to see you," Mrs. Simkins said, relief strong in her voice as she took Sarah's coat.

"Is he much worse?" Sarah asked anxiously, loosening the ribbons of her bonnet and slipping it off.

"He's wild with rage, my lady, and there's nothing any of us can do with him this time. Not even Dawson can manage him."

Dawson was the marquess's valet and, next to Sarah, the person most able to coax her father to do what he should. It had been Dawson's message that had been sent to London. A note that had languished one whole day at her father's town house before someone thought to see if she were in residence at her husband's.

That delay was not something she could regret, no matter how disturbed the household might be about her belated arrival. If Dawson's message had reached her on Christmas Eve... She took a breath, thanking providence it had not. Because then, of course, she would not have last night to remember.

"What happened?" Sarah asked, laying her bonnet and reticule on the hall table.

"No one knows, my lady," Mrs. Simkins confessed. "Dawson come downstairs for his nuncheon while your father was napping. When he went back up, his lordship wasn't there. By the time we found him, wandering the grounds, he was in a rage, swearing and raving enough to frighten a saint. I haven't seen him like this since before your sister died,'' Mrs. Simkins said.

They would probably never get to the bottom of whatever had overset her father's delicate mental balance. There were days when he seemed almost himself, although lost in events from the past, of course. Then there were periods like this, when he was virtually a madman. Luckily, he had never hurt anyone, perhaps because the servants were wise enough to avoid him when he was in one of his fits.

"Where is he?" Sarah asked.

"In his rooms, my lady. What's left of 'em," Mrs. Simkins added almost under her breath.

Sarah knew what that meant. Her father had always had destructive tendencies in his anger, but during the last three years, these rages had grown increasingly more violent.

"I'll see to him," Sarah said, ignoring the last comment. "May I have your keys?" And when the ring had been handed over, she smiled at the housekeeper before she dismissed her. "Thank you, Mrs. Simkins. That will be all, I think."

Sarah waited until the woman retreated toward the kitchen before she allowed herself to react. She closed her eyes tiredly, dreading what she would find when she went upstairs. But this was why she had come home, she told herself, and putting off the confrontation wouldn't change anything. At least Andrew wasn't here to witness what went on.

Unconsciously she placed the tips of her cold fingers against her lips, pressing them there tightly to still their trembling. She was a coward, she thought in disgust, opening her eyes. And she had never in her life been called upon to face real disaster. Not like Justin.

The catalogue of what her husband had endured would have defeated a lesser man. Her supposed betrayal of their love and the broken engagement. Surviving years of war and the loss of friends, and then, at the very end, suffering such a devastating injury. And finally coming home to face the loss of his entire family and the threatened loss of everything he held dear.

Still, when she had found him last night at the foot of those treacherous stairs, Justin had managed to jest about the cause of his fall. That was the kind of man she had married. The kind she had chosen to guide Drew to manhood. And here she was, surrounded by a house full of servants, afraid to face her own father. Trembling with dread over what lay ahead—which would be nothing more than a few moments of unpleasantness.

Justin was looking after Drew. He would keep him safe. The rest of it was up to her to deal with. Her father. And David Osborne. Little enough, she told herself again. Resolutely, she walked to the stairs and then slowly began to climb them.

Sarah knocked on the door of her father's room, putting her ear against the solid wood. There was no sound. And, although she waited, perfectly still, there was no answer to her tap. She wondered if her father had finally fallen asleep, exhausted by what had, according to Dawson's message, been three days of almost endless ranting and raving.

"Papa," she called, listening again for a response. There was nothing. She found the right key on the housekeeper's huge ring. After she had unlocked the door, she laid the keys on the hall table and put her hand over the doorknob, saying a silent prayer before she forced herself to turn it.

The room was dark and still. There were no candles, of course. And no lamps. Her father's tendency to throw things precluded those. Although it was twilight, there should have been some light coming in from the tall windows. Instead, the draperies had been pulled across them, making the chamber almost as black as night. And as silent.

Gathering her courage, she stepped inside and closed the door behind her. There was a thick stench to the darkness, a combination of unwashed body and unemptied chamber pot. She swallowed against her nausea, although the smell was not unexpected. Or unfamiliar.

She stood a moment, trying not to breathe too deeply, her back against the door, and allowed her eyes to adjust to the dimness. Eventually they did, but she was able to distinguish the features of the room and its furnishings only because she was very familiar with them.

She put her hand on the massive chest that stood beside the door, the solid wood reassuring under her fingertips. She could make out the tall, old-fashioned bed with its hangings. And her father's desk and chair, which stood near the shrouded windows.

"Papa," she called again.

She knew her voice wouldn't awaken him if he were sleeping. The exhausted slumber he fell into after one of these episodes was as deep as a coma. He seemed unaware of noise or light around him. Once he had slept for three days, awakening, she remembered, uncharacteristically docile, almost childlike.

She walked toward the windows, intending to draw the curtains just enough that she could make sure her father was all right. As she moved, broken glass or porcelain

crunched under her feet. Once she stumbled, tripping over
an object she hadn't seen and couldn't identify. When she
reached the windows, her fingers hesitated only a second
before she reached up and pulled the drapery aside.

A murky twilight filtered into the devastated room.
There was nothing standing on the tops of any of the
tables or chests. Every object had been thrown or swept
off onto the floor. There was an overturned tray of food,
obviously left from the last time Dawson had tried to get
her father to eat. Clothing had been scattered across the
room. Some of it appeared to have been cut or torn to
shreds. Knowing her father's unnatural strength at times
like these, she did not doubt the latter.

Steeling herself, she walked toward the high bed. She
had hoped her father would be there sleeping, but he
wasn't. The bed seemed almost the only undisturbed fea-
ture of the room, its damask cover bizarrely smooth amid
the chaos.

"Where is the whoreson bastard?"

Sarah jumped at the question. She turned, guided by its
sound, and found her father coming toward her from the
darkest corner of the room, blue eyes peering out from
under thick brows. His face was contorted, spittle trailing
from the corner of his mouth. *Drew?* she thought. *My
God, he means Drew.*

"He isn't here," she said, trying to pitch her voice to
be low and calm. "There is no one here but me, Papa.
It's Sarah. I've come to take care of you."

"You're the one who brought him here," he said.

In spite of her resolution, Sarah shrank from the men-
ace of his tone. He looked frail and thin, and he was both
barefoot and coatless, but his voice seemed as strong as
it ever had.

"There's no one else here, Papa," she said again. "No one but you and me."

"You're hiding him from me. All of you are hiding him."

"No one's hiding."

"They're all hiding," he said. "They're hiding because they know what I'll do to them."

"No one's hiding," she said again.

She took a step nearer, and he lunged toward her. Instinctively, she dodged the object he thrust at her like a rapier. It was a cane, she realized. A fine ebony walking stick with an etched silver head—one her mother had given him. He was using it as if it were a foil, the classic positioning of his body making the mimicry obvious.

"It's Sarah, Papa," she said, regretting that all she felt was terror. She wanted to do what she had done last night—run away from something she didn't understand. From something that frightened and confused her. Something unknown.

But this was her father. Who had once loved her. Who had loved her mother. He had loved her so much that he had never been the same after her death. Never again the man she and Amelia had adored when they were children.

"I'll kill him," the old man said. "I swear on your mother's grave I'll skewer him like the whoreson bastard he is."

"He's not here, Papa," Sarah said softly, taking another step nearer to him. "No one else is here. Why don't you let me help you into your bed? You must be tired."

"You won't fool me with your sweet ways, whore," he said. "You won't ever fool me again."

He turned the cane, executing another perfect fencing maneuver. It was a grotesque ballet. A mad old man, barefoot, performing, with what seemed to Sarah a nearly flawless precision, moves he had learned more than half a century before.

"Let me turn down your bed," she said, moving still closer.

He thrust the point of his imaginary sword toward the center of her chest. This time she stood her ground. She could see his eyes, pale, watery, and almost luminescent in his fevered insanity, shining at her through the dimness.

"Take me to him," he demanded, the tip of the cane poised, if it *were* a blade, to pierce her heart. "Take me to him *now*."

"Papa," Sarah whispered, holding his eyes, trying to find something of her father still within them. "It's me, Papa. There's no one else here. If you'll lie down, I'll call Dawson. He'll see to everything," she promised. "He'll make it all better."

He cocked his head, as if evaluating her tone. She forced herself to remain motionless. She was near enough that she could smell him, the odor of an aged, unwashed body sickeningly combined with the scent of the perfume he had worn since the days he had spent at court, when he had been one of the old king's favorites.

"Aren't you tired, Papa?" she asked softly.

Moving slowly and very carefully, she put her hand up and touched the tip of the cane, which was only inches from her breastbone. His eyes, feral as an animal's, watched her. He was like an animal, she thought, wild and untrusting.

"Let me take this," she said.

She gripped the cane more firmly and tugged on it. Surprisingly, he released the handle, and then he straightened from the fencer's lunge. As she watched, his body slumped, losing the youthful swordsman's grace it had assumed.

"Aren't you tired?" she asked again. "It's been so long since you've slept. Dawson told me. Your bed is here."

Still gripping the end of the cane, she turned, using it to point toward the inviting smoothness of the counterpane. Her father's eyes followed the movement.

The bed did look inviting, she realized. And once he was there, he would fall asleep. That had always been the pattern before. She had no reason to doubt that after a three-day-long rampage he wouldn't follow it again. As soon as he had closed his eyes, she would dispatch Dawson to see to the room. Dawson really would take care of everything.

Except getting her father to calm down. Sarah was the only one who had ever had any success at that when he reached this stage. This had been the easiest of her encounters with him, but her father's strength had been exhausted in the time it had taken the message to reach her and for her to get home. Never before had she allowed him to go on as he had this time. She had always tried to intervene before his rage had run its course.

She had been afraid that to do otherwise would lead to apoplexy or stroke. Then, when his fit was all over, she would wonder if it wouldn't have been better to let fate take its course. Death seemed preferable to this madness. It would have been preferable for her father, if he had been in his right mind.

"Come to bed, Papa. It's time to rest," she said.

She held out the hand that was not encumbered by the walking stick. Almost as if he couldn't resist its invitation, her father put his spotted, vein-gnarled hand in hers. It was trembling, she realized. And hers was not.

She was no longer afraid of him. She was the one in control now. She was the parent, luring the tired, fretful

child to his rest. She closed her fingers around his hand
and pulled. He shuffled toward her, and she led the way
to the bed.

She wished she could bathe him and put him into his
nightshirt. Of course, none of that mattered now. He
would sleep, and as he slept, the servants would clean up
the devastation he had wrought. She bent, laying the
walking stick on the floor beside the bed.

With the hand that had held it, she pulled back the
covers. Obediently, the old man stepped past her, up onto
the first of the two low steps that had been placed beside
the high bed. He crawled under the covers she had lifted,
and then Sarah drew them back over his body.

He was shivering. For the first time she became aware
of how cold the room was. The bed warmer that was
always placed between her father's sheets each night
wasn't there, of course. Dawson would see to the fire
when he came up, but for now she tucked the covers
around her father's shoulders.

"Cold," he whispered, his body trembling.

"I know," she said. "I know you are."

With the hand that had warded off the thrust of the
cane, she smoothed back the wildness of his hair. It was
almost as long as Drew's now, she thought, because he
hated to have it cut and so she didn't force him to.

"Dawson will see to the fire while you sleep. Close
your eyes, Papa, and when you wake up again, it will be
warm," she promised. She was talking simply so he
should hear the sound of a human voice. Perhaps he
would even recognize it as hers.

His eyes were on her face. They seemed as unseeing,
as unknowing, as those of Meg Randolph's baby. Sarah
smiled into them, wondering if he would ever know her
again. If he would ever speak her name.

"Go to sleep," she whispered.

"A good child," her father said.

Given the context, Sarah wasn't certain of his meaning, but she smiled at him again, her hand stroking his hair. Slowly his eyelids drifted downward. His eyes opened once or twice more, holding on hers a moment, before the lids fell and stayed closed, finally hiding the lost emptiness that was in their faded blue.

Sarah bent and put her lips against his forehead. His hand stirred beneath the cover, fighting its way outside. It patted her shoulder awkwardly, and when she lifted her head to see his face, his eyes were open again.

His fingers, cold and trembling, cupped her cheek. "You're a good child, Mellie," he said distinctly.

Mellie. It was what her father had called Amelia when she was small. His sweet Mellie. And she had been, of course. His baby girl. His favorite.

Sarah put her hand over his, holding it there a long heartbeat, and then she lifted his fingers, limp and unmoving, and put his arm back under the covers. His eyes were closed, sunken under the discolored, paper-thin skin of their lids.

She waited a long time beside his bed, keeping watch over him until the last of the fading daylight had slipped away into night. Then, stiff with the cold and with her long journey, she straightened.

She did not look back at the old man who had once been her father. She crossed the debris-strewn room and opened the door, taking a long deep breath before she picked up Mrs. Simkins's keys and went downstairs to find Dawson.

Chapter Ten

"Sarah!" Drew shouted. "We're home, Sarah! We're home!"

He scampered into the estate office almost before the sound of the words had faded. Sarah had only had time enough to move around her desk before he was in the doorway. Suddenly he was in her arms, his small body flung against hers as if it had been months since he had seen her, instead of days.

She hugged him fiercely and then held him away from her, a hand on each shoulder, so she could look at him. His cheeks were reddened from the cold, and his eyes were bright and clear. And happy, she realized. Incredibly happy. Sarah pulled off his cap, running her fingers through the disordered curls and feeling the burn of tears. She hugged him close again to hide them.

"Are you very glad to see me?" he asked.

"More glad than you can ever imagine," she said truthfully.

"Wynfield said you would be. He said you would hug me to pieces, and you are."

Drew struggled a little, and she released her hold, allowing him to step back. "You've grown a foot," she said.

He did seem taller. And older. Of course, it might be that when she had had him constantly at her side, she hadn't noticed his maturing. Not even when "I'm no longer a baby" was his most frequent rejoinder to her every comment.

He wasn't, she realized. He was a little boy who was growing up. And growing away from her as he did. Away from her and toward Wynfield, which was exactly what she had wanted.

"Look," Drew said, ignoring her hyperbolic comment about his size as too ridiculous to answer. He held out for her inspection a small leather crop, its stock well-worn. "It was Wynfield's," he explained, the words rushing over one another in his hurry to get them out. "His very own first crop, which he has given to me for Christmas."

He looked up from his treasure, eyes widened and mouth opened in amazement, waiting, she knew, for her equally excited response. She wouldn't have disappointed him for the world.

"His very own?" she said, her tone properly awestruck.

Solemnly, Drew nodded.

"Oh, my goodness," she breathed.

She reached out and touched its smooth handle, running her fingers admiringly over the surface.

"And just my size," Drew said.

"It does seem to be," Sarah agreed.

"What a lucky boy I am, Sarah. Don't you think I am?"

She almost missed the question. She had been listening instead, as she had been since Drew's precipitous entrance, she realized, for the sound of the uneven footsteps that were now coming down the hall. Her eyes lifted from the crop and over Drew's head to focus on the doorway. Again, her heart seemed to beat in her throat, its pulse strong enough to be visible if anyone were looking. A sweet rush of moist heat stirred in her lower body as the limping footsteps came closer.

And then Wynfield was in the doorway, wide shoulders almost filling the frame. His hazel eyes found her face before they considered anything else in the room. Like Drew's, his cheeks were touched with red. He had taken off his hat, a tall, handsome beaver, which he held in one hand, leaving his thick chestnut hair almost as tousled as Drew's.

"Hello, Sarah," he said softly.

She fought the urge to throw herself into his arms as wildly as Drew had sought hers, the urge to tell him how much she had missed him and had longed to hear him say her name. Instead of doing any of those things, she said, "Did you have a good trip?"

He nodded, almost imperceptibly, his lips compressing a little before he answered. "Considering the season."

"It's been snowing here for three days," she offered.

She realized she was still on her knees, looking up at him as they discussed the weather. She put her hand on the floor and pushed herself up. Her knees were trembling as she walked back behind the desk and sat down again in her chair.

"Then I wonder how work at the Park is progressing," he said, his tone matter-of-fact, the question practical.

"I'm afraid I haven't had time to inquire," she admitted. She hadn't. There had been too much to do here.

Justin glanced down at Drew, who was snapping the loop of the crop against the corner of the desk, obviously enjoying the small pop of sound, and then up at her. "How's your father?" His eyes made their own apology for not having inquired before.

"He's much better, thank you. He usually is for a period of time after..."

"I'm glad," Justin said.

Then there was a small silence, unbroken except for the crack of the miniature whip. Sarah wanted to ask if he were well, but it was obvious he was much better than when he had gone up to London. She had gleaned from some of the things the earl's staff had said that he had gone there to seek medical treatment. She wasn't sure what that treatment involved, but she had surmised that's why he hadn't worn the artificial foot while he was in London. Now he was wearing it again.

And so, she reasoned, he *must* be better. She resisted the strong inclination to allow her eyes to trace down the straight line of his trouser leg. She concentrated instead on the improved color in his face. On the fact that he was no longer so thin and drawn. Much more like the man he had been before he had gone to Spain.

More like her Justin, she thought. Her beloved Justin.

"I think I'll check on their progress," he said.

Their progress? The workers at the Park, she realized.

"Of course," she said.

"Shall I go with you?" Drew asked.

"Not this time," the earl said, smiling at him.

His words fell almost on top of Sarah's protest.

"You've only just arrived," she said. "I haven't had a moment alone with you."

That was not what she meant to say. It seemed to imply that she didn't want Justin here, and of course, that was the furthest thing from her mind. And from her heart. Even Drew's eyes widened over her unthinking statement.

"Another day, Drew," Justin promised softly.

Before Sarah could formulate protest or apology, he had turned away. The doorway was suddenly empty, and she listened to his steps retracing the path they had followed only a few minutes before. The anticipation that had been in her heart turned to disappointment.

"Don't you like Wynfield?" Drew asked. "Don't you want him here with us?"

She forced her eyes to focus on Drew rather than on the doorway from which Justin had disappeared. Her cheeks burned with regret and embarrassment. "Of course I do," she said.

Drew's eyes examined her face, seeking confirmation of that. It was no wonder he was skeptical, given her choice of words. And if he doubted her feelings, then what must Justin think?

"I'm very glad you're home. I've missed you both," she said.

"He's going to teach me to ride."

"I thought he would," Sarah said, smiling at him.

Just as he will teach you all the other things you must know. The things that will make you the same kind of man he is. And if nothing else ever comes of this marriage... She broke off that thought, a possibility she didn't want to admit. Considering the impediments the specter of their past relationship brought to this one, however, it *was* a possibility.

If nothing else ever came of her marriage, she forced herself to conclude, then the place Wynfield had assumed in Drew's life was quite enough return on her investment. Quite enough return on *all* her investments.

"Hello."

Andrew looked up at the sound of the unfamiliar voice.

He had been cracking the thong of the crop along the paddock fence, waiting for Wynfield. It was already twilight, on another one of the winter's short days, but the earl always tried to return to Longford before nightfall, preferring not to take Star through the forest in the dark.

A good horseman protects his mount, he had said. Drew was confident, therefore, that Wynfield would be back soon. They could walk up to the house together, and he would ask when they could begin his riding lessons. He had been wishing the earl would hurry, and shivering, despite his heaviest coat, as the sky grew grayer. And then the stranger had spoken to him.

"'Lo," Drew said.

The man was leaning against the wall of the stable. Not a groom. His clothes were too fine. They seemed finer even than Wynfield's, who was a peer.

"Are you Andrew?" the man asked.

His eyes were smiling, as was his mouth. Drew smiled back at him, liking the way the skin wrinkled around the corners of his eyes. They were dark blue, he realized. Like his. And like Sarah's.

"I'm Andrew," he agreed. "Drew if you like."

"I like that very much."

The stranger straightened away from the wall and began to move closer to where Andrew was waiting. He was as tall as Wynfield, Drew realized, but...thicker. Bigger, he amended, watching the stranger saunter across the frozen ground of the paddock. He didn't limp like the earl, of course. Perhaps that meant he hadn't been a soldier.

"What's *your* name?" Drew asked. He forgot to pop the crop against the fence, watching the stranger's approach instead.

"My name is David."

"Like in the Bible?" Drew asked.

David laughed. The sound of it was as nice as his smile. Neither Sarah nor Wynfield laughed very much, Drew realized. On Christmas Eve, of course, but they hadn't today. Today...

"Very much like the David in the Bible, I'm afraid."

The man was now standing beside him, his hand held out, palm up. "That's a fine crop," he said. "May I see it?"

Although his present was still very new and special, since it had once belonged to the earl, Drew's good manners managed to overcome his reluctance to let the crop out of his possession, if only for a moment. He laid it on the outstretched palm and watched, fascinated, as the stranger's eyes smiled at him again before examining the whip.

"A very fine crop," he said finally. "I had one much like this when I was with the army in India."

"India," Drew breathed.

"A very long time ago," David said. "Would you like to hear about India?"

"And about the army," Drew exclaimed, his eyes wide.

Sarah had told him not to talk to Wynfield about the war because she was afraid it would make him sad, but this gentleman was obviously not sad about the time he had spent in the military. His eyes were still smiling.

"And about the army, of course," David agreed easily, holding out the crop.

Drew's small, gloved fingers closed around it, his eyes on his new friend's face. *Another soldier,* he thought excitedly.

"Do you know Wynfield?" he asked.

"The earl? I don't believe I've had the pleasure of his acquaintance. Is he a friend of yours?"

Drew nodded. He glanced over his shoulder, expecting at any moment to see Star, carrying Wynfield home on his back. The path that led from the woods was very dark, however. And still empty.

"Is there somewhere we could go to talk?" David asked. "It's a bit cold out here. Nothing like the cold in the mountains of Tibet. Nothing at all like that. Of course, it was the contrast to the heat that made it worse, I suppose. The heat in India is terrible in the summers. Why, I remember one campaign...." David hesitated in his reminiscence, looking across the paddock toward the stables.

The grooms would be there, Drew knew—waiting, just as he was, for Wynfield to return. "It's warmer inside the stables," he suggested. "There's always a fire in the tack room."

David's eyes came back to his face. "Then you should be there. Or inside the Hall," he said. "I've kept you standing in the cold too long. Sarah will never forgive me, I'm afraid."

"Sarah knows I come here," Drew said.

David laughed. "Running away from her skirts? Good for you."

For some reason Drew was stung by the laughter, despite the compliment that followed. It made it sound as if he were still a baby, clinging to Sarah as he had once done.

"I don't have to run away," Drew protested. "I always come here in the afternoons to wait for Wynfield."

"Waiting for the earl, are you? Then I'd better not keep you from your duty," David said. Smiling, he put his heels together and snapped a smart salute. "We'll talk another day when you aren't so busy."

"You were going to tell me about India," Drew reminded him.

"And I will, but…" The well-shaped lips pursed a little. "Not tonight. You wait for the earl if you wish. I'll tell you my stories another day."

"When?" Drew asked.

"Tomorrow afternoon?" his new friend suggested. "If you are free then."

Eagerly Drew nodded, his eyes shining.

"There are braziers in the conservatory," David said. "It should be warm enough there. Do you know where that is?"

"Beside the gardener's bothy," Drew said quickly.

"I should have known that a boy like you would know every nook and cranny of this estate," he said. "I'll be in the conservatory at four o'clock tomorrow. If you meet me, I'll tell you all about that campaign. As well as any other things you should like to know about India."

"All right," Drew said.

David's long fingers fished in his waistcoat pocket. He extracted a watch, detaching it from its chain. "Can you tell the time, Drew?" he asked.

"Of course. I'm not a baby, you know."

"No, you're not," David agreed readily. "With this, you will know exactly when to come for our appointment."

He held out the watch, but Drew didn't reach for it. He had never held a watch before, although he really could tell time. Sarah had taught him.

"Do you see this dent?" David asked, leaning closer to show him a small crease in the metal. "That's a scar made by a bullet," he said, his voice very low, sounding almost as full of wonder as Drew felt. "This watch saved my life. Which, as I'm sure you can imagine, makes it very special to me. Take good care of it, Andrew. But of course, I know you will. After all, you aren't a baby.''

Unable to resist, Drew gathered the pocket watch off the stranger's palm before he looked up into the face of the man who had trusted him with the very thing that had once saved his life.

David was still smiling, even his eyes. ''Until tomorrow,'' he reminded. ''A secret meeting,'' he suggested. ''A rendezvous between just the two of us. We won't tell anyone else, not even Sarah. Is that all right, Andrew? To keep it our secret?''

Drew nodded, only half listening, his eyes again on the treasure he had been entrusted with. He laid the crop on top of the fence and, holding the watch carefully in his right hand, ran the thumb of his left slowly along the crease.

The mark of a bullet, he thought. And tomorrow he would have a secret rendezvous. Just like real soldiers. He envisioned red-clad units standing against the foe. He could almost feel the beat of the tattoo and see the ensigns snapping in the hot, dusty air of India. David, his new friend, had really been there. And he was willing to tell him all about it.

When Drew looked up again, he realized it was almost fully dark, and the stable yard was empty. The stranger had gone, seeming to have vanished into the shadows.

David had been right, he thought, shivering again. It was very cold out here. And there was not enough light to thoroughly examine the watch and the scar the bullet had made in its case.

He would go back to Longford, Drew decided. He could just as easily wait for Wynfield there. That way Sarah wouldn't be worried if she were looking for him to have his supper.

He wished he could tell someone about the watch. He wished he could show it to Sarah. Or even better, show it to Wynfield, who would certainly recognize that this was a military watch. He couldn't do that, of course. He had been sworn to secrecy. A military secret. Just like the rendezvous tomorrow, when David would tell him about India.

Andrew began walking across the paddock, but before he reached the gate, he was running, the watch carefully clutched in his right hand. The crop Wynfield had given him for Christmas, which he had so excitedly shown to Sarah only yesterday, lay forgotten on the top of the paddock fence.

Sarah had been expecting some communication from David Osborne since she had come home. She had even consulted Mr. Samuels to find out how much capital would be available when David finally made his demand. And had been frightened by the answer. She had known Justin's withdrawals were enormous, but she truly hadn't realized how little remained in the accounts.

As the days went by without any word from Osborne, however, her sense of fear and dread began to ease. So much so that when Sarah received his note, two weeks after Drew and Justin's return from London, it was almost a shock to hear from him again. The passage of time had lulled her into a sense of false security, she supposed. That and the fact that Justin was back.

There was no demand in the note except for a meeting, which was not to take place at Longford, but in the woods that ran along the estate's western boundary. There was a small clearing on the other side of the brook where, Amelia had once confided, she and David had met in the weeks prior to their elopement.

Sarah understood why Osborne wouldn't want to chance an encounter with Justin. However, she wasn't looking forward to meeting him in such a secluded spot. It didn't seem as if she could avoid it, however, since he had given her no indication of where he was staying or of how she could reach him to arrange a change. His message assumed she would do what she was told.

And she would have to, she realized. She had no other choice. She would go and hear his demand, and then she would have to find some way to give him whatever he wanted. She was desperate to get the threat David Osborne represented out of their lives. At least until the next time he ran out of money, she thought bitterly. And maybe by then…

Her eyes lifted from the letter, focusing on the doorway of the estate office. She remembered Justin standing there, his eyes locked on hers. Maybe by the time Osborne came back for another payment, she would have someone at her side who could put an end to his blackmail.

Sarah pulled the hood of her woolen cloak closer against her cheek, trying to keep the cold wind from her face and throat. David was very late, and the shadows in the forest around her were lengthening. She had thought about riding out here this afternoon, and now, as the light was beginning to fade, she wished she had.

Instead, she had put a few items from the kitchen into a wicker basket and told Mrs. Simkins she was going to call on one of her elderly tenants. If the housekeeper thought it strange she should be making a charity call so late in the day, she had thankfully held her tongue.

Sarah had set the heavy basket on the ground as she waited. She crossed her arms over her chest, her shoulders hunched under her cloak. Her eyes searched the woods around the clearing. She was impatient to get this over. Impatient to find out the worst.

It had been such a temptation to confide in Justin last night. She had wanted to seek him out and ask for his advice. But again, she couldn't think of any way to frame an explanation that would not violate her oath.

So she had come alone to meet a man she didn't trust. Which made her even more foolish, she supposed, than poor Amelia had been. After all, Sarah understood very clearly the kind of man David Osborne was, and her sister had not.

"Ah, Sarah. I should have known you'd be punctual."

It was almost as if by thinking about him she had conjured David up out of the misty shadows. She turned in the direction of his voice and found him propped against the trunk of an oak, arms akimbo, and his ankles, covered by highly polished boots, gracefully crossed.

A pose he had probably practiced, she thought cynically. Still, she had to admit he was striking. No wonder he had been able to turn Amelia's head. Handsome and charming to boot. And interested only in himself, she reminded herself.

"What do you want?" she challenged, keeping her voice as frigid as the darkening January air.

"You know what I want, Sarah. I made that quite clear, I believe, during our previous meeting. I want my son."

"You're not interested in Andrew. You never have been."

"So quick to judge, Sarah. What makes you certain I have no father feeling for the boy?"

"Perhaps the fact that you've had nothing to do with him since he was born," she said. Her reply was deliberately biting, although she hadn't raised her voice.

"I'm set on turning over a new leaf. Correcting my

unconscionable behavior. You should applaud that, I would think, since you have been very free with your criticism of my previous relationship with Drew."

"You haven't *had* a previous relationship," Sarah said.

"Now I intend to rectify that," Osborne countered smoothly.

"How much?"

"How much?" Osborne repeated, as if he had no idea what she was talking about.

"To leave. To leave Drew alone. How much money will it take to make you go away?" .

"Sarah," David chided, his tone full of shock and dismay, both of which were patently assumed. His eyes were amused. "I should think you'd welcome my desire to get to know my son."

"Why should I?" she asked. "You are not the kind of man I want Andrew to know. I wouldn't want him to know you exist."

"I suppose you prefer his hero worship of the earl."

"Wynfield? Actually, I much prefer that. Which is convenient, since Drew *does* worship him."

David smiled. "What a shame, then, that he isn't Andrew's father. And he isn't, Sarah. You really should remember that."

"I also remember that you, who are, didn't want anything to do with Drew. Not until you thought of a way it might benefit you to claim to be his father."

"Not *claim,* Sarah," Osborne said softly. "I *am* Drew's father. Surely you don't intend to deny that?"

Sarah hesitated, knowing she couldn't. He had proof. And the courts would be forced to consider it.

"You don't really want to be saddled with a little boy," she said instead. "Why don't you tell me what you *do* want? The sooner you do, the sooner we can put an end to this farce.''

He laughed, the sound ringing in the thin air, grating on her nerves, which were already stretched to the screaming point. Suddenly, he straightened away from the tree and took a couple of long strides, which brought them face-to-face.

''You can't afford to make me angry, Sarah,'' he said. ''This time I hold all the cards. And there is no one who can stop me from doing whatever I want to do with them. Not your insane father. Not your so nobly crippled husband.''

Sarah's mouth tightened over the words she wanted to fling at him. She managed to hold her tongue, but she held his eyes as well, forcing hers not to reflect her fear.

''Tell me what you want,'' she demanded again.

''Something I wanted more than five years ago.''

Since she had been thinking only of money, his movement caught her off guard. He took a step forward, his right arm snaking around her back. He pulled her roughly against him. With his left hand, he grasped the back of her neck, effectively imprisoning her.

At first she was too shocked to struggle. By the time she realized what he intended, it was too late for her efforts to have much effect. Her arms were pinned between their bodies, imprisoned by his hard chest and the folds of her own cloak. As his head lowered, she saw he was still smiling.

His lips ground into hers. Her hands, palms flattened against his chest, tried to push him away. Her strength was not enough, and he simply increased the pressure of his mouth, forcing her head back until her hood fell away.

The rush of cold air had the same effect as if someone had poured water over her. It galvanized her into a more frantic resistance. She finally managed to force her hands up from where they had been imprisoned, fighting free of the restraint of her cloak. She battered at his head and face with her fists, determined to make him turn her loose.

Eventually he did, raising his arm to ward off her blows. His eyes were alight with amusement, but he had been forced to take a step backward. "You haven't changed a bit, Sarah," he said, laughing at her indignation. "Still the innocent."

Blushing, hand at her throat, she watched his eyes change. But then no one had ever accused Osborne of not being shrewd. Or of not knowing women.

"Good God," he said. "You are, aren't you? Still the innocent."

She wanted to hit him again. To drive that knowing smile from his face. To destroy the words that seemed to hang, frozen in the air, between them.

"And I wonder why," he said, his voice musing. He almost sounded as if he cared. As if he really wanted to know.

"How much do you want?" she said. She was breathing as if she had been running, almost panting in her fury.

"Why doesn't your husband kiss you, Sarah? Exactly what kind of marriage do you have with our gallant earl, my dear?"

Sarah could think of nothing to say. She would know later what a mistake that had been, but unnerved, she couldn't think of any way to explain the kind of marriage she and Justin had. And when she didn't answer, David came up with his own conclusions.

"That's why you were willing to meet me out here. You're the kind of woman who needs to be kissed, well and often. The passionate kind of woman that poor, bloodless Amelia, try as she might, could never be.''

''Don't you talk about my sister,'' she warned him.

''You're right,'' he said agreeably. ''You're a much more interesting subject. You always were. But you were so bloody enamored of your soldier....''

He stopped, his eyes studying her face, which felt stiff, not only from the cold and her anger, but from trying not to reveal anything of what she was feeling. David would use any weapon she gave him.

''And you still are,'' he said, his voice almost hushed with surprise and speculation. ''And yet for some reason...'' Suddenly, the perplexity that had been in the handsome face cleared, and he laughed again, the sound mocking. ''You haven't told him,'' he said, reveling in his conclusion. ''Like everyone else, he thinks Drew is your own darling little bastard. And you haven't told him any differently because you won't besmirch precious Amelia's name. My God, do you know how funny that is?''

''Stop it,'' Sarah said, her voice hard and cold.

''And in his self-righteous nobility, Wynfield won't touch you because he thinks you're spoiled goods. The pair of you deserve each other. Both of you too damned virtuous for your own good,'' he accused, laughing again. ''And *that's* why you're so hungry for a man's touch.''

''Not yours,'' she said, not even bothering to deny the rest.

''Because your beloved thinks you're a whore,'' he continued, ignoring her insult.

At this moment she hated Osborne almost as much as she had hated him when he'd walked out on Andrew in Ireland. Almost as much as when Amelia had died, all alone except for her sister.

"*My* whore," he added softly.

Something was happening, some idea obviously forming, but Sarah didn't know what he was thinking. All she knew was that her instincts had been correct. She should never have come out here to meet David Osborne. She had been a fool to put herself this much into his power.

"So why did he marry you, I wonder?" he asked, his voice full of speculation. "Simply for your money?" he suggested. "And for what it could do for him, of course."

Lips tight, Sarah continued to look at his handsome, hateful face, determined to tell him nothing.

"Then he's not nearly as noble as I thought," David said. "No more noble than I am. So I was right before. You really *did* buy yourself a husband. But you didn't get what you'd bargained for, did you, Sarah? You must be very disappointed."

Again his voice was genuinely amused.

"This is the last time I'll ask you," Sarah said. "How much will it take to make you go away?"

"And it seems a shame for all of this to go to waste."

His hand lifted, and with one long finger, gloved in thin, supple calfskin, he traced a line down her cheek, from her eye to the corner of her lips, and then slowly across the bottom one. She reached up and grabbed his hand, intending to push it away, but he was too strong for her. His fingers closed around hers instead, carrying them to his lips. He pressed a kiss onto the back of them, and then, smiling, released her.

"I'll be in touch, sweet Sarah," he promised softly. "I will definitely be in touch."

David turned and walked across the clearing, disappearing into the same darkness under the trees from which he had materialized. Behind him, Sarah drew a shuddering breath. She was so angry she was trembling. He had again bested her. Despite her demands and ultimatum, she was no closer to getting rid of David Osborne than she had been before.

He had been back almost two weeks, Justin realized, as he guided Star at twilight through the woods that joined the two estates. And in that entire time, he had barely seen Sarah.

He had kept to the terms of their agreement, returning each evening to Longford. During the short daylight of the midwinter days, however, he had buried himself in the ongoing renovations at his own estate. While he was supervising the work there, he didn't have to think about his marriage. Or about Sarah.

He still didn't understand what had happened that night in London. He would have staked his life on what he had seen in Sarah's eyes just before he kissed her. He would have gambled his immortal soul that she had *wanted* him to kiss her.

He had gambled it, he acknowledged grimly. And from the moment his lips had closed over hers, from the moment she had melted against his body, it had been lost.

He had once before fallen in love with Sarah Spenser, and she had betrayed him. So he had gone into this marriage with his eyes open, assuming she wanted from him exactly what she had bargained for—his guidance of Andrew and acceptance for her son in society. Nothing more.

Then, when she had shown up in London, he had let himself begin to believe Sarah wanted something else as well. Something that had to do with the emotions that had once flared so strongly between them. Even knowing that she had once before chosen another man over him, Justin had fallen into the same trap. The trap of letting himself think Sarah Spenser could care for him. And apparently he had again been a fool.

Suddenly, he became aware of distant voices, the words indistinct, but the sound of them loud enough to carry through the thin, cold air. He slowed Star, wondering if the boys from the village had ventured into his woods again.

At least Drew wouldn't be anywhere around, he thought gratefully. Then he realized with a deep sense of surprise that he had also seen less and less of Andrew. They had been together almost constantly in London. Now that they had returned to Longford, Drew seemed to have found other occupations.

He had not even asked about the riding lessons he had been so eager to begin when they left London. And he no longer waited at the stables each evening for Justin's return. Lost in his own perplexities over his and Sarah's relationship, Justin had not thought until now to question the little boy's absence.

He had ridden close enough to see part of the clearing, revealed through gaps between the tall, straight trucks of the winter-stripped oaks. He pulled Star up, eyes straining in the fading light to identify whoever he had heard.

A woman, and not the village boys, he realized, carefully guiding Star closer, although they were still hidden by the trees. She was wearing a cloak that served to disguise her build, but the hood had fallen back. Even in the dimness, he could see that her hair was fair. And the shape of her classic profile familiar.

His first thought was that Sarah and Drew might have come out to wait for him. And then, catching a glimpse of the other figure through a break in the thicket that separated him from the clearing, he realized the person with Sarah wasn't Drew.

Justin dismounted, his movements furtive, more by instinct than by design. Leaving Star behind, he moved closer to the pair, who seemed deeply engaged in conversation. Their voices were much lower than they had been before, the sound no longer carrying through the twilight stillness.

Justin didn't recognize Sarah's companion, not even when he was near enough to distinguish the man's features. As he watched, the stranger touched Sarah's face, running one finger slowly down her cheek and then across her lips, the gesture obviously tender.

She caught his fingers in her own, and the man carried their joined hands to his mouth, pressing his lips against the back of Sarah's. Then he turned and disappeared into the shadowed woods.

Sarah stood perfectly still for a long moment, her eyes fastened on the place where her companion had vanished. Justin didn't move, either—scarcely breathed as a cold sickness stirred in the pit of his stomach.

Finally unable to look at her any longer, he closed his eyes, fighting a wave of desolation and despair far stronger, despite the blows of the last six months, than any he had ever known.

Chapter Eleven

When Sarah got back to the house, she was still trembling. She was not certain whether that was from the dregs of her anger or from the cold. Either would have been excuse enough.

She sent word to Mrs. Simkins that she had returned, and then she retreated to the sanctuary of her rooms to deal with what had happened. She had sorely overrated her ability to maneuver Osborne. To employ the analogy he himself had used, she had badly misplayed her hand. As a result, he understood more about her marriage than she would have wished anyone to know. And she had no doubt he would use that knowledge in any way he thought could benefit him. David Osborne wouldn't care who he hurt, as long as he got what he wanted.

She had been so sure that she knew what that was, and then he had seemed to imply that money wasn't all he was interested in. To imply that he was still interested in her, which was ridiculous, of course. He was simply prolonging the agony. *I'll be in touch,* he had said, and again the sense of threat hovered over everything she loved.

She jumped when a knock sounded at her door. Maybe it was Drew, wanting to tell her all about his day's adventures, she thought. But he hadn't done that in a long time, she realized. He was obviously making those revelations to Justin now. She was delighted, of course, that they had grown so close while Drew had been in London, but she missed him. Missed the closeness they had always shared.

When she opened the door, Mrs. Simkins looked past her, eyes skimming the room, before they returned to Sarah's face. "The boy's not with you then, my lady," she said.

"Drew?" Sarah questioned. Her pulse quickened, anxiety growing as she considered her housekeeper's expression.

"He's not come in for his supper," Mrs. Simkins said. "And he's not in the nursery. I thought he might be here." Again the housekeeper checked Sarah's room, as if hoping she had been mistaken in her first survey.

"He must be with the earl," Sarah suggested. Drew always waited for Wynfield, and although it was now later than Justin usually returned—

"The earl hasn't come in, either." The housekeeper destroyed that comforting possibility. "I checked with his man before I came to speak to you."

Sarah glanced at the clock on the mantel. It was only half past six, but it had been fully dark for more than an hour. And she knew Justin's habits as well as Mrs. Simkins did.

"Have you sent to the stables? Perhaps the earl has been detained, and Drew is still waiting for him there."

"I thought I should check with you first. I can send one of the footmen."

Sarah took her cloak off the back of the chair where she had laid it when she came in. "I'll go myself. I'll probably meet them coming up the path," she said reassuringly, although her own heart rate had not slowed since the housekeeper's first inquiry. "Please don't worry, Mrs. Simkins. And I promise I shall speak to Drew about being late for supper."

"Don't you go scolding the child on my account, my lady. His supper can wait. It's just such a bitter night...." The housekeeper's voice faded, the worry clear in her dark eyes.

Sarah was worried as well, but not about Andrew. She was sure she would find him safely ensconced by the tack room fire. She was now far more anxious about why the earl was late. Drew was simply waiting for his hero. The question of why he was having to wait loomed in her mind, far more important right now than Andrew's being a little late for supper.

"They haven't seen hide nor hair of him, my lady," the head groom told her regretfully after he had put the question to his lads. "Neither of them have been here this afternoon. Neither the boy nor the earl."

"Then I shall need the coach to go to Wynfield," she said. "Don't worry, Riley. I'm sure Andrew is with his lordship."

Again she found herself reassuring others, when her own inclination was to panic. She remembered, however, the number of times Drew had gone across the boundary stream and to the Park without permission. Obviously, he had done it again. Probably because Justin was so late and Andrew, too, had been worried.

"I'm sure he's there, my lady," the groom said comfortingly. "You know lads when they get a notion in their heads. He'll be at the Park, as sure as anything." In his eyes, however, was the same unspoken concern that had been in the housekeeper's.

"Have them search the grounds, Riley," Sarah ordered

softly. "Just to be sure. And send word to Wynfield if you find him."

That he had been a fool was something for which he could hardly blame Sarah, the earl of Wynfield had finally decided. It had taken him two hours of steady drinking to arrive at the conclusion, but he was satisfied that it was not only accurate, but eminently reasonable. After all, he had known full well what Sarah Spenser was. What she had done five years ago had given him no room for doubt about that.

And from the beginning she had told him exactly what she wanted from this marriage. There had been no equivocation on her part. Hers had been a straightforward business proposition, made through her banker. *Make my son acceptable to society, make him a gentleman, and I'll pay your debts.*

That should have been clear enough for anyone's understanding, Justin thought, as he poured another splash of his father's very excellent French brandy into his glass. Clear even for someone so besotted with a woman that he was ready to forgive all her past indiscretions. Ready to make her bastard son his own. Ready to bare his soul—*and* his body, Justin thought bitterly—for her amusement.

And she would surely have been amused at how completely she had taken him in. He was. He had been pining for Sarah like a lovesick schoolboy, while she had already selected her next lover.

He lowered his empty glass to place it carefully on the table beside him. Carefully because neither his hand nor the table seemed particularly steady. For a man who had indulged in drink only twice in the last six months, it hadn't taken him long to remember how to get drunk. *Foxed,* to use Sarah's word. Except this time he really was.

He hadn't quite accomplished what he had set out to do, however. He hadn't yet managed to destroy his capacity to think. Or to remember. The images from the clearing—as vivid and as painful as they had been this evening—were still in his head. Along with those very different ones from Christmas Eve.

Sarah, glancing up at him over Drew's curls and smiling that small, secret smile. The two of them, standing together in the open doorway, laughing at the mummers' antics and at Drew's delight in them. The outline of her slender body, revealed by the candlelight. And her lips, moist and softly parted, opening under the demand of his.

He deliberately destroyed those memories, replacing them with the more recent one, which seemed burned into his mind's eye as if it had been branded there. The man in the clearing brushing Sarah's hand with his lips. Touching her face with one long, gloved finger. Touching Sarah as if he had the right. His Sarah.

Except she had never been that, of course. Never *his* Sarah. That had always been his mistake, his fantasy— the thought that she cared for him. Not then and not now. And the sooner he got that through his thick head, the better off he would be.

He would put a stop to what was going on, of course. Sarah was his wife, and whatever the situation between them, he wouldn't play the cuckold. He would demand that for Andrew's sake, if for no other reason....

For Andrew's sake. Despite the effects of the alcohol, those words impacted on his brain. And slowly Justin realized their significance. Why would Sarah jeopardize the very thing she had professed to desire so much that she was willing to pay off his enormous debts and refurbish his properties to accomplish?

There was no doubt about what would happen to Andrew's chances of acceptance if the district discovered

what his mother was doing. If anyone found out about
those meetings in the clearing, the gossip would begin
anew, and it would be even more virulent this time.

And eventually someone *would* find out. After all, he
had. It seemed Sarah wasn't very wise in carrying out her
affaires. Or not very lucky, perhaps. This time her own
husband had seen them. And the first time—

The thought was sudden, swimming up into his consciousness out of the alcohol-induced haze. The more Justin considered it, however, the more sense it made. He
supposed that during his absence, Sarah might have found
a new object for her affections. It seemed much more
likely, however, now that the idea had finally occurred to
him, that the man in the clearing and the man to whom
Sarah had given herself years ago were one and the same.

Andrew's father? Justin recreated the stranger's features, which had been dimly visible in the twilight. And
then, just as deliberately, he destroyed them. Andrew was
a Spenser, through and through. He looked far more like
Sarah than he did the stranger. And there was no way to
prove Justin's theory.

Perhaps that was the reason he had seen the boy so
infrequently during the last two weeks. Maybe Drew was
busy reacquainting himself with his real father. Perhaps
he and Sarah both were, welcoming the prodigal home.

Apparently welcoming him with open arms, Justin
thought, remembering the scene in the clearing. Unerr-
ingly, his hand found the neck of the bottle and poured
another measure of brandy into his glass. In London he
had drunk the port because thoughts of making love to
Sarah had filled his head. And tonight...

It was better *not* to think about the reasons he was
drinking tonight. It was better not to think at all. Trying
to arrange that, the earl of Wynfield raised his glass to

his lips and then, closing his eyes against the images that would not stop haunting him, tossed down its contents.

The house was so dark that Sarah wondered if Justin had dismissed his staff during the course of the renovations. Finally, however, someone opened the door and someone else was hurriedly dispatched to fetch Blevins. Sarah stood in the entrance hall, much as she and Drew had huddled together in the foyer of the London town house. It seemed she was destined to stand outside the earl of Wynfield's doors, demanding admittance.

"Lady Wynfield," Blevins said.

She glanced up to find the old man watching her from the end of the hallway. "I'm looking for my foster son, Blevins," she said. "I think he has come to see the earl."

"I'm afraid you have been misinformed, my lady. No one has called tonight. No one but you, of course."

"Andrew isn't here?" she asked. All the reassurances she had given herself began to crumble.

"I'm afraid he is not, my lady."

"Then I should like to see the earl," she said.

"I believe his lordship is...indisposed."

The butler's response seemed full of genuine regret. Sarah, however, was beginning to feel just as she had in London—out of place and very unwelcome. Perhaps the same solution she had employed there should be used here.

"I'm afraid I really must insist that I be taken to my husband," she said softly.

Blevins considered her a moment before he inclined his head. "Then if you'll come with me, my lady," he said.

Blevins had led her to the library, Sarah realized, standing beside him in the doorway. The room was lit by a single candle, which stood on a table beside a worn wing chair. Both were positioned invitingly in front of the fireplace. The grate was empty, however, except for a mound of cold, gray ashes.

Her gaze circled the room, which appeared to be empty as well. She had already turned, intending to question Blevins about why he had brought her here, when he stepped back into the hall, closing the door behind him. Sarah released the breath she had taken, and again her eyes examined the room, searching the shadows more carefully. "Justin?" she called softly.

The inflection was questioning, since she had already decided Blevins must have made a mistake. She had placed her fingers on the handle of the door when a hand reached out of the darkness and grabbed her wrist. Gripping it tightly, Justin pulled her around to face him. Startled by his uncharacteristic action, she tried to twist free. His fingers tightened.

"What are you doing here?" he asked, his voice very low.

He was so close she could smell him. An aroma compounded of starch and leather and the scent of the sandalwood soap he used. Completely masculine. Undeniably appealing, especially to her. And underlying those fragrances was a whiff of brandy. Justin had been drinking, which was probably what Blevins had meant by "indisposed."

"I guess it really doesn't matter *why* you're here," he continued, before she had time to formulate an answer. "I've given up on the whys of you. They're far too taxing. Too cerebral. Maybe that's always been the trouble between us."

"The trouble?" she whispered.

His eyes were very dark, shadowed by long, thick lashes. As her vision adjusted to the room's dimness, however, his features became more distinct. His smile was as mocking as David's had been—an expression she had never before seen on his face, not in all the years she had known him. And it made her afraid.

"I've never understood what you wanted from me," he said.

She shook her head, having no idea what he was talking about. She held his eyes, wary of what was in them, but compelled to stillness by the depth of emotion in his voice.

"But if *this* is what you want, Sarah…if this is what you've wanted all along…"

He had leaned so close his breath was warm against her cheek. And she found the aroma of the brandy heady. Exciting. As was the feel of his hand, his fingers rough and slightly callused as they encircled her wrist, demanding and possessive. She had never known Justin in this mood. He had always been the perfect gentleman, except that one night in London. She had run away from him then, and she had regretted her action ever since.

"If it is, then there isn't any reason why I can't be as accommodating as the next man," he finished softly.

She couldn't remember exactly what he had said before, but these words seemed out of context, their tone almost accusatory. He caught her other wrist, holding both shoulders high as he pushed her against the door. He was still watching her intently, almost daring her to resist. Except she had no desire to resist. No desire but to let this play out, as she had so often wished she had that night in London.

Then his head began to lower, the downward sweep of his lashes hiding the indictment that had been in his eyes. With the first touch of his lips against her throat, Sarah lost any sense of unease. Her own eyes closed, and her head fell back, resting against the door behind her. Her breathing deepened.

His tongue trailed languidly over the soft skin under her jaw and then down her throat until it encountered the barrier of the high neck band of her cloak. He released her right wrist and, one-handed, untied the strings, pushing the cloak apart with his fingers. She gasped as his thumb touched her skin, slid down into the neckline of her gown. His hand was warm in contrast to her coldness, its movement so knowing.

Her free hand cupped the back of his head, fingers spreading through his hair. It felt like silk, and it curled around them just as Drew's did. As warm and alive as Justin's mouth, which had somehow replaced the slow caress of his thumb.

"Is this what you want?" he whispered. His lips were so close that the words left a trace of moisture on her skin. She couldn't reply, lost in the flood of sensation.

"Answer me, Sarah," he demanded. "Is this what you want from me?"

"Yes," she whispered, knowing now that it was. The fear she had felt in London was gone, burned out of her by this terrible longing and by her need.

She needed Justin's touch, just as she had needed his strength. The fiasco of this afternoon's confrontation with Osborne had reinforced what she had known when she made her offer of marriage. She needed Justin. So she had buried her pride and proposed to a man who had every reason to despise her. And now, finally, she knew that he didn't.

His mouth had moved into the valley between her breasts. No man had ever touched her like this. Her knees were trembling, and a searing heat curled through her body like flame, flickering over nerve endings that had slept, unawakened, her entire life. Until this moment. Until Justin's touch.

His fingers found her breast, enclosing its softness. Still demanding. Their hard strength seemed almost as erotic as his trailing tongue. Daringly, her own hand touched the front of his shirt, the starched lawn slightly abrasive under the sensitive tips of her fingers. She moved them over the hard contours of underlying muscle and bone, recognizing their powerful contrast to her own body. Her fingers explored until they encountered the small, pebbled nub of his nipple.

She heard his intake of breath. She liked hearing it, she realized. So she moved her fingers back and forth, feeling the nipple begin to harden under their stroke.

He released her other hand, freeing it as suddenly as he had grasped it. Before she understood what was happening, he leaned back, his upper body moving away from her even as his hips pushed hers against the wall, holding her prisoner as effectively as he had before. He stripped his shirt over his head in one quick, fluid motion and dropped it to the floor.

He took her hands and placed them on his chest, inviting the exploration she had thought so daring. He wanted her to touch him, and that was almost as exciting as had been the movement of his lips against her bare skin.

She obeyed, her palms slowly moving over the hair-roughened strength of his chest. Moving in unison. His face was hard, almost set. His eyes were closed, his head tilted slightly back, his breathing irregular.

The same thing she had felt happening to his body in London, which had sent her running in panic, was happening again. And this time there was no fear. Justin wanted her. Despite what he believed about Drew. Despite what everyone had told him. Despite the gossip and the lies, he still wanted her.

From there it would be only a small step to what *she* wanted. To the relationship she had always dreamed of. She knew she could eventually make him love her, because she loved him so much.

She leaned forward, putting her mouth against the smooth muscle of his shoulder. She pressed a kiss into the heat of his skin, and then ran her tongue along the protrusion of bone. More daring now, her lips found the hollow of his collarbone, and she caressed it, too.

In response, his hand pushed aside the fabric of her crossed bodice. His fingers began to slip inside the opening he had created, moving over the bare, highly sensitized skin of her breast. And then, suddenly, they hesitated.

It took a moment for her to understand why. A moment to realize his hand had fastened around the strand of pearls he had given her for Christmas. She felt him lean back, away from her, and when she looked up into his face, his eyes were open, fastened on the worthless necklace she had worn against her heart since she had returned to Longford.

He had wrapped the string of misshapen pearls around his fingers, pulling them out into the light. He didn't meet her eyes, although they were still fastened on his face. The silence grew and expanded until finally he broke it.

''Who is he, Sarah?''

His voice was very soft. Almost too soft. She was disturbed by the tone of the question, although she hadn't understood it. It seemed to have nothing to do with the pearls he had given her. His mother's pearls.

His eyes, cold and infinitely distant, despite the very intimate positions of their bodies, were on her face at last. Waiting for her answer.

"Who...is he?" she repeated hesitantly.

"The man in the clearing," he said, stepping away from her without releasing his hold on the pearls.

Her heart stopped. She honestly hadn't known what he was talking about. She had separated the problem Osborne represented from her feelings about Justin for so long that there had seemed to be no connection between them. But of course, there was. There always had been.

Justin had seen them together. She should have thought of the possibility, but she had agreed to the meeting because she had been so eager to get rid of David. Eager to find out what he was demanding and then put an end to his threats. So confident that she could do that simply by offering him enough money. And instead...

If only David had been on time, she thought. But there had been so many if only's. If only Amelia had never eloped... If only her father had been in time to stop them... If only she had not been given the responsibility of caring for Andrew...

Instantly, Sarah dismissed the bitterness of that regret. No matter what it had cost her, she could not regret having Drew as part of her life. Not even if protecting him cost her Justin.

"His name is David Osborne," she said, her voice low, her eyes bravely meeting the coldness in his.

She had lied to Justin once. Lied to free him from the scandal that had broken her heart and stained her reputation. Lied to him because she loved him too much to hold him to an engagement that would bring him that same disgrace.

"Drew's father?" Justin asked.

A simple question, which required only one word to answer. The truth or another lie? She didn't make that decision, however, because finally, finally she remembered why she was here. "Where's Drew?" she asked him instead.

It wasn't what he had been expecting. She could see the puzzlement in his eyes. Which meant Blevins had been right. Andrew wasn't here. And Justin had no more idea where the little boy was than she did.

"Drew?" he repeated.

"He's not at Longford."

"What the hell are you talking about?"

"He's not there. I came here because I thought he would be with you. I thought he had waited for you, and when you didn't come home... Why *didn't* you come home?"

As soon as she said the words, she knew. That's what Justin had been doing when he had seen her with David. He had been coming home. Never once had she even considered that he would ride through the darkened woods rather than take the road that connected the two estates. Never once, although she knew that crossing the brook was Drew's preferred route of travel between the two estates.

"*Home,* Sarah?" Justin questioned bitterly.

"What you saw... It wasn't what you thought."

"Then tell me what it was," he suggested coldly.

She hesitated, trying to decide what she could tell him. Before she had, however, he freed his hand, unwrapping the necklace with a quick twist of his fingers, and took a step backward. He bent and picked up the shirt he had dropped. Then he turned away from her, walking over to the fireplace.

He's tired, she thought, not even conscious that she had learned to gauge the depth of Justin's fatigue by the severity of his limp. She watched as he put his hands on the mantel, long fingers gripping the edge, still holding his shirt in one hand. He leaned forward, his head lowered as if he were looking down into the nonexistent flames.

"If Drew's not here—" she began.

"Maybe he's with his father," Justin said bitingly.

And with his words, everything fell into place.

"Oh, dear God," Sarah said softly.

He turned at her tone, and she watched his face change, his eyes reflecting the fear she knew must be in her own. David had told her he wanted Drew, and she hadn't believed him. But if Drew wasn't at Longford, and he wasn't here...

"You think that's where he is?" Justin asked. "With Osborne?"

Slowly, she nodded. "He said he wanted Drew. I didn't believe him because..." Her voice faded, as she thought about everything she knew about David Osborne. Justin waited through the silence. "He doesn't care about Drew. I think somehow he found out about my father's illness and saw his chance to blackmail me."

"You've been paying him money?" Justin said disbelievingly.

"I intended to. He said Drew was entitled to a share of the estate. Because he was Brynmoor's grandson. He threatened to take his case to the courts. I knew that if he did that, there would be more scandal. At least a revival of the old one. And Drew..."

"Would be at the center of it," he finished for her.

She nodded. There was so much more that she hadn't told him. Not only would Drew be at the center of any case Osborne brought, but so would Amelia. David would show the priest's document to the court, and it would destroy Amelia's reputation, which Sarah had tried all these years to protect.

More importantly, of course, it would destroy any claim Sarah might have to guardianship of Drew. Even if

David didn't succeed in getting control of her father's money, he would still have control of Drew. "He doesn't really *want* Andrew," she said, almost to herself. That was one thing she had held on to in the midst of David's threats. No matter what else happened, he wouldn't really want to take the little boy with him.

"He wants your father's money."

"That's all he's ever wanted," she said bitterly.

Justin's eyes considered her, and since he knew nothing about Amelia's elopement, she wondered what he thought she meant.

"The courts won't give him that," Justin said after a moment.

"How can you be sure?"

"Because the only rights illegitimate children have are those that are accorded them *if* they are legally recognized. Your father has never done that."

It wasn't a question. He knew as well as she did that Brynmoor's pride wouldn't allow him to recognize a bastard grandson, not even had he been competent to do so. He would ignore Drew's existence, just as he had buried the daughter who had shamed him, long before her death.

"David has proof," Sarah said hesitantly, knowing she was treading dangerously near to breaking her oath.

"What kind of proof?"

"Something I signed. Verifying Andrew's...paternity."

Justin's eyes had hardened again, still focused on her face. "Since you will be your father's heir, Osborne might believe he can use that paper to force you to acknowledge the child's rights to the estate after your father's death," he said, "but obviously he can't use it to threaten Brynmoor. Even if he tried, such a threat would have no effect on your father. Osborne can't possibly use his proof to get part of the estate until after his death. And only then if you acknowledge the boy as your heir.''

"Then why has he taken Drew?''

"What better way to make sure you'll give him whatever he wants?'' Justin asked softly.

Justin was convinced David would be staying in the district, somewhere close enough that traveling to and from Longford would be practical. Because, of course, that was one thing they had discovered from their questioning of the stable boys.

Osborne had been seen on the estate on two different occasions. Once he had even been seen with Drew. And no one had thought to report the matter to Sarah. Or to the earl. That wasn't a mistake any of her servants would ever make again, Sarah thought. The fury with which Justin dealt with the grooms was another aspect of his character she had never seen before.

It was not until he ordered the carriage brought around that she realized what these frantic preparations reminded her of—that terrible night her father had discovered Amelia's elopement and gone out to find her. The horses' breath, mingling with the cold air, had been visible then as well, drifting thick and white in the ghostly light of the lanterns.

"I'm going with you,'' she had said then. Her father had ignored her, the crack of his whip against the backs of his bays his only answer. Justin looked down on her a long moment as she stood beside the carriage, uttering the same words she had said that long-ago night. His eyes were still cold, his face set.

"I'll travel faster without you,'' he said.

"Please, Justin,'' she begged. "Whatever you think about what I've done, please let me come.''

"What if you're wrong?'' he asked.

"About David?"

"Maybe Drew's fallen asleep somewhere."

"If you really believed that, you'd be searching for him here."

"I'll leave that to you and the servants," Justin said.

"What if he's already taken Drew away?"

"He hasn't," Justin said. "That isn't what this is about. You said it yourself."

"And what if *I'm* wrong about that?" she asked. "Please take me with you. I can't bear to stay here, waiting and not knowing."

His eyes studied hers a long time, and then he held out his hand. Her throat closed with gratitude and relief. She put her fingers into his and felt them tighten firmly.

"If we find them... *When* we find them," he amended, "I'll handle Osborne. Is that understood?"

He gave her no choice. Reluctantly, she nodded, and he pulled her up into the carriage. Almost before she had time to settle on the seat beside him, Justin touched the leader with the tip of his whip, sending the bays thundering into the darkness.

They found Osborne at the third of the posting inns they visited. They would have found him sooner had the two estates not lain in such close proximity to several well-traveled roads. They had simply chosen the wrong ones to search first.

Justin was just as effective in dealing with innkeepers as with stable boys, Sarah discovered. They answered his questions without hesitation, accurately reading what was in his eyes. He would brook no nonsense, and they knew it. A sense of mastery he had obviously learned during his years as an officer under Wellington, and he had not forgotten how to convey it.

Sarah didn't know what would happen when he confronted David. Justin hadn't told her what he planned. In fact, he had barely spoken to her. Nothing beyond the questions necessary to extract every bit of information he thought might help them locate Drew. She had told him everything she knew. And nothing at all that was important.

"He's here," Justin said.

Sarah had followed him inside, waiting by the banked fire in the parlor, since the lad who opened the door for them had had to wake the innkeeper. She had done the same thing when Justin questioned the hosts at the first two inns. And by the time Justin had pulled the team up here, she was beginning to think he had been wrong about David's motives in taking his son. And beginning to be afraid.

"Is Drew with him?" she asked.

"The host didn't see Osborne this evening, so he couldn't confirm if he had anyone with him when he returned."

"Then—" she began.

"One of his serving girls took supper up to Mr. Osborne's room. He asked for mulled wine. And a glass of cider."

Cider for Drew, she realized. "I want to go with you," she said. "I want to see him."

"Someone is coming to build up the fire. I'll bring Drew to you here."

"What if David won't let him come?" she asked.

She watched Justin's mouth move, the change in its alignment slow and subtle. It took a few seconds for her to realize that what she was seeing was a smile. A parody of the one she was heartbreakingly familiar with and had seen far too seldom since he had returned. This expression was something very different from that. It was as cold as his questions to the stable boys had been. As hard as his eyes when he had asked her to tell him about David.

"If Drew *wants* to come home, Sarah," he said softly, his gaze holding hers, "then I'll bring him."

"If he *wants* to come home?" she echoed.

"Osborne *is* his father."

"And Drew barely knows him."

"Drew has a hunger for masculine attention. Who better to supply that need than his own father?"

You, she thought, just as she had from the beginning. She didn't say it, however, because there was already enough pain inherent in this situation. If Drew chose to stay with David, it would be as much a rejection of the attachment he had formed to Justin as it would be of his feelings for her.

Drew wouldn't do that, she told herself. He adored Justin. And he loved her. There was nothing—no one—she thought fiercely, not even the charming David Osborne, who could break the bonds they had formed. "He'll want to come home," she said.

Justin's lips tightened, and he held her eyes. Finally he nodded. "Then I'll bring him to you," he promised.

"I want no trouble," the innkeeper whispered as he pointed to the door. "I run a respectable house. And I don't want my guests disturbed."

"Nor do I," Justin said.

The less gossip about tonight's events the better, he thought. He had known the truth of that from the moment Sarah realized where Drew must be. And with whom. Questioning the staff at Longford couldn't be avoided, but for all they knew, the man he had asked them about was really a stranger. There was no way they could connect Osborne with the old scandal.

The countryside abounded with apocryphal tales of stolen children. Small boys forced into the cruel slavery of the sweeps. Children snatched by Gypsies or even, according to the locals, by fairies. Nothing he or Sarah had said in front of the servants had indicated Osborne's kinship to Andrew.

Sarah had lived with her secrets so long they were second nature to her now, he supposed. And he... He had been protecting her. And protecting Drew, of course. He had done the same thing for his father's and his brother's reputations. Sarah was his wife, and the vows he had sworn in this marriage of convenience had included one to love and protect her.

He wondered how willing he would have been to do that had his hand not brushed across that strand of misshapen pearls. When Sarah had shown up at his door tonight, protection had been the last thing on his mind. He had been prepared finally to claim what was his. His at least legally. Determined that this time, no matter the circumstances, Sarah wouldn't evade him.

Instead, he was standing outside the door of the man who had taken her away from him, about to demand that he return Sarah's illegitimate son. Despite what he had said to Sarah, Justin knew he had nothing to use as leverage against Andrew's father. Nothing but Sarah's conviction that Osborne didn't really want Drew. And his own acknowledgment of how much he *did*.

"You can go," he said to the host, without even glancing in his direction. Then, not waiting to see if he had been obeyed, he raised his fist and pounded it against the heavy oak that was all that separated him from David Osborne. And from Sarah's son.

Chapter Twelve

The features of the man who opened the door were even more pleasant than they had appeared in the fading light of the clearing. Especially when he smiled.

"What an unexpected honor," David Osborne said.

"Unexpected?" Justin questioned.

The smile widened. "I expected Sarah, of course. I must confess *your* arrival is a surprise. Would you like to come in, my lord?" David stepped back, gesturing toward the chamber behind him.

Not the landlord's best parlor, Justin decided, but there was a brisk fire. The remains of the supper Osborne had ordered was spread out on a table before it. A small mound disturbed the smoothness of the bed, visible in the darkest corner of the room.

"We can talk in the hall," Justin suggested.

"Whatever you have to say," David said, his eyes amused, "you may say in front of my son. He isn't a baby, you know."

The mocking phrase struck a chord. Justin had heard Drew make that claim a half dozen times, usually about something Sarah had said or done. Or about something she had forbidden him to do.

Osborne had probably used Drew's desire to be seen as more mature than he really was in order to bring this off. His mockery was almost an admission of that. And a warning that in the short time he had been around Drew, he had gleaned a great deal of understanding about the child.

"No?" David said, when Justin hesitated. "Then I'm afraid I must bid you good-night, my lord. We have a long journey tomorrow. And whatever *your* custom may be, I don't conduct business in the hallway of a public house."

He began to close the door, but the earl's hand, fingers spread, flattened against it, then pushed, widening the opening.

"Changed your mind?" David said agreeably. He released the door, apparently choosing not to engage in a show of strength this early. "The wine's still warm," he continued, moving back into the room. "You'll find the bottle on the hearth."

Again the sweep of his arm invited, almost theatrically. This time, Justin reluctantly stepped over the threshold. He limped across to the fire, ignoring the stone bottle that held the mulled wine. He needed nothing else to drink. His head was reminding him of the brandy he'd consumed earlier tonight.

He turned around to face the door and found Osborne's eyes focused on his right foot, the artificial one. Slowly the blue gaze lifted to Justin's face. That same mocking smile played about Osborne's lips.

Too obvious, you bastard, Justin thought, almost amused by the blatant attempt to unsettle him. He was surprised at how little effect it had. And that misjudgment made Osborne seem far less clever than Justin had given him credit for being.

"Vitoria," he said easily, holding Osborne's eyes. "Since you're curious."

"Drew told me all about it," David said. "I understand you were very heroic. My humble congratulations, to go along with the thanks of a grateful nation, of course." His eyes were as derisive as his voice.

Ignoring that provocation as well, Justin asked the question that had brought him here. "What do you want?"

"I want my son. I should think that would be obvious by now. Even to Sarah."

"It seems rather late for your paternal interest to have manifested itself."

"I knew nothing about caring for an infant. I told Sarah as much. Now, of course…" He shrugged.

"Drew and nothing else?" the earl asked softly. "Would you be willing to sign a paper to that effect?"

Osborne laughed. "I'll tell you exactly what I told Sarah. Drew is entitled to his rightful inheritance. I want no more than that. Only what is due the boy as Brynmoor's grandson."

"*His* inheritance. Which *you* intend to oversee for him."

"Of course. Brynmoor is no longer capable of administering his assets. Sarah may try, but I doubt the courts will find her a proper steward for holdings that vast and diversified."

"Sarah employs a competent man of business," Justin said.

"As well as having recently acquired a husband," David suggested, smiling. "Whose needs, if you'll forgive the reminder, have proven to be quite a drain on her resources. Or should I say on her father's resources?"

The earl considered the point of that digression. "And Sarah's husband may therefore be considered by the courts *not* to have Andrew's best interests at heart," he said. "Or at least not the best interests of his…rightful inheritance."

"I had heard you were astute," David admitted, his tone complimentary.

"You want Drew because you want control of Brynmoor's wealth."

"Of my son's inheritance," Osborne corrected. He was still smiling.

"Your son. Of course, you can prove that."

"I told Sarah I could. I showed her the documentation. Which bears her own signature, by the way."

"I don't suppose you would like to show it to me?"

Osborne's eyes considered him a moment. His lips pursed, and then he said, "Sarah can verify the validity of my claim."

"The courts will demand more than her verification."

"*I'm* perfectly willing to let the courts decide the issue," Osborne said. "The question is whether Sarah will be or not."

"You must know that unless Byrnmoor acknowledges the boy as his heir, Drew *has* no claim to the estate."

"What are you arguing about?" Drew asked.

The earl's gaze quickly moved to the bed. Drew was sitting up, his small face pale against the backdrop of the dark wall.

"I'm sorry, Drew. We didn't mean to wake you," Justin said.

"What are you doing here, Wynfield?" Andrew asked softly.

The little boy seemed more subdued than at any time since Justin had met him. Perhaps that was because he had been awakened out of a sound sleep by the sound of angry voices. Or perhaps it was for some other reason.

Was he already missing his mother? Having second

thoughts about what he had done? Drew's instincts about people were usually very good. And Justin was now convinced that Sarah had been right about Osborne's motives. He was not interested in his son, other than in how he could make use of him. Perhaps Andrew was beginning to have doubts about his father as well.

"Are you all right?" the earl asked. His eyes, however, had come back to examine Osborne's face. He noticed that David hadn't even turned toward the bed when Andrew spoke, and he didn't look at his son now.

"I'm all right," Drew said. "I'm not a baby, you know."

The statement lacked its usual surety, repeated almost as a matter of habit. Whistling in the dark, perhaps.

"I know," Justin said.

"Were you looking for me?" Drew asked almost hopefully.

"Sarah was worried. She didn't know where you were. I thought we had an agreement that you wouldn't run away again."

"I didn't run away," Drew said with a hint of indignation.

"But you didn't tell anyone where you were going. That's the same thing as running away, whatever your intent."

"*He* was supposed to tell Sarah."

He. Osborne, Justin realized, feeling a surge of anger.

"He didn't," Justin said. "Sarah didn't have any idea where you were. She's been very worried."

"You said you would send Sarah a message," Drew accused. "You said you would tell her where we were going."

"She simply hasn't received it yet," David said calmly. "Messages are often delayed."

There was no guilt in his voice. And no regret over the

worry he'd caused. Of course, Justin believed that had been his intent. To warn Sarah about what might occur if she didn't give him what he wanted.

"Sarah's downstairs, Drew. She's waiting to take you home," Justin said. "Home to Longford. To your own bed."

There was a long silence. Behind him, the earl could hear the hiss and crack of logs on the fire. From the small figure on the other side of the room, however, there was no sound at all.

"Don't you want to go home?" Justin asked.

"I'm going to India," the child said. "My father was once posted to India. They have tigers there."

Justin took a deep breath. At least that question had been answered. With it, however, a trap had opened at his feet. He would have to be very careful about how he proceeded.

"Have you ever seen a tiger, Wynfield?" Drew asked.

"No," Justin said softly.

"Neither have I. But I'm going to. You can come with us if you wish," he offered magnanimously.

Justin could imagine Osborne's reaction if he accepted *that* offer. Of course, he had no intention of going anywhere with Osborne. And no intention of letting Drew go with him. No matter what he had suggested to Sarah about legality and rights.

"What about Sarah?" Justin asked. "What shall I tell her?"

"That I have gone with my father to see the tigers in India," the child said. It was almost as if that answer had been rehearsed. Almost like the rote phrases Drew repeated about his grandfather.

"India is a very long way away, you know," the earl said. "I should miss you very much if you went so far. I know Sarah would miss you, too. I imagine you would miss her as well.''

Again, there was silence from Andrew.

''You're no longer a baby, Drew. I know that. But you *are* still just a boy,'' Justin continued, his voice reasonable, but carefully not patronizing. ''I think such a long and dangerous journey might well be delayed until you are older. After all, your father didn't travel to India until he was a grown man.''

''Is that true?'' Drew asked his father. ''Were you a man when you went to India?''

''I wasn't still clinging to my mama's skirts,'' Osborne said coldly.

''I'm not clinging to Sarah's skirts,'' Drew protested. ''But…I have never been so very far away from home. Except when we went to visit Wynfield in London. That was with Sarah, and it was a Christmas journey. Did I tell you about London?''

Osborne's lips had tightened, his eyes still meeting Justin's. And then, with practiced control, they relaxed into a smile as he turned to look at his son for the first time.

''You told me *all* about London,'' he said, his voice assuming its previous pleasantness. ''But you and I are going much farther than that, Drew. And we'll see more wonderful things than you can even imagine.''

''Could Sarah come with us?'' Drew asked.

Osborne laughed. ''I'm amenable to that…arrangement. Why don't you ask the earl if he is?'' he suggested maliciously, his eyes returning to Wynfield's face.

''Sarah can't go to India, Drew,'' Justin said. ''She must look after Brynmoor. She has to look after everything at Longford. You know that.''

''Rather dog in the manger, my lord,'' Osborne said,

his voice deliberately low enough not to carry across the room. "If you don't want her..."

At the taunting words, a wave of fury roiled through Justin's body. There was only one way Osborne could know the dynamics of his relationship with Sarah. Sarah herself must have told him.

"If Sarah can't come with us, then perhaps..." Drew's voice faded.

It was obvious to Justin that he feared Osborne's scorn. And obvious as well that he was not eager to leave the only home he had ever known. Or to leave the people who loved him and accepted him for what he was—a very small boy trying desperately to acquire the qualities he had been taught to admire: courage, honor, truthfulness. None of which his father, with whom the child was presently enamored, seemed to possess.

"Let me take you to Sarah, Drew," Justin urged.

"I think that would be best," Andrew agreed, his voice hesitant and very soft. "I can go with you to India another time," he offered to his father, and then he added, "but I think it would be best if I went home with Sarah tonight."

Osborne's mouth curved. "We can talk about this tomorrow, Andrew," he said patiently. "You need to go back to sleep. Things will look different in the morning. I'll tell you some more about what we'll see in India.

"But...Sarah is waiting for me," Drew said.

"Sarah..." David began, the edge of anger in his own voice quite clear before he made an almost visible effort to modify it. "Sarah isn't in charge of you, Drew," he said. "*I* am. And *I'm* the one who will decide what you will and won't do. And you will *not* be returning to Longford tonight."

"But—"

"No arguments," Osborne ordered. "You'll never be a man if you let a woman rule you."

"Come, Drew," Justin said quietly, deciding this wrangling had gone on long enough. Despite what he had told Sarah, he didn't intend to leave here tonight without the child, who obviously wanted to come home. "Your father may come to Longford tomorrow if he wants to talk to you. But for tonight—" Justin's eyes didn't falter before the sudden fury in Osborne's "—for tonight, I'm taking you home."

"Don't begin something you aren't capable of finishing, my lord," David said. The anger was again controlled, replaced by the earlier derision.

"Come, Drew," Justin said without raising his voice. He started to walk across the room toward the bed.

The little boy had already begun to scramble out of the tangled sheets. He was wearing one of Osborne's shirts. The sleeves had been rolled up, and the child's thin wrists were barely visible under their fall.

Suddenly Osborne moved, taking a step to the side, which put him directly in Justin's path. "I'm warning you," he said, fists raised.

Justin laughed. He couldn't help it. Osborne's forte, it seemed, was melodrama.

"Afraid, my lord?" Osborne challenged.

"Bored," Justin said succinctly. Then his tone hardened. "Don't be a fool, Osborne. There would be no quicker way to bring the magistrates down on our heads."

"I'm not opposed to that. After all, I'm in the right here. You are trying to steal my son."

"Who is Sarah Spenser's son as well," Justin said. "And Brynmoor's influence is enough in this district to call your claim into question, I should think, no matter what your paper says. And I'd be willing to bet if I spent a few pounds in the right places, I could discover some things in your past that you'd rather not have reach the ears of the authorities.''

"Blackmail, my lord?'' Osborne said mockingly, but it was apparent by the delay in his answer that he had thought about the validity of the threat.

"Why not? It's only what you're trying to do.''

As he spoke, Justin took another step toward Drew, who was now standing beside the bed. He looked lost and a little forlorn in the too-large shirt, which swallowed his thin frame and was so long it fell over his small, bare feet.

In response to the earl's advance, Osborne's right fist stabbed out. Justin moved his head so that the blow whistled harmlessly by his ear. That avoidance had been by instinct alone. Or perhaps through some unconscious memory of those long-ago hours spent under Gentleman Jackson's excellent tutelage. The earl straightened his head, considering the man before him, and allowed one brow to lift in question.

"Still bored?'' Osborne asked softly, smiling at him. He raised his fists in front of his chin, just as if he were in a sparring ring. His feet danced, again putting himself directly in Justin's path. "Or don't you enjoy boxing anymore?'' he continued sarcastically. "Andrew claims you were quite good. At one time, of course.''

"Good God,'' Justin said, his voice full of genuine amusement. "Are you actually proposing that we fight? For control of the boy? Or to prove to Drew which of us is the better man, perhaps?''

Again, a fist shot forward. The earl dodged, but not quite quickly enough. Osborne's knuckles grazed his cheekbone, a glancing blow that was still powerful enough to leave a reddened mark on his skin. Suddenly, the hazel eyes no longer reflected either boredom or amusement.

"I'm willing to let Drew make that evaluation," Osborne said. "Aren't you? After all, my lord, *you* are the heroic one. At least in Andrew's eyes."

"You don't have to fight, Wynfield," Drew said. "It doesn't matter. I know—" He stopped, the words cut off too abruptly.

"What do you know, Drew?" Osborne asked. His fists were still raised, ready to place the next punch.

"That it wouldn't be fair," the child said very softly.

"And why not?" Osborne asked. "Why wouldn't it be fair for his lordship to fight me?"

His eyes had never left Justin's face, and he was smiling. Enjoying himself. Drew said nothing, however, refusing to explain what he had meant, even in the face of his father's goading. Of course, it was obvious to what he had referred. And just as obvious that Osborne cared nothing about the fairness of this contest.

Again, his right darted out. Justin moved in time to avoid it, and the blow sailed by. But almost without any conscious decision, Wynfield lifted his own hands, which had tightened into fists. It had been years since he had hit anyone, in anger or otherwise, but suddenly he thought it would be very satisfying to plant his left, once justifiably famous for its speed and power, into David Osborne's handsome nose.

His opponent had begun to move in earnest, weaving and bobbing around him, one fist and then the other stabbing the air almost tauntingly. Justin's eyes followed him, although he moved more slowly, shifting just enough to keep himself face-to-face with his enemy. He was taking infinite care with the placement of his feet. The awkwardness of his artificial foot and the amount of brandy he'd consumed earlier demanded that.

When Osborne landed his next blow, Justin was more than ready to respond. It was as if all the rage and frustrations he had denied expression for the last six months had finally boiled to the surface, directed now at the mocking face in front of him.

The earl had always had a good eye, and his right connected with Osborne's chin, just where he'd aimed it. Osborne's head recoiled from the force of the blow. There was something very satisfying about the surprise in the depths of his opponent's eyes, Justin realized.

Especially since he immediately followed up that successful right with a left cross. It, too, found its target. And for the first time, Wynfield's lips tilted in enjoyment.

He stepped back, feeling his balance falter briefly, but he recovered in time to dodge a left hook thrown at his head. He took the solid right to the body that followed it, however. He had known it was coming, but was unable, or unwilling to push his luck by trying to move fast enough to get out of the way. With that strike there was again a gleam of triumph—and perhaps even anticipation—in Osborne's eyes.

Justin feinted with his left and then followed with an uppercut that opened a gash beside Osborne's brow. The sight of blood was satisfying, although his knuckles stung from their encounter with solid bone.

He could probably manage to trade blows like this for a long time. This was how he had been taught. It was the standard of bare-knuckle fighting—simply to stand up and exchange punches with one's opponent until one or the other was worn down. Justin knew he would be at a great disadvantage, however, if Osborne were smart enough to use his lack of mobility against him.

He dodged the next right, but took a hard left to the ribs. He countered with a one-two combination of his own, and heard the whoosh of expelled air as he landed a blow to Osborne's solar plexus. That was a deeply satisfying sound, just as the sight of that thread of crimson over his opponent's eye had been. It gave him confidence that in this battle he could hold his own—at least for a time.

"What are you doing?"

The words were touched with fear. Justin turned his head, automatically reacting to the sound of Sarah's voice. She and the innkeeper were standing in the open doorway, watching them.

Her eyes should have warned him. Their dark pupils dilated suddenly, but Justin didn't understand why until Osborne's fist exploded against his temple. He staggered, falling into the table that stood before the fire. Hands back, Justin caught himself before he could go down. The table tilted under his weight and a couple of pieces of crockery fell onto the hearth and shattered.

"Here now!" the innkeeper shouted. "Stop this, you two. I told you, I run a respectable house."

Wisely, Osborne had ignored everything but his opponent. He charged Justin now, fists windmilling in an attempt to follow up on his advantage.

Fighting to regain his balance and to shake off the effects of the blow to the head, which had left a ringing in his ears, the earl pressed his elbows inward, protecting the vulnerable center of his body. Osborne got in three or four good hits, but they fell on his arms and shoulders.

Since he was trapped by the table, however, Justin had nowhere to go to escape the barrage of blows his opponent had launched. He finally managed to shove Osborne away, and staggered a few feet to the side, his movements awkward and unbalanced, hampered by his foot. Dimly, he could hear voices raised in the background, despite the ringing in his ears.

Sarah's voice, he thought, and even Drew's, higher pitched than the others. Justin was also aware peripherally that the host had started into the room, obviously intending to put an end to the fight before more damage to his property could be done.

Then Osborne moved between Justin and the door. Ignoring the activities of the others, he renewed his attack, raining blows again on Justin's upper arms, neck and shoulders, driving him back.

The earl kept his hands up and his chin down, protecting himself as well as he could, concentrating on keeping his balance as he staggered backward. He couldn't afford to move out of his defensive posture, he knew, not even long enough to direct his own punches at the man who was pummeling him. The longer this went on, the more likely it was he would go down. Stubbornly, he determined not to let that happen. Not in front of Drew and Sarah. He knew he needed to end this as quickly as possible.

Giving up his protective posture, and suffering for it, he drove his right fist, the weight of his whole body behind it, into his opponent's chin. When it connected, Osborne's head snapped backward.

When it righted again, all the amusement had disappeared from the blue eyes. They were filled now with rage. And with blood lust. Justin had seen this same hatred, this same desire to kill in the eyes of hundreds of men he had fought. He moved forward, knowing he had to finish this now, before David, consumed by that black rage, could realize how truly vulnerable he was.

Suddenly, Osborne stuck out his foot, deliberately thrusting it between Justin's legs. Justin stumbled, his left hand reaching out to grab at the wall, trying desperately not to fall. At the same time, Osborne raised his right fist, coming in high and hard from above, with a move that was popularly known, for painfully obvious reasons, as the pickax.

Justin dodged, turning his face away and hunching his

shoulder. The blow landed on the side of his neck instead of on his nose. Already off balance as he was, the force of the blow drove Justin to his knees.

This was what he had dreaded since the beginning. And it had probably been inevitable. "Don't begin something you aren't capable of finishing," Osborne had taunted. Justin had, however, goaded by those smiling eyes, and now he would pay the price. His opponent charged, obviously intending to take advantage of the fact that he was down. Intending to put an end to his resistance.

Justin somehow got his left foot under him and drove upward, his head slamming into Osborne's stomach. Again, the involuntary exhalation of air was enormously satisfying. He locked his arms around his opponent's body and let his forward momentum carry both of them down. He landed on top of Osborne and began pounding his ribs while he had the chance.

Osborne's left arm was under him, but he slapped his right fist and forearm again and again against the side of Justin's head. When that didn't have the desired effect, he suddenly poked his stiffened fingers at the earl's eyes. Justin recoiled, his upper body automatically jerking back, away from the stabbing fingers. Taking advantage of that reaction, Osborne somehow managed to get his knees up, throwing Justin to the side. Unencumbered, David quickly scrambled to his feet.

As soon as he had, he kicked out, his booted foot connecting with the earl's shoulder. Justin rolled, trying to get away from the vicious kick, but he was too near the fire, still cheerfully blazing in the grate. He attempted to push himself up, at least to get to his hands and knees, but David kicked him again, in the ribs this time, effectively putting an end to that fledgling effort.

"Stop it!" Drew screamed, rushing across the room. He put his hands on Osborne's arm, trying to pull him away. Angered at the interference, David shook the boy off. Then he drew his foot back again, aiming this time at Justin's head.

Andrew threw himself at his father, wrapping his arms around his thigh. Osborne turned toward him, trying to push the child away. And in that split second, Justin realized, his concentration was on Andrew and not on him.

Trained by years of war to take advantage of any weakness the enemy displayed, of any opening he was given, Justin pushed up onto his knees, his hand fastening around the neck of the thick stone bottle on the hearth. As he swung it upward, he was aware that Sarah was running toward them, trying to protect Drew.

David had succeeded in pushing the boy away and was turning back to deal with him. At the top of its arc, the bottle connected with Osborne's jaw, wine spilling out of its neck and cascading over them both in a warm crimson shower.

Osborne fell backward as if he'd been poleaxed, landing at Drew's feet. His skull hit against the wooden floor, bouncing a little. And then he was still.

"You've killed him," Drew said breathlessly, his eyes widened in horror. "You've killed my father."

They all seemed frozen by Drew's accusation. No one moved until Sarah knelt, putting her fingers on the pulse in David's neck. Then she laid her ear against his mouth. "He's breathing," she announced, her voice full of relief. Straightening, she turned to look into Justin's eyes.

Only with that look did he realize he was still on his hands and knees, swaying like a hurt animal. He straightened his torso and then, reaching out blindly with his left hand, found the mantel. Using its support, he pulled himself to his feet.

He could feel the blood trickling from his nose. He could even taste it, a salt-copper tang in the back of his throat. He wiped at the stream with the cuff of his shirt. And instead of meeting Sarah's eyes again, or Drew's, he looked down on the mingled stains of blood and wine that soaked the material.

"Get your son," he ordered. Then, stepping over Osborne's legs, he limped past the landlord toward the door.

"Who's going to pay for all this?" the man said. "That's what I want to know. You can't come into an honest house and break up things without paying."

"I'll pay," Sarah said.

She was crying, Justin realized. He turned again when he reached the door, one hand resting high on its frame for support. Sarah and Drew were still kneeling, one on either side of Osborne's body. One of Drew's small hands was cupped gently around his father's face.

"I'll have the horses brought around," Justin said, feeling sick. "Have Drew downstairs in five minutes."

Sarah's eyes moved from the angry face of the host back to his. Wordlessly, she nodded. He knew she was still watching as he limped out of the door of Osborne's room, but despite that knowledge, he never looked back.

Chapter Thirteen

The earl of Wynfield had been sitting before the fire in his rooms, almost unmoving, since they had returned to Longford. He had removed his coat, but he was wearing the same shirt in which he had fought Osborne, its sleeve stained by blood and wine.

Occasionally he shivered, but he wasn't really aware of being cold. Just as he was no longer aware of the aches and pains in his battered body. The memory of those matching pairs of eyes, looking up at him in shock from either side of an unconscious David Osborne, was so powerful it outweighed any physical sensation.

He had sent his valet to bed. Someone had knocked on his door much later, but he hadn't responded. Tomorrow would be soon enough to face what had happened. And he would, of course, because it must be faced. Something still had to be done about Osborne. What had happened tonight had accomplished nothing. Except to create the accusing look he had seen in Drew's eyes.

The knock that sounded on his door this time was very soft, and although he didn't give permission, eventually the door opened. He turned his head and found Sarah standing in the doorway. Her right hand, holding a ring of keys, was still on the knob. She held the handle of a wooden box in her left.

"May I come in?" she asked.

He looked away from her, focusing on the flames instead. Involuntarily, his mouth tightened, the painful movement reminding him of the number of times Osborne had gotten in under his guard. Justin didn't want to deal with Sarah tonight. The effects of the brandy had worn off, leaving him with a headache and a foul taste in his mouth. Of course, both might just as easily be explained by his self-disgust.

He heard the door close. Knowing Sarah, he understood that she would not be standing outside it. Still he didn't look at her. He didn't want to see what was in her eyes.

He had a half second's warning, the familiar fragrance of roses suddenly surrounding him. Then she set the wooden chest and the keys she had been carrying down on the table beside him.

When he felt her fingers touch his chin, he didn't fight their pressure. He looked up, lifting his face into the pitiless exposure of the light. He watched her eyes widen, the pupils dilating just as they had before Osborne hit him. He could imagine what he looked like. He had seen the evidence of innumerable fistfights among the ranks. Broken noses and blackened eyes were common sights among His Majesty's finest.

Sarah's fingers released their hold on his chin, but her eyes held his a few seconds longer. Then, opening the box she'd brought, she removed a brown bottle from one of its neat compartments and took off the glass stopper. Laying that aside, she tipped the bottle, pouring some of the liquid it contained onto a piece of lint she had taken from another compartment. An acrid, medicinal smell replaced the evocative hint of rose water that had been in the air. Justin looked back at the fire, regretting that loss as well.

"Drew?" he asked.

"He's finally asleep," Sarah said.

She put her forefinger under his chin this time, tilting his head upward again. Although she was holding the soaked lint in her left hand, she didn't apply it to the scrapes and abrasions. She held his eyes instead. And then she bent, moving very slowly, giving him every opportunity to turn his head. When he didn't, her lips touched his. She applied no pressure to his bruised mouth, her kiss as insubstantial as the fog he had driven through on the way home. When she lifted her head, his questioning eyes followed, still fastened on hers.

"Thank you," she said softly.

He laughed, the sound little more than a breath. "For what?" he asked. The words were as bitter as his laughter.

"For finding Drew. For bringing him home."

"I did more harm than good, Sarah. You know that. More harm in dealing with Osborne. Certainly more harm in my relationship with Drew."

She hesitated a moment, and then she laid the lint on top of the open bottle and knelt beside his chair. She took his hand in hers and, looking down on it, ran the tips of her fingers over the cut and swollen knuckles.

When she finally looked up again, she said, "Thanks to you, Drew is home. Back at Longford where he belongs. Away from David's influence. And I assure you, that can only be good, however it came about."

No matter how she tried to rationalize what had happened, Justin knew he had accomplished nothing, except perhaps to harden Osborne's resolve. Maybe to insure that he would really do what he had only threatened before and take his case to the courts. For revenge, if not for profit. Whatever Osborne did, Justin knew it would be designed to make them all suffer for the confrontation tonight.

"Osborne will be more determined than ever to extract his pound of flesh," he warned. "You may now add a quest for revenge to the greed that drove him before."

"I know," she said. "But at least now he understands…" She hesitated, taking a breath that was deep enough to be visible, before she continued. "At least he knows that we're not alone. Or unprotected."

"I didn't make things better, Sarah," Justin repeated. "If anything, what happened tonight simply made everything worse."

"I'm not sure it could have been *made* worse," she said. "David has always held all the cards in this game because he *is* Drew's father. And he has always been greedy and unprincipled, uncaring of who he uses or who he hurts by what he does. Nothing you did tonight changed any of those things. Or could change them. Nothing ever really can, I suppose."

Justin thought again of Drew's shocked words, and of the brief surge of elation he had felt when he'd heard them. Brief because killing the child's father had never been an option. It would have legal repercussions, of course. And it would forever alienate Drew. As it was, the damage that had been done to Justin's relationship with the little boy might be irrevocable.

"No matter what happens," Sarah continued, her voice still low, but filled with a mother's instinct to protect, "I *won't* let David have Drew. I can't. Not knowing what he is."

Which must mean, Justin realized, that whatever hold the man had once had on her emotions was broken. She had told him that what he had seen in the clearing was not what he had thought. And her behavior tonight seemed to confirm that. *Knowing what he is…*

"There are things Osborne had just as soon not have made public," he said, remembering the Irishman's re-action to that threat. "Going to court may expose his own past as well as..."

He hesitated, and she finished it for him, her voice soft, but steady. "As well as expose the details of Drew's birth."

It wasn't Drew's past Justin had been thinking about, of course, but hers. "If Osborne does what he threatened, Sarah, it will revive the scandal. There will be no help for that."

"And Drew will suffer for it," she acknowledged.

As would she. And he would suffer as well, watching them dragged through the mud of what would be a very public censure. He wondered if Osborne were sensitive enough to realize what a very apt revenge that would be for the injuries Justin had inflicted on him tonight.

If David *were* determined on that course, however, it seemed there was nothing Justin could do to protect them. Nothing except blame himself for mishandling the situation, as he had been since he'd returned to Longford.

"How much can you offer him?" he asked. He had finally come to the same conclusion Sarah had reached— the only way to get rid of Osborne, short of killing him, was to pay him off.

She released his hand. She put both of hers in her lap, holding them tightly entwined.

"Sarah?" he prodded after a few seconds of silence.

"As long as my father is alive, I can't sell Longford or any of the attachments or even the furnishings. They don't belong to me. I'm not sure what David will demand, but I'm afraid..."

Her voice faltered, but Justin knew very well what she feared. After all, Osborne had reminded him. Justin had drained her accounts to save his lands and his family name. To save Wynfield. To save his heritage.

Brynmoor's wealth was more than able to bear those expenditures, but they had taken almost all of the estate's available capital. Justin was confident that a renewed Wynfield Park, no longer neglected, mismanaged, or robbed by an addiction to gambling, would eventually generate more than enough to repay the money that had been used to save it.

Eventually, he thought. He knew he could do that, given enough time. If his reading of Osborne's character was correct, however, he wouldn't be allowed any time at all.

"Perhaps he'll let me send him the money," Sarah said, her eyes searching his for confirmation of that hope. "I could have Mr. Samuels set up some way to make a transfer of funds to David's bankers at regular intervals."

"Blackmail by installment," Justin said mockingly. "Do you think he'll agree to that?"

His sense of frustration was growing with the knowledge that they had little choice. And even if Osborne accepted that unlikely premise, they would be held hostage to him for the rest of their lives.

"I'm going to try to persuade him to. I'll do *whatever* I have to to keep him from taking Andrew," Sarah said, ignoring his tone. "My greatest fear has always been that I would see something of his father in Drew. But there is nothing of him there. You know that. You know Drew—courage and honesty at the very core. A genuine love and concern for others. But if I give him over into his father's hands…" She shook her head, still holding his eyes. "I can't do that. I will *never* do that."

"If you knew what Osborne was—" he began, the question that had haunted him since the beginning finally given voice, almost torn from him by the depth of her despair.

"Don't," she whispered, putting her hand quickly over his to stop the words. "Please don't ask me that."

His mouth tightened against the need to pour out the long bitterness. The need to tell her what her betrayal had meant. Especially what it meant now—to all their lives. Blaming Sarah would change nothing, however.

"Then tell me why you wore the pearls," he said instead.

Her eyes widened a little before they fell, again seeming to examine her locked fingers. When she looked up, her lips were curved in the smallest of smiles.

"Because you had given them to me," she said simply.

It was the truth. He could read that in her eyes as well as in her voice. There were things Sarah was determined not to tell him. Determined not to explain. What she had just said, however, he found he could not doubt.

"And that meant something to you?" he asked. "That I had given them to you?"

"It meant," she said, her eyes clear and open, still meeting his, "finally I could hope."

"Hope?"

"That someday…you might really forgive me."

His heart hesitated, breathing suspended, as a vacuum of silence surrounded them. Those soft words echoed again and again through the void.

"And you want my…forgiveness?" he asked.

"I want what I once had," she said.

She was smiling at him again, the movement of her lips so sweetly familiar it tore at the bitterness her betrayal had wrapped around his heart. A bitterness he had denied for years and had then been forced to confront when he again came face-to-face with Sarah Spenser. *I want what I once had.*

"And what is that?" he asked, his voice very soft.

"I want you to love me," she said.

Again the silence grew and then expanded. She waited through it, her eyes calm and serene on his face.

She had made no defense. She had offered no explanation for what she had done. No contrition. And no promises. Only a desire, as simply stated as her comment about the pearls.

Because you had given them to me. He had known that was the truth. And his heart, using the same measure he had applied to that, found this was true as well. *I want you to love me.*

He had no reason to believe her. No reason to trust her again. She had betrayed him. She had rejected what he had given her, which had been true and unsullied, for the tawdry, worthless charm David Osborne had offered in its place.

She had borne another man's bastard and had then asked Justin to teach that child to be a man. She had lain in another man's arms and had then asked Justin to love her again. In doing those things, however, she had forfeited the right to ever ask anything of him. He knew that. And she knew it as well. That knowledge was in her eyes, raised to his. Still waiting.

No explanation. No apology. Nothing but the truth that was so palpably sincere he could not doubt it. *I want you to love me.* His throat closed, hard and tight, aching with the force of what he felt for her. What he had always felt. His eyes burned with tears he had never shed, not once in the horrors of the last six months. He denied them now, but somehow she knew.

Her own eyes filled at what she saw in his. Her hand lifted, thumb tracing compassionately over the fullness of his bottom lip as her fingers shaped the contour of his cheek. No words had been spoken. Nothing of the past. Or of the future.

Slowly he raised his own hands. They were stiff, and the swollen fingers ached with the movement. He put his palms on either side of her face, pulling her to him. His mouth lowered over hers, which opened, welcoming his touch. Responding without hesitation to the invasion of his tongue.

Her hands fell, caressing his shoulders and then his chest. He wanted to feel them against his skin. He wanted her to touch him as she had before, her fingers moving over his body as if she still found it desirable. *I want you to love me.*

He held the words in his mind, shutting out any doubts. Denying any fear of how she might react to his injury. The fire was dying. And in the darkness…

She put her hand on his knee, pushing away from him. His lips clung, reluctant to release hers, however briefly. He had waited too long for this moment. Too long to be denied. He knew, however, by her own reluctance to end the kiss, even as she was moving, that this was not rejection.

Finally she lifted her head, breaking the heated contact of their lips. His eyes opened in time to watch her stand. She took two steps away from him, her back still to the fire. He was afraid that if he released her eyes, if he lost hold of what was in them, she would disappear, and all this would be a dream. A fantasy created by the long, lonely years of loving Sarah.

She held out her hand. An invitation. And to accept it, he had only to stand. To walk across the distance that separated them and put his hand into hers. *I want you to love me.*

There was no wine to give him courage. Not yet enough darkness to hide the imperfection of his body. No more bitterness for him to brandish like a shield between them. Only her hand, reaching out to his.

With the courage that had served him so long, the earl of Wynfield rose from his chair and took the two limping steps that would bring him to his wife. He put his hand into hers. And when she smiled at him, all the fear that had gathered around his heart shattered like the skim of morning ice that gathers over the dark surface of a pond.

He turned, her fingers still resting in his, and led her to the high bed where he had slept alone throughout their marriage. And where he knew he would never sleep alone again.

He had removed the bloodstained shirt, pulling it off over his head. He threw it onto the foot of the bed, and then he hesitated, his eyes finding Sarah's in the too-quiet dimness of the bedroom.

She had been watching him. Suddenly, she stepped nearer, her eyes tracing over the bruises, already beginning to darken, that marred his chest and stomach. She pressed her lips against each discoloration, kissing the places where David's fists had struck him. And when she finished, she lifted her head, smiling at him again. Still he didn't move.

She would understand what he dreaded. She was probably preparing herself as well, determined to hide whatever shock she might feel when he removed the rest of his clothes.

"I've played valet for my father on more occasions than I care to remember," she said. "Would you like me to help you with your boots?"

Her tone was commonplace, deliberately lightened from what had been in it when she knelt by the fire. He took a breath, wondering if her courage would be enough. If his would.

"Sarah," he said softly. And nothing else.

His lips had flattened, compressed so that all the things he wanted to say to her could not escape. And he would never be able to say them, he knew, not unless they got past this. Past his fear. Past her horror. Or her pity.

"Don't worry," she said, smiling. "I'm not like Drew."

Justin tilted his head, questioning the non sequitur.

"I'm not fascinated by the bits and pieces of you that are missing. I confess I find myself far more interested…" She hesitated, her chin lifting a little before she finished, "*Far* more interested in the bits and pieces that aren't."

She was trying to put him at ease. To tell him that it didn't matter. He acknowledged the kindness, but still, the words didn't destroy his sense of dread. Perhaps nothing could.

"And which bits and pieces are those?" he made himself ask, carefully controlling his voice, his tone as light as hers.

"All the others, I guess," she said, a deliberately wicked gleam in her eyes.

"I've never had a female valet."

"Then," Sarah said softly, "you really have no idea what you've been missing."

"Just…a few bits and pieces," Justin suggested.

"*Not,*" Sarah answered, smiling at him again, "any of the important ones."

She held his eyes, and in hers he read nothing of the apprehension he felt. None of the fear. Only the same love he had seen when she had held out her hand by the fire. And trusting her love, because he understood that if he truly wanted Sarah, he had no other choice, Justin sat down on the edge of the bed and held out his left leg.

She tugged the boot off by straddling his ankle and

gripping the heel, exactly as his valet would have done. Apparently her claim about having helped her father had not been the generous untruth Justin had assumed it to be.

"And now the right," she suggested quietly.

He realized she was waiting for him to hold out his right leg, the one that now ended midcalf, so she could remove its boot. No more hiding. And not nearly enough darkness.

Steeling himself, he straightened his knee, holding out the gleaming Hessian. After only a heartbeat's hesitation, she turned her back to him again, straddling his calf and putting both her hands around the heel of the boot.

He should have warned her, he realized belatedly. Due to the inflexibility of the artificial foot, this one was always much more difficult to take off. She took a firmer grip, obviously determined not to admit defeat. Unable as he was to bend the ankle to help the boot slide off, there seemed nothing he could do. Except, of course…

Just as Sarah made another valiant effort, Justin put his left foot on her slim, rounded derriere, temptingly right in front of him, and pushed. It was what he did to assist his valet in the difficult removal. This time, however, his attempt to help didn't have quite the same effect.

The boot suddenly flew off, taking Sarah with it. She stumbled forward, dropping the Hessian and throwing her hands out to break her fall. She succeeded, ending up rather inelegantly on her hands and knees in front of him.

She looked at him over her shoulder. "You did that on purpose," she accused, her eyes alive, filled with laughter that he hadn't seen in them in far too long a time.

"Why, whatever are you doing down there, Lady Wynfield?" he asked, laughing with her.

"Looking for more port, perhaps?" she answered tartly.

"You didn't believe me," he said, realizing only now that she had known he wasn't foxed that night in London.

He held out his hand, which she ignored. She turned around instead, settling comfortably cross-legged at his feet, her shirts disarrayed enough to display slim, stocking-covered ankles and neat kid slippers.

"I will. I promise I *will* believe you," she said. "I'll believe whatever you say about that night…if you'll tell me why you *really* went to London." The laughter was gone. Her voice had softened, no longer teasing.

"To see the king?" he suggested lightly.

And then, when her eyes refused to respond to that lightness, the hand he had held out fell back against his leg.

"You had made yourself ill," she said. "Because you were working too hard?"

"My…recovery wasn't as far along as I had hoped."

"What does that mean?"

What *did* it mean? He could tell her, of course, about the constant irritation the ill-fitting foot had been to the newly healed stump. Explain that he'd been determined to work as many hours as possible—no matter the pain—so that he could delay coming back to Longford. Back to where she was.

He had done the same thing today, of course. Refused to come back to Longford after he had seen her with Osborne in the clearing. And then there had been the hunt for Drew. Another long day of being on his feet, so that among the assorted discomforts that had resulted from the fight with Osborne was the dull, familiar ache of the stump.

"What does that mean?" she had asked. Without giving himself time to think about it, no time at all to examine the very good reasons for *not* answering that question—or for not answering it in this particular way—he stood and began unfastening his trousers. Sarah's eyes now seemed locked on his fingers, watching his hands rather than his face.

Finally he stepped out of the trousers and stood before her, clad only in his knee-length knit underdrawers. Her gaze fastened on what the removal of the trousers had revealed—the cunningly carved foot and ankle and the leather harness that attached it to his leg. He held his breath, an eternity it seemed, before her eyes lifted again to his.

"How does it work?" she asked.

He could read nothing but curiosity in the question. And, more importantly, nothing beyond that in her eyes. Simple curiosity—as natural as that Drew had displayed from the first.

And so Justin began to breathe. One slow breath and then another. Until finally, the familiar pattern of breathing seemed restored enough to provide air to form an answer.

"Not as bloody well as one might wish," he said truthfully, his voice deliberately laced with a shaky attempt at humor.

"Show me," she said, her eyes still on his face.

He didn't move for a long time, but her eyes never faltered. And they never changed. "You *are* like Drew," he said finally.

The banter was only a bridge, a joint conspiracy created to carry them beyond the things they couldn't afford to talk about. At least they had found a bridge they could use to get them through this. And when it was over…

He sat down on the side of the bed, and although his fingers trembled, hurrying over the now-familiar task, he unfastened the harness that held the artificial foot in place, and laid the contraption on the floor. Her eyes fell, but he didn't even look down at the reddened stump. Its ugliness was clearly imprinted on his mind's eye, so he knew exactly what Sarah was seeing.

When she looked up again, she smiled at him. And her eyes were still the same. He had expected revulsion. Or perhaps, because she was Sarah, only pity. There was nothing of either in the clear calm blue.

And then she touched him. The hand he had so often watched caressing Drew's curls brushed now, with the same obvious love and compassion, over the reddened skin that the surgeons had drawn tightly downward and gathered to cover the end of the shattered bone they'd sawed away. Her fingers lingered tenderly over the places that had been rubbed raw by the long hours he'd worn the foot today.

"I told Drew not to talk to you about this," she whispered, her eyes lifting again to his. "I'm sorry I did that. I know now it was wrong."

"Not...wrong," he denied softly.

He tried to remember how he had felt before he had seen her eyes. The overwhelming flood of relief made it hard to remember how much he had dreaded this. He had dreaded having anyone see what had happened to him. Especially Sarah. But Drew's curiosity had always been less painful than the carefully averted eyes of adults. More honest. And far more natural. As were Sarah's openness and her questions tonight.

"This is part of you," she said. "It will always be part of you. And there is no reason not to talk about it. No reason not to let Drew ask his questions. You never minded them."

"I never minded *Drew's* questions."

"But..." she whispered, hearing the caveat.

"I was afraid of what you'd think," he admitted. "Of how you'd feel. Or maybe afraid of what I'd feel."

"How *do* you feel?" she asked.

It was darker in the room. The fire was burning itself out, but neither of them had thought to add more wood. Nothing mattered tonight, of course, but being together. And for that they didn't need light.

Only time. And space. And one another. And it seemed finally that they would have all of those. At least for tonight.

"No different," he said softly, and was aware with a deep sense of surprise that that was true.

She had given him that—the surety that to her he was the same man she had fallen in love with. Whether she saw him sprawled at the foot of a staircase or stumbling awkwardly, trying to escape David Osborne's punishing fists, in her eyes he was still the man she had loved so long ago. Still the same.

As she was to him. She had borne another man's child, and he knew now that what she had done truly made no difference to him. She was still Sarah. And she was his. No matter how twisted the path that had brought them here tonight, he could not doubt Sarah was his. Or that she should always have been.

"Love me," she whispered, perhaps seeing that realization finally in his eyes.

They had been robbed of what should have been the first joyous culmination of their love. Robbed by time. And distance. Her trusting innocence had played a role, of course. And David Osborne's poisonous charm. Maybe even Justin's stubborn pride.

He found it no longer mattered to him *why* Sarah had done what she had done. He had accepted, without any explanations, that she had. And tonight he could regret nothing that had brought them, finally, to this place.

He held out his hand again, and this time she took it, allowing him to pull her up from where she had been sitting at his feet. She stood before him a moment, and then her fingers began to loosen the bodice of her gown. His heart faltered and then began to race, the blood it had dutifully pumped through his veins now rushing instead, hot and heavy, to his groin.

She slipped one sleeve of the gown off her shoulder, exposing smooth ivory skin, brushed now with gold by the low fire. And then she lowered the other and slipped her arms out of the sleeves. With one hand she held the dress in place over her breasts a long moment, her eyes on his.

Finally she released it, pushing the garment down over her hips. It fell to the floor, pooling around her feet. The chemise followed, a small foam of white lace centered against the darkness of the fallen wool. She stepped out of them and bent, gracefully somehow, at least in his eyes, to remove her slippers and then the thin silk stockings. When she straightened again, her eyes found his once more.

Her hands did not lift to hide the small perfection of her breasts. She stood straight and tall, almost proudly. The fire highlighted softly rounded curves and darkened secret places that finally—finally—he would be allowed to know.

Despite what he believed about her relationship with Osborne, Justin did not hurry her. He was as patient as he had always been with Drew, she thought. There had been no sense of urgency conveyed in the slow glide of his fingers. He touched her as if she were delicate, fragile and infinitely precious.

His hard, callused hands moved so knowingly against areas of her body she had never dreamed a man could want to touch, producing feelings beyond anything she might ever have imagined. They coursed along the network of nerves and veins and arteries that spread sensation throughout her whole body.

From the beginning, despite her trembling, she had refused him nothing. She had no guides where he had taken her. Little knowledge of what would happen. No expectations. Nothing to hold on to except her love for Justin and her unwavering trust.

With endless patience and unquestioned skill, he had begun to coax from her untutored body responses that left her gasping his name in the fire-touched darkness. His lips moving against her throat. His fingers drifting over the small, hardened nipples of her breast. His tongue... His tongue exploring in ways that caused her bones to melt and her blood to flow in a thick molten stream through her veins. A hot river of need and desire, its source the very center of her aching body.

Soon, after all these long years of lies and deceits, he would know the one truth that mattered. He might not understand that truth, but it would mean as much to him as his hand, placed in hers tonight, had meant to her. Hope restored. Trust and faith renewed. And the knowledge that no matter what David Osborne threatened, they would somehow deal with it together.

As he caressed her, her own fingers moved through the curling mat of hair on his chest, her breathing uneven, her skin flushed and damp. Occasionally she scored his skin with her nails, unable to bear, it seemed, the sweet, mindless ecstasy of what he was doing. Sometimes she felt that if he touched her again, she would shatter into a thousand pieces and each would beg anew for his touch.

When she began to tremble, her body's inner eruption was totally unexpected. She had no guide, except his love. The heat of need gave way to a sudden cascade of moisture, scalding through her loins. Without her volition, her hips arched, hands grasping at Justin's shoulders as he began to move over her.

His weight was suddenly on her chest and stomach, her breasts pressed into the hard, unyielding wall of his. She could feel the roughness of the hair that covered those muscular thighs, trembling now against the smoothness of hers. His hands caught either side of her head, forcing her to look at him. And what she read in his face caused another involuntary upward surge of her hips, bringing her into contact—shockingly direct contact—with the hard strength of his erection.

Her eyes widened as he began to push into her, his own hips rocking forward just in time to meet the next uncontrollable arch of hers. Flesh met flesh, seeking that most intimate of all positions, trying to fulfill the perfect design nature had intended for man and woman.

She gasped and her head fell back as the pressure increased. More than pressure. Beyond it now. She wanted to tell him that he was hurting her, but the words refused to form on her lips. Then again, more powerfully this time, he pushed downward into the heat and wetness he had so carefully created.

She watched his eyes as realization penetrated his passion-drugged mind. They widened, pupils expanding quickly, and then they closed, involuntarily it seemed, as he pushed against the barrier he had never expected to find. A downward thrust so strong it succeeded in tearing through. As it did, the pulsing jet of his hot seed poured into her body. His head was back, eyes still closed, as his own body was racked with the same shuddering ecstasy he had created in hers.

She held him, understanding nothing except that he loved her. Held him until the convulsive movements of his body finally stilled, and he lay against her breasts, like a spent swimmer who had ventured too far into a strange ocean and been barely able to return to shore. Finally his breathing eased, returning to something approaching normality.

He pushed away from her, onto his elbows, and looked down into her face. His eyes traced over her features, studying each for a long time. In a silence that was too long. And frightening.

"Why didn't you tell me?" he asked.

She wanted to tell him now—especially hearing what was in his voice—but she had given her word, her most solemn oath, and even this... Even this...

"I can't," she whispered. "Please, please don't ask me."

She raised her head enough to touch her lips to his. Trying to soften her refusal. Or perhaps to let him know, without words, how much she had always loved him. Even when she had written that letter four years ago. Maybe more then than at any other time. Except this.

"Drew isn't your child," he said, not a question, of course. Not after tonight.

"No," she whispered.

"But David Osborne *is* his father?"

Not against her oath, and the part she had feared most about Osborne's threat, the important part that she could never tell Justin. David had a true parental claim to Drew. And she, who had loved him, who had raised him since his birth, had none.

"Yes," she said.

"And you won't tell me—"

"I can't," she interrupted. "Please don't ask me anything more. Please, Justin. No more questions."

All the questions she had forbidden him to ask were reflected in his eyes. There were only so many possibilities and explanations, of course. Eventually he might discover the right one, but her father's vindictive and premature funeral for Amelia made the chance of that very slim.

"It didn't matter to you tonight," she said softly, fighting against the tightness in his face. "Why should it matter now?"

"If Osborne goes to court—" he began.

"We'll live through it together," she said. "You and I and Drew. He won't take Drew away unless he can get my father's money, too. That's what he really wants. And my father will never recognize Drew as his heir. He can't. So we'll only have to endure the gossip a little while and then…"

The words faded. His face had hardened, becoming almost as cold and set as when he had swung the stone bottle. She wasn't sure if the anger was directed at Osborne, at the possibility of a renewed scandal or at her.

"What is it?" she whispered. Her fingers found his face, running coaxingly over the late-night whiskers. "It doesn't matter. Nothing matters but this. You and I. And Drew. Nothing else is important."

Finally, very slowly, the tension around his mouth relaxed. He lowered his head, his lips finding the small pulse at the side of her neck. Her eyes closed, feeling the spiraling heat start again, low and deep within her body.

Whatever happens, she thought. It was almost the last coherent thought she had, because his hips had begun to move again, slow and sure and powerful. *Whatever happens we'll handle it together, my darling. Whatever happens…*

Chapter Fourteen

By daylight the following morning the earl of Wynfield had finished the messages that he would have dispatched as soon as the servants began to stir. He had also completed the documents, writing them by candlelight, his pen scratching across the foolscap in the silence of the room where his wife still slept.

When he had folded the messages, pressing his seal into the hot wax, he set them aside and walked across to the bed they had shared for the first time last night. A bed he had deserted more than two hours ago, dressing quickly in the darkness, because suddenly he had known exactly what he had to do. As soon as the decision was made, he had been eager to put it into effect.

And he had no regrets, he thought, looking down on Sarah. Unconsciously, his lips tilted, remembering her unladylike sprawl last night as she had pulled off his boot. Of all the women he had known, only Sarah would have had the mettle to make that offer. And the courage to carry it out.

He should not be surprised, of course. It had taken incredible courage to do what she had done so long ago. After an absence of several months, Sarah Spenser had brought a baby home to her father's house, an infant who looked enough like her to be her son. She had to have known what the gossips would suggest. When they did, she had written him, breaking off their engagement. Then for four long years she had kept her silence, enduring scorn and scandal she had never deserved. And she would never have to endure it again, he vowed.

His eyes found the telltale bloodstains that marked the tangled sheets. Not that he needed their evidence. Until he had taken her virginity last night, Sarah had been as untouched as when he had left for Spain. Pure and unsullied, just as her love for him had always been. And he wouldn't stand by and let Osborne drag her name through the mud again.

One day she might be willing to tell him the secret of Drew's birth. To explain why she had begun this long deception. One day. But for now…

For now Justin had realized there was one other thing he needed to do. One other chasm that must be bridged, as he and Sarah had managed to span all of those that lay between them last night. Because, of course, there was another person who was involved in what he planned.

Someone who had thus far had little say in the events that had unfolded around him during his short life. And who, if asked, might not approve of the decision Justin had come to after those long dark hours of holding Sarah against his heart. In spite of the bitterness that had once choked it, Sarah had found her way there again. Against all his defenses. And so, he acknowledged, had her son.

Who was not her son at all. Not by any of the standards the world understood. Only by those too infrequently recognized was Drew Sarah's child: the love they shared, the hours she had devoted to his care, and her unending concern for his happiness. Judged by those, Drew *was*

Sarah's son, far more than those children who were given over to the care of servants at birth.

Sarah's son, he thought again. And his. That last realization had been a shock. But when he had made it, he knew how true it was. Osborne wanted to use Drew for his own benefit. Justin, like Sarah, wanted only to love him.

And to be loved in return. It had seemed in London that he might have accomplished that. Then, in his preoccupation with what was between him and Sarah, Justin had let his relationship with Drew wither for lack of attention. Drew's father had stepped willingly into that breech, which would never have been there for Osborne to take advantage of if Justin had treated the child's adoration with the respect it deserved. He hadn't, and now he would have to pay for that failure. Something else to face. Another duty to be performed.

But not all duties turned out to be unpleasant, he thought, his lips relaxing into a smile. He bent to press a kiss against Sarah's bare shoulder. She stirred in her sleep, breath sighing out of parted lips. He stepped back, away from the bed, waiting for her to return to the deeper slumber from which he had unintentionally awakened her. *Tonight,* he promised silently, his lips again curving, and then he turned away from the bed and slipped out of the room.

He entered the nursery as quietly as he had left his bedroom and found Drew still asleep. After the late night the little boy had had, it wasn't surprising that Justin's entrance hadn't awakened him. And he didn't choose to wake him now.

Instead, he stood looking down on the sleeping child, just as he had looked at Sarah, feeling the same rush of love. Sarah's son. That was one reason it was so important that what he had planned be successful. For Drew. And for Sarah.

And for himself as well. His eyes lifted, unconsciously seeking the location where the crop he had given Drew for Christmas had hung above his own bed at Wynfield for all those years. He realized he hadn't seen the whip in several days. But then he hadn't really seen Drew, either. Not for almost two weeks. The same two weeks Osborne was enticing the child with promises of trips to India, irresistible for a boy like Drew.

Something on the table by the bed caught his eye. It was a pocket watch, gold case reflecting the light beginning to filter in through the narrow windows. Justin picked it up, wondering idly if it were Brynmoor's, since it was obviously old.

"That crease, the one on the left side, is the mark of a bullet," Drew said.

Justin's eyes came up to find that Andrew, propped on one elbow, was watching him. Drew was wearing his own nightshirt and seemed none the worse for his misadventure last night.

"A bullet mark?" Justin repeated doubtfully. His gaze fell again to examine the case lying on his open palm. He turned it over, but there was no mark on its surface that looked to him as if it might have been put there by a ball, not even a spent one.

"It saved my father's life," Drew said.

"I see," Justin said. He was beginning to. One of Osborne's colorfully entertaining stories. And Justin was fairly certain that's all it was. A story. Of course, its truthfulness wasn't relevant. Drew's reaction to it was what was important. Justin laid the watch back on the table, allowing none of his skepticism to show in his face.

"It's very special to him," the little boy said.

"And it meant a great deal that he gave it to you."

"Yes." The single word was very soft, almost hesitant, but Drew's eyes seemed as clear and open as Sarah's had last night.

"Is that why you decided to go away with him?"

"He *is* my father," Drew said, his voice still subdued. "I have always wanted a father, you know."

Justin nodded, understanding that if he had been more forgiving—or more giving, he amended—he might have fulfilled that longing, so that when Osborne showed up with his charm and his tales of derring-do, Drew would not have been so easily seduced away from the people who really loved him.

"I know," Justin said. "I know you have."

"I thought that perhaps…" The childish voice faltered, but Drew's eyes were still on his face.

"What did you think, Drew?"

"When you married Sarah, I thought you might want to be my father. And when you didn't—"

"Whatever made you think I *didn't* want that?" Justin interrupted, his tone sharper than he'd intended.

"You never *said* you did. I had hoped you might say it to me for Christmas. Saying it would have been just like Sarah says presents should be."

Something of you in them. He remembered what Drew had told him, and now he knew he hadn't really understood, after all.

"But you never said it," Drew said.

"And it's too late, I suppose," Justin said softly.

The blue eyes, which were so much like Sarah's, considered the question. And then they clouded with anxiety. "I have a father. A *real* father," Drew said softly.

Justin nodded, acknowledging a truth that neither of them could ever change, no matter how appealing it might be to try.

"I'm sorry I fought with your father last night, Drew.

What we did...what *I* did was wrong. Fighting isn't the way to settle disputes. It isn't the way a real gentleman does things."

"Because you hit him with that bottle?" Drew asked. "Because that isn't the way a gentleman fights?"

"Yes," Justin admitted.

He couldn't afford to criticize Osborne to Drew, no matter what David had done, even if it were totally unacceptable by the unwritten code that governed such activities. He couldn't mention that gentlemen also did not kick their opponents when they were down. Or deliberately trip them to make them fall.

"That's one reason," Justin said simply, not voicing any excuse for what he himself had done.

He was not responsible for Osborne's behavior, of course, but he *was* responsible for his own. Hitting an enemy in battle with any weapon that came to hand was one thing, especially if you did so to save your life. He knew very well, however, why he had hit Osborne with that bottle. And it had more to do with the woman he had left sleeping downstairs than with a fear of death. And more, of course, to do with this child. Both of them had been watching as Osborne tripped him and then kicked him like a stray cur when he was down.

"He didn't fight fairly, either," Drew said.

Perhaps the weeks he had spend with Sarah's son had not been in vain, Justin thought in relief. Some of those lessons he had tried to instill had apparently had an effect.

"It was like the boys from the village," Drew continued. "You said they didn't fight fairly. And what he did—making you fight him..."

The child's voice faded, and the silence stretched, the accusation unspoken. Justin was afraid he knew, however, what Andrew thought had been unfair, and it had nothing to do with Osborne trying to break his ribs or his skull by using his boots.

"He shouldn't have made you fight," Drew said finally. "It was...one-sided."

"Because of my leg," Justin said, his voice almost without emotion. Almost. Because the blue eyes that had fallen, perhaps in embarrassment over what his father had done, quickly lifted again to Wynfield's face. The child said nothing, sensitive enough to recognize that what he just said had not been well received.

Drew was only repeating the lessons about fair play that he himself had taught, Justin realized. Repeating them with the flawed understanding of a four-year-old. An understanding that, left uncorrected, made Osborne as guilty as Justin felt himself to be. For some reason, however, Justin couldn't leave Drew's impression uncorrected.

"I never wanted *that* to make a difference to him," he said.

"Then it was all right for him to make you fight?"

"Fighting is not the way gentlemen conduct their affairs," Justin said again, "but one has nothing to do with the other."

The blue eyes were puzzled. "Then..."

"It doesn't matter, Drew," the earl said quietly. "That isn't why I came. Not to discuss what happened last night."

The boy nodded, his eyes still on Justin's face.

"I was wrong at Christmas," Justin said. "I thought I understood what Sarah meant about presents, but I didn't. I gave you something that had belonged to me. Something *I* had loved. I thought that was the right kind of present, but I know now that all along what you really wanted was my love. I had already given you that, but I'd forgotten something very important."

"What did you forget?" Drew asked, his eyes unwavering.

"I forgot to tell you. I forgot to *say* how much I love you. And sometimes that's the most important gift of all. Just saying the words aloud. Even if you think someone understands."

Drew took a breath, the depth of it lifting his narrow shoulders. "And you do?" he asked. "You do love me?"

"More than you can ever know," Justin said. "Until one day you have a little boy of your very own."

"But...I am not your very own boy."

"Perhaps not," the earl agreed, "but if you ever want me to be then...I would very much like to be your very own father."

Drew nodded, his eyes wide.

"Because I love you very much," Justin added. "And I have loved you for a very long time. Long before I told you. And whatever happens, I want you to promise that you will always remember that. Will you promise me, Drew?"

"I promise," the child said.

Justin smiled, and then, turning, limped across the room and opened the door. Before he stepped through it, he stopped and looked back at the child, who was still watching him from his bed.

"And Drew?" he said softly, smiling at him again. "Merry Christmas."

"The deed to Wynfield Park, which is unencumbered and free of debt," Justin said as he laid the paper on the desk. "The deed to my London property." Justin laid another sheet on top of the first. "Our agreement would include everything that is within them, as well. However, there are a few family mementos I have listed here...." He placed a third sheet on top of the rest. "They are without monetary value, I assure you, but with your permission, I should like to keep them, along with my personal mount. Other than those exclusions, it's all yours. Everything I own. According to the terms I outlined, of course.''

The earl of Wynfield looked up from the stack of documents and into the eyes of David Osborne. Into one eye, at least. The other was swollen shut. For some reason Justin had been pleased to find Osborne's face as heavily marked by their encounter last night as his was.

''And all you want in exchange is the document Sarah signed in Ireland?'' David asked.

''And your signature on a statement saying that Drew is not your son.''

''Drew *is* my son,'' Osborne said.

''And if Drew is what you want…'' Deliberately, Justin let the rest of that sentence trail off. He had already made Osborne's choices quite clear to him.

He could have Drew and press the child's claim to Brynmoor's fortune in the courts. Even if he won recognition of Drew as the marquess's illegitimate grandson, however, he would probably receive nothing for his trouble. Brynmoor was incompetent to name Drew his heir, and Sarah, who had not yet inherited and would not do so until Brynmoor died, owned nothing.

Or, if he so chose, Osborne could have everything Justin owned, which was, thanks to Sarah, free and clear of debt and in much better condition than it had been when the earl had taken possession of it. Justin had agreed to have both properties sold immediately, the money to be given to Osborne. All he had to do in exchange was give over the document Sarah had signed at Drew's birth and deny in writing any paternal claim to Andrew.

''You could live like a king in Ireland,'' Justin said softly. ''Or at least like a prince,'' he added, when Osborne's still functioning eye came up from the stack of documents to meet his.

He was thinking about it, Justin realized in relief. David's mouth began to purse, and then he winced, obviously feeling the soreness of the dark bruise that marred his jawline.

"What do you stand to gain?" Osborne asked.

"Probably nothing you could understand," Justin said.

"My understanding is as great as anyone's."

"Apparently…not about this."

"You're doing this to keep me from taking Drew from Sarah?"

"You don't want Drew. You never have. So it shouldn't matter to you what my motives are. I haven't questioned yours."

"When a man does something I don't understand, it makes me suspicious. As this does. Did she put you up to this?"

"Sarah has nothing to do with my offer. This is between the two of us. You accept it or you do not."

"What offer?"

Sarah was standing in the doorway of the estate office, in which Wynfield had chosen to conduct the interview because it was away from the rest of the house. Not, evidently, far enough away, he thought in disgust.

Sarah walked across the room, stopping at the end of the desk on which the documents Justin had written were spread out for Osborne to read. Sarah scanned them, obviously seeing quite enough in that assessment.

"What are you doing?" she asked, her voice expressing shock.

I'm buying Drew. The words formed in Justin's head because they were the essence of this. He couldn't say them, of course, since he didn't know his opponent well enough to be sure what effect they might have. He only knew what Sarah had told him. And he had trusted her insight. Osborne didn't want Drew. He wanted money. Which was exactly what Justin was offering him. A great deal of money. Everything he owned, to be precise.

"I'm trying to reach an agreement with Mr. Osborne."

"What kind of agreement?" Sarah demanded. Her eyes fell back to the papers, again quickly looking over each of them.

Justin waited until she had, and when her eyes lifted, he said, "An agreement that he will give up any claim to Andrew. Now and in the future."

"In exchange for these?" she asked softly.

All she had not said was in her eyes, and so he smiled at her. "A fair exchange, I believe."

"Justin," she whispered, but it was not a protest.

"Mr. Osborne?" he said, pulling his gaze from Sarah's face and back to the battered one before him.

"No tricks?" Osborne questioned.

"You see the documents yourself. I have written out the deeds, as well as the instructions, which I have already signed. My banker will sell the properties and give the proceeds to you. What trickery could there be in that? I have also written out the statement you are to sign. When you have done that, and have given me the proof you showed Sarah, I will arrange for you, and my instructions, to be conveyed to my man of business in London. He will handle the sale and have the money turned over to you."

"And that's all?" Osborne said, his tone still skeptical.

"That's all," Justin agreed. One small boy in exchange for everything he owned. Everything he had once thought important.

Without another word, Osborne picked up the pen that lay by the well and dipped it into the ink. He scrawled his name across the bottom of the agreement and pushed it across the desk toward Justin. In almost the same motion he reached toward the deeds. The earl's hand came down on top of them.

"Mr. Samuels has agreed to convey you *and* the documents to London," Justin said. "When the sales are complete, he will then escort you on board ship, at which time he will hand you a bank draft for the full amount."

David's eyes met his and held for a long moment. Then he nodded and stepped back, away from the desk. "When do we leave?"

"As soon as you're ready. Unless, of course, you wish to say goodbye to Drew." Justin had thought a long time about making that offer, wondering if it would be better for Osborne to disappear out of Andrew's life or to give them some time together. Finally, he had decided to leave that up to Osborne.

"I see no need for that," Osborne said, his eyes without regret, perhaps even amused at the sentimentality that had prompted that proposal. "Since he is now no longer my son."

"Mr. Samuels is waiting in the parlor," Justin said. "I thought it better if he were not party to our negotiations."

"Then I hope you won't mind if I bid you good-day, my lord. It's a long journey, and as I'm sure you can understand, I'm eager to begin it." His eyes left Justin's face and sought Sarah's. "I always thought you were an extraordinary woman," he said softly, "I didn't really understand exactly *how* extraordinary until today."

For a moment the undeniable charm was back in place, both in Osborne's eyes and in his voice, deep and touched with the lilting cadence of his homeland.

"I believe you've forgotten something," Justin said, fighting a surge of jealousy that was patently ridiculous, considering what had happened between Sarah and him last night.

"Ah, yes," Osborne said. Smiling, he fished in his

pocket and produced a sheet of paper. He held it out to the earl.

"Sarah," Justin said quietly. When she looked at him, he nodded at the document. "Would you verify that this is the paper you signed, please."

She hesitated a moment, and then her fingers closed around the single sheet. Both men watched as she opened it. "This is what I signed," she said, her eyes coming up to meet her husband's.

"And there was only one?" he asked.

"There was only one," she agreed softly.

"Then you may throw it into the fire," Wynfield directed.

Sarah didn't obey him. She held his eyes as the silence built around them until David Osborne finally broke it.

"And perhaps you have married a man extraordinary enough to deserve you," he said softly. "I'll wait for you in the parlor, my lord." He turned on his heel and crossed the room to the door, leaving another, somehow different silence behind him.

"Why?" Sarah asked when he was gone, the paper in her hand still held out to her husband.

"Because it doesn't matter," Justin said.

"You gave away your heritage for a child—" Her voice broke suddenly, but she swallowed the emotion and continued, "For a child who can mean nothing to you. Who is not your son. Who is not even *my* son. You know that now, and yet...you don't even want to know who he is?"

"I know who he is," Justin said simply. "He is your son. And he is mine, Sarah. And whatever the secret of his birth, you may take it with you to the grave, for all I care."

Her eyes held his a long time, and then Sarah walked to the fire and laid the document her husband had given his fortune to buy, the document that would forever have cleared her own name of scandal, on the blaze. It had already begun to blacken and smoke when they heard the first shouts, distant and indistinct, until two familiar words rang clearly. "Whoreson bastard!"

"Drew," Sarah said, already running for the door through which David Osborne had just disappeared.

"I knew you were hiding him," Brynmoor accused, his dark eyes, full of savage cunning, swinging briefly to Sarah's when she ran into the parlor.

Her eyes circled the room, looking frantically for Drew. Mr. Samuels cowered against the wall beside the fireplace, but the marquess was paying him no attention. His entire focus was on the only other person in the room. The man who had besmirched his youngest daughter's honor more than five years before.

The point of the foil the old man held was pressed against Osborne's throat, a trickle of blood already running onto the white cravat. David didn't move. Only his eyes had reacted to Sarah's entrance. They pleaded for her help.

She heard Justin enter the room a few seconds behind her. She had outrun him, of course, and thankfully realized she was between him and her father. Between Justin and the threat of the rapier. She remembered how skillfully Brynmoor had used the cane against her, just as if he had forgotten nothing his fencing master had taught him as a youth.

"Papa," she said, working hard to control her quivering voice, trying to make it calm and reassuring. By now she understood that David was what had set off his Christmastime rage as well. Osborne, whom he must have seen on the estate, was the "whoreson bastard" her father had been looking for, and not Drew.

"I have him, Mellie. He won't ever hurt you again. Or any other innocent woman," Brynmoor said. His voice was triumphant. The insult apparently still rankled within the chaos of his madness when he remembered nothing else, not even her name.

"It's Sarah, Papa," she said softly. "That man never hurt me. You are mistaken. You've made a terrible mistake."

She took a step nearer. The floor creaked under her weight, and Osborne's eyes stretched wide with fright. The trickle of blood suddenly increased, running in a thick rivulet into the knot of lawn at his throat.

"Don't," Justin ordered from behind her.

Sarah had already stopped, aware now that anything that upset her father could result in David's death. She had never believed Brynmoor would be capable of hurting anyone, not even in the depths of his most insane rages. Now it seemed she must face the reality that she had been wrong.

"I will take him off your hands, sir," Justin said, pitching his voice loudly enough to carry across the room. It rang with an authority he had learned on some distant battlefield, she supposed. And he moved confidently nearer as he talked. "The magistrate will have to be called for, of course. I can lock him in the pantry until he arrives."

"I don't know you," Brynmoor said. His gaze traveled back and forth between the earl and Osborne.

"I'm Wynfield," Justin said. "I've come to help you." His voice was calm, but decisive. Byrnmoor seemed confused by his certainty, his eyes flicking between his victim and Wynfield. "If you'll give me the sword, sir, I shall take him off your hands," Justin said again.

He was near enough to touch the marquess, and still, unbelievingly, the old man had not made the final thrust with the rapier. Sarah wanted to close her eyes, to shut out the image, but she couldn't. As horrified as she was by what was happening, she was more terrified by what might occur. It was possible that Brynmoor, enraged over his interference, might direct the sword at Justin instead.

"Give me the sword," Justin commanded.

"Take it from him," Osborne begged.

It was a mistake. It refocused the old man's attention on him and on his grievance. "The whoreson can speak," Brynmoor said maliciously. "What words did you speak to my daughter, jackal? My sweet daughter that you made your whore. What words did you use to trick her from her father's house?" Osborne's face was without color, the tip of the rapier lost in the crimson swell of blood. "She's dead, you know," the old man whispered. "I buried your harlot. Buried her where you'll never find her."

"I never—"

Those two words were as far as Osborne got. The pressure against his throat suddenly eased as the marquess pulled back his elbow, withdrawing the sword for a final, obviously fatal thrust. Justin lunged, arms extended. He wrapped them around the marquess, throwing his full weight against the old man.

They both fell, the point of Brynmoor's rapier leaving a thread of crimson all across Osborne's neck. A shallow thread, judging by how quickly Osborne leaped away from the wall, both hands clutching his throat.

Brynmoor's enraged curses filled the room. Somehow in his fury he managed to break Justin's hold, jumping to his feet with the alacrity of a far younger man. He slashed downward at the earl, who was still on the floor, the sword making a hissing sound before it struck, and Sarah's heart stopped. Then, eyes murderous and face purpled with engorged blood, he turned to find his original victim.

Belatedly, Osborne realized his danger. He tried to climb over the sofa that stood between him and the door. The marquess of Brynmoor drew back his foil, in preparation this time for plunging it into the back of his fleeing victim. Before he could complete the move, however, Justin was there.

He grabbed at the old man's coat, all he could reach in time, jerking him backward so that the sword missed its mark. Brynmoor whirled, bringing the rapier around with him. He hit the earl in the face with the metal guard. Justin staggered back, losing his balance. Both hands on the hilt now, the marquess raised his sword high above his head, preparing to bring the point of it down on the defenseless man at his feet.

"Papa," Sarah screamed, her voice echoing against the walls.

It halted the movement of the marquess's hands. They hesitated at the apex, his eyes finding hers. Suddenly, they widened, a circle of white around the Spenser blue. His mouth opened and then closed spasmodically, like a dying fish. His hands relaxed their grip on the sword, which fell, tip briefly embedding itself in the thick Oriental carpet, before it toppled.

Brynmoor clutched at his temples. Eyes closed now, his face distorted into a mask of agony, the old man slipped to his knees, and then, like a felled tree, slumped forward onto the rug, one thin, liver-spotted hand coming to rest beside his rapier.

Epilogue

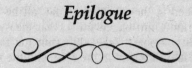

When Justin opened his eyes, Drew was standing beside the bed watching him. Despite the burning pain in the arm Brynmoor had slashed from elbow to shoulder, the earl reached out his hand, palm up, to the little boy.

Small fingers slipped into his, and Justin squeezed them tightly. It seemed almost too hard to do any more than that. Certainly too difficult to formulate the right things to say.

"I'm supposed to tell Sarah when you're awake," Drew said.

Justin nodded, fighting the urge to close his eyes again and drift into that peaceful world halfway between waking and sleeping, which he had occupied since the surgeon had bled him. He had never been able to understand why, when one had already lost a great deal of blood, the surgeons wanted to let more. He vaguely remembered being assured that he'd rest easier. And perhaps that was even true. It seemed he'd done nothing but rest since he'd stopped Brynmoor from skewering Osborne.

"Sarah says you aren't going to die," Drew said. "Do you think that's true?"

Justin managed a laugh, his fingers again tightening reassuringly over the small ones enclosed in his. "Very true," he said. "I'm not so easily gotten rid of."

"You've been wounded much worse than this," Drew said hopefully, "and you didn't die then."

A rote repetition of what Sarah had said to him, Justin imagined, repeated like a talisman. Exactly as Drew had done with her assurances about his grandfather.

"I'm not going to die," the earl said softly. "I swear to you I'm not, Drew. We have some riding lessons to catch up on," he added, and was rewarded with a slight relaxation of the fear that clouded the blue eyes.

"I'll go get Sarah," the child said. "Don't go away."

Without waiting for an answer, he released Justin's hand and ran from the room. Despite Drew's admonition, the earl's eyelids drifted downward again. He lifted them a couple of times, looking toward the door, but they were far too heavy for him to stay awake until Sarah arrived.

He wasn't sure how long he had slept when he opened his eyes again, but the light had faded and the shadows had lengthened, hiding the corners of the room. He turned his head restlessly on the pillow and found Sarah reading in a chair she had pulled up beside his bed. Without speaking, he simply watched her for a long time, thinking about the wasted years that lay behind them. And about all those, of such promise now, that lay ahead.

She turned her head finally, and when she realized he was awake, she smiled at him. Just as he had done earlier with Drew, she offered him her hand. He took it and brought it to his mouth to press a kiss against her fingers.

"Where's Drew?" he asked.

"Having his supper, but you should expect another visit before bedtime. He's convinced he's going to lose you, too."

"Too?" Justin questioned.

"David left this afternoon," Sarah said.

There was something in her voice he didn't understand. Some hint of...regret? Because Drew was upset? Osborne's departure was, however, what they both had wanted. David had given up all claim to Drew and was permanently out of their lives, no longer a threat. Nor, of course, was Brynmoor. No longer a threat to anyone.

"I'm sorry about your father," he said.

"Maybe...maybe it's better this way. Maybe Drew was right to be afraid of him."

"I don't think he would have hurt Drew. I think that somehow, all these years, he never forgot what Osborne had done to Amelia."

"You know," she said softly.

"That Drew is Mellie's son?" Justin said. "I know."

The old man had said enough to make that obvious. Justin didn't understand everything, of course, but there was no doubt in his mind about the essential part of the mystery. Or about why Sarah had done what she had done. After all, she had always protected Amelia, at least since their mother's death.

The long silence stretched between them, but there was no discomfort about it. It seemed instead that after a tiring and dangerous voyage they were at peace. Together at last, all the things that had held them apart of no importance. The room was almost dark when Sarah finally spoke again.

"I have something for you," she said.

"For me?"

"A belated Christmas present, I suppose. I never gave you one."

Justin smiled. "I never expected you to."

"I know," she whispered, "but... These aren't your mother's pearls, not nearly so valuable, but I think you will like to have them, all the same." She reached to light the lamp beside the bed.

"Should we wait for Drew?" he asked, trying to think what Sarah might want to give him. Something of Brynmoor's, perhaps? That would somehow even seem fitting.

"I think this might be better with just the two of us. Later on…" She hesitated, her eyes on his again. "Later on, I'll tell Drew. I'm not sure I'll be able to explain everything to him. I'm not sure I even understand it all, but…I don't believe many little boys are lucky enough to have so many people who love them."

She picked up a packet that was lying in her lap and placed it on the bed near his hand.

"What's this?" Justin asked.

He touched the paper on top of the stack, and then he opened it, his fingers trembling weakly over that simple task. When he had, he realized it was the document Osborne had signed renouncing his parentage of Drew. Justin's eyes lifted to Sarah's, questioning.

"Look at the rest of them," she said.

He laid the first sheet aside and opened the second. And for a moment, his brain couldn't seem to comprehend what he was seeing. "This is the deed to the Park," he said, his eyes lifting again to Sarah's face.

"And the last is the one to the town house," she said.

"I don't understand," Justin said, his eyes falling again to the papers that represented his entire heritage, all that was left of his family.

"He said it was the only noble thing he'd ever done in his life. And he didn't want you to spoil it by trying to send them after him. If you are really determined to give them away…" Her voice broke, and Justin looked up to find that her eyes were awash with tears. "If you are really determined, he said you could give them to Drew."

"Why?" Justin asked again, mentally reviewing all he had thought he knew about the character of David Osborne.

"Maybe because of what you did today. You put your own life at risk to save his, even after what he had done. Maybe he finally realized..." She hesitated again, and when she went on, it was to say something different. "He said you were an extraordinary man. And you are. A far better man than David could ever be. A better father for Drew. Maybe...maybe he was wise enough to realize that."

"You think he's gone for good?"

"There's no reason for him to come back. There are no claims he can make against the estate. No way he can hurt us."

"And Drew?"

"His father has gone to India, which is a very long way away," she said, smiling at Justin, as she recited his own words. "And perhaps someday when Drew is a grown man—"

The door opened, and they both looked up to see Drew peering around it. "May I come in?" he asked.

"I should be very unhappy if you didn't," Justin said. "I've been wanting to see you."

"And I have been wanting to see you," Drew said, walking across the room to stand shyly beside Sarah's chair. His eyes carefully examined Justin's face, and then he took a deep breath.

"Still here," the earl said softly, reading quite accurately the relief in those blue eyes. "I promised you I would be."

Drew leaned against the bed, laying his crossed forearms on the high mattress and putting his chin on the top one. "Do you want me to tell you a story?" he asked.

Justin controlled the urge to smile, his eyes meeting Sarah's above the small, curly head. "I should like that very much."

"A once-upon-a-time story or a real one?" Drew asked.

"I'm not sure," the earl said truthfully. "Which is the better kind?"

"I like them both," Drew said. "They both end happily ever after."

"How every good story should end, I think," Justin said.

"My father told me some stories about India. Would you like to hear one of those?"

"If you'd like to tell it."

Drew hesitated, and then he drew another breath and released it all at once, almost a sigh. "I don't think he will be back for a very long time," he said softly. "Perhaps not even until I am a grown man."

"You may be right," Justin said. "After all, it's a very long way to India."

"Do you suppose…" Drew began, and then he paused, his eyes seeking Sarah's. "If it's not a Christmas present," he asked, "*then* can you tell the other person what you really want?"

"What you want to be given?" she questioned, and waited until he nodded agreement. "I think you might tell. If it's something very important," she added.

"Or something you want very much?" Drew suggested.

When Sarah nodded permission, the little boy's eyes cut quickly to Justin's and then came back to hers. "You called Brynmoor your papa," he said.

"He was my papa," Sarah said. "And when my sister and I were little girls, just about your age, I thought he was the best papa in the whole world."

"And you loved him very much."

"I loved him very much," Sarah said.

"Because he was your *real* papa?" Drew asked.

Sarah's eyes found Justin's face, and then they returned to meet that set of matching Spenser blue. "I loved him because he loved me," she said. "That's all that matters, Drew. That's all that's ever real."

"Then..." The child turned to face the man who was watching them both. "Then I would like for you to be my papa," he said. "That's what I would like more than anything else."

"And that's what *I* would like more than anything else," the earl of Wynfield said softly.

"And now," Drew said happily, apparently relieved to have that settled to everyone's satisfaction, "now I shall tell you all about the tigers."

* * * * *

Please watch for Gayle Wilson's next book,

EACH PRECIOUS HOUR, in
THE McCORD FAMILY COUNTDOWN,

*a new multiauthor series
from Harlequin Intrigue.*

*STOLEN MOMENTS by B.J. Daniels,
available in October 1999*

*MEMORIES AT MIDNIGHT by Joanna Wayne,
available in November 1999*

*EACH PRECIOUS HOUR by Gayle Wilson,
available in December 1999*

*As the days and hours count down to the dawn of
a new millennium, the McCords of Star County,
Texas, seem poised to fulfill their dreams—until
long-buried secrets threaten not only those dreams
but the family itself.*

This season, make your
destination Great Britain with
four exciting stories from

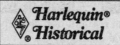
Harlequin®
Historical

In October 1999, look for
LADY SARAH'S SON #483 by Gayle Wilson
(England, 1814)

and

THE HIDDEN HEART #484 by Sharon Schulze
(Wales, 1213)

In November 1999, look for
ONE CHRISTMAS NIGHT #487
by **Ruth Langan, Jacqueline Navin and Lyn Stone**
(Scottish Highlands 1540, England 1193
and Scotland 1320)

and

A GENTLEMAN OF SUBSTANCE #488 by Deborah Hale
(England, 1814)

Harlequin Historicals
Where reading is truly a vacation!

HARLEQUIN®
Makes any time special™

This season,

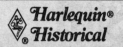

is proud to introduce four very
different Western romances that will
warm your heart....

In October 1999, look for

COOPER'S WIFE #485
by Jillian Hart
and
THE DREAMMAKER #486
by Judith Stacy

In November 1999, look for

JAKE WALKER'S WIFE #489
by Loree Lough
and
HEART AND HOME #490
by Cassandra Austin

Every Man Has His Price!

HEART OF THE WEST

At the heart of the West there are a dozen rugged bachelors—up for auction!

This December 1999, look for *Hitched by Christmas* by **Jule McBride**

Luke Lydell was supposed to be Claire Buchanan's last fling before her Christmas wedding—a gift from her bridesmaids. But Claire told herself she didn't want him…not in that way. She didn't need his hard body, she didn't need the passion that sizzled between them. She needed him to find her missing fiancé.

Each book features a sexy new bachelor up for grabs—and a woman determined to rope him in!

Available at your favorite retail outlet.

HARLEQUIN®

Makes any time special™